Calls at one in the morning usually meant trouble, but when her mother said "I love you," something was definitely wrong...

Dana's cell phone squawked loudly. She ground the heels of her palms into her eyes and swore under her breath. Who the hell was calling her at...she squinted and looked at her watch...one o'clock in the morning?

She stretched across the bed and grabbed the phone. Its green screen light glowed in the dark like some alien homing beacon.

"Dana Sinclair," she announced. "Hello?" Silence. "Hello." She ran her hand through her tangles. Another crank call? Seriously?

"Dana?" It was faint, but she recognized the voice immediately.

"Mother? Is that you?"

"I'm so sorry." Mother sounded exhausted, and Dana wondered if she was ill.

"What's wrong?"

"I only—did it—" her mother wheezed, "—because I—love you." There was a dull clunk, then silence.

"Mother?" Dana shouted. "Mother!"

Still nothing.

"Hang on, Mother," she said, ripped off her slippers, and reached for her hoodie. "I'm on my way."

A dead father's heroism is difficult to live up to, but an embittered mother is even harder to live with. Orange County Sheriff's Deputy Dana Sinclair longs for just two things: more action on the job, so she can earn a promotion like her father before her, and a better relationship with her estranged mother. When her partner is killed, she wonders how she'll get along without him. But when her own mother is murdered shortly thereafter and it appears that her dead father has come back from the grave to do it, she does everything she can to uncover the truth, despite warnings to the contrary from her boss. Then there's the bouquet of English daisies a mysterious man hands her at her partner's funeral—the very same flowers Daddy gave her the night he was murdered. So, are the flowers a gift…or a warning?

KUDOS for *Murder in the Family*

In *Murder in the Family* by Lisanne Harrington, Dana Sinclair is troubled. Becoming a cop like her father, who died heroically in the line of duty—or so she thinks—Dana is estranged from her mother who doesn't like her choice of career. But when her mother is killed, Dana begins to unravel a dark family secret that calls her father's death into question, as it appears that he has come back from the dead to kill her mother. As Dana struggles to uncover the truth, she puts everything on line—even her own life. Well written, suspenseful, and intriguing, this mystery will keep you on the edge of your seat all the way through. ~ *Taylor Jones, The Review Team of Taylor Jones & Regan Murphy*

Murder in the Family by Lisanne Harrington is the story of a young woman who wants to follow in her father's footsteps and be a cop, something for which her mother can never seem to forgive her. When Dana Sinclair's partner is killed, Dana gets a bouquet at his funeral from a strange man. The flowers are pink English daisies, ones that have a special meaning for her. Then there are the photos of her childhood that someone sends her, but who? After her mother is brutally murdered, Dana starts to wonder if what her mother told her about her father dying heroically is true or if it was all lies. She suspects her father has returned from the grave and is responsible for the murder. But how can she prove it? Although *Murder in the Family* is a completely different genre than her first three books, Harrington proves that she can handle the mystery/thriller genre equally well, crafting a tale of betrayal, deceit, and greed that will keep you turning pages as fast as you can from beginning to end. ~ *Regan*

Murphy, The Review Team of Taylor Jones & Regan Murphy

ACKNOWLEDGMENTS

Dana is a composite of quite a few characters, real and fictional. Author Alex Kava's character, FBI Agent Maggie O'Dell, was a huge inspiration. While Dana isn't a lot like Maggie, my hope is that her personality draws the reader in the way Maggie's does.

My family, as always, was patient and more than willing to overlook my faults and forgetfulness while I was writing this, even if not all of them truly understand what I do. Or that I *must* do it to survive. It's like breathing.

Huge thanks to Lieutenant Dennis Parker, (Ret.) of the El Reno Police Department for answering my endless questions about police procedure, guns, squad cars, and all things law enforcement. You rock, buddy!

My team at Black Opal Books, however, *do* understand me, and work hard to help me create the very best story I can, because some stories just have to be told: Faith, my amazing editor, who patiently encouraged me; Lauri, who saw potential in the story, and in me; and Jack, who worked so diligently to once again create a cover that was exactly what I envisioned, despite my being so frustrating a client, although he never let on. Thanks, guys.

And as always, my special thanks go out to you, my Most Important Reader, without whom all this wouldn't mean a thing. I hope you enjoy helping Dana solve the murder. You can contact me through my website:
http://www.lisanneharrington.com
or shoot me an email at Lisanne@lisanneharrington.com.
I would love to hear from you.

OTHER BOOKS
BY
LISANNE HARRINGTON
AND
BLACK OPAL BOOKS

Moonspell

Moon Watch

Moon Shadows

MURDER

IN THE

FAMILY

Lisanne Harrington

A Black Opal Books Publication

GENRE: MYSTERY-DETECTIVE/WOMEN SLEUTHS/SUSPENSE

This is a work of fiction. Names, places, characters and incidents are either the product of the author's imagination or are used fictitiously, and any resemblance to any actual persons, living or dead, businesses, organizations, events or locales is entirely coincidental. All trademarks, service marks, registered trademarks, and registered service marks are the property of their respective owners and are used herein for identification purposes only. The publisher does not have any control over or assume any responsibility for author or third-party websites or their contents.

DEDICATION

For my beloved Tod,
who encourages me to write,
even if he doesn't understand what I do.
Love you, Sweet T.

CHAPTER 1

Gunfire exploded somewhere close by. Two rapid shots. Then a third. Close enough to make Orange County Deputy Sheriff Dana S. Sinclair's heart jump into her throat and her hand go automatically to her sidearm. It was right here, right in the McDonald's parking lot. Right where she had left her partner, José Ramírez, talking to a young boy not two minutes ago. She sprang out of the food line and pushed through the crowd already rushing in the doors, trying to get out of the way of whoever was shooting.

"Shots fired," Dana shouted into her shoulder radio mic as she burst out the door. She gave their location and ducked behind an old Mustang convertible parked about thirty feet away from the squad car. José's legs stuck out from behind the cruiser.

They didn't move. She'd give anything to go to him and make sure he was still alive, but he'd be pissed if she let the shooter get away.

"Officer down. Officer down!"

A boy in a black hoodie ran away from them, and she raced after him.

"Down," she commanded the few gawking bystanders who hadn't scattered when the shots were fired. "Everybody get down."

The boy turned and fired two rounds. Dana crouched, took aim, and returned fire. The bullet hit him in the fleshy part of the shoulder. He looked wide-eyed at the wound as blood flowed down his chest. She went to him quickly but cautiously and took the 9-mm Ruger out of his hand.

"Better sit down and put some pressure on that." She snapped her handcuffs around his wrist and got a better look at his face. Asian, about fifteen. She frowned. He resembled the composite sketch the department had recently released of one of a trio of home invasion suspects. Was this boy involved? Was that why he shot José? She secured the suspect to the door handle of the car next to him and ran to her partner's side. He had two holes. The one in his hand was minor. The one in his thigh worried her. She spoke into her radio mic again. "This is officer three-two-four-seven-nine. Sinclair. Shots fired. Repeat, shots fired. Two casualties. Officer down. Hurry!"

Dana dropped to her knees and applied pressure on the largest wound. She scanned the crowd and spotted a young man wearing a faded Angels T-shirt, with a battered leather backpack slung over his shoulder. "You." She pointed at him. "Anything in that pack of yours we can use as a compress?"

The man took off the bag and rummaged inside. "Napkins?" He tentatively held them up for her inspection.

"What's your name?" she asked him.

"Matt."

"Okay, Matt." She pointed in the direction of the boy who'd shot José. "Take the napkins to that kid over there. Hold them in place on his wound. Press hard. Understand?"

He nodded, and Dana turned back to her partner. "Hold on, José." She tried to ignore the blood. There was so much of it. She pressed down on his thigh. "You'll be okay." Her hands were quickly drenched. She increased the pressure. That damn kid must have nicked the femoral artery. This was bad. Really, really bad. "It's okay, buddy. You're okay," she said. "Just hold on. Help's on the way. Stay with me."

The bleeding wasn't going to stop on its own. Dana ripped a wide strip off the bottom of her uniform shirt and shook her partner softly to make sure he was still conscious. "This is going to hurt," she told him, and wound the fabric tourniquet tightly around his thigh. She knotted it as securely as possible, wincing when a semi-conscious José moaned. "Sorry, partner," she whispered.

"S'okay, kiddo." His eyes momentarily rolled back in his head, then cleared. Dana leaned close. She didn't want to miss anything he might say. "Don't let this change you." He grimaced, his eyes flickering as he struggled to stay awake. A faint smile formed on his lips. "Stay crotchety."

She smiled back. "Ha ha. You'll be barking orders at me again before I know it."

"Not this time." José's eyes fluttered shut, and his breathing slowed to almost nothing.

"No, wait." She scanned the crowd. "Where's that damn ambulance? Someone get a doctor!" She turned back to her partner. "Hang on, José. Just hang on!"

Tears streamed down her face and splashed onto her hands as she tightened the makeshift tourniquet. She glanced over her shoulder when she heard the faint sounds of a siren, then smiled down at José.

"Hold on just a little longer, buddy. Help's on the way." But it was no use. He was bleeding out. There was nothing more that she could do. Her partner, her friend, her brother in blue was going to die. That punk had killed him. "Aw, José," she whispered. "Stay with me. Please. I can't make it without you."

He opened his eyes. "Watch after my kids," he said, and his faint smile slowly faded.

"Don't leave me," Dana cried and shook him angrily. "Don't you dare, you son-of-a-bitch."

But he was already gone.

CHAPTER 2

The funeral was three days later. Dana had never been to the Cathedral Memorial Gardens in nearby Garden Grove before, but she was well aware of the turmoil the congregation of the Crystal Cathedral had suffered years before. Dana was surprised it was to be José's final resting place. Final resting place. She still couldn't believe he was gone.

Protocol stated that the ceremony couldn't begin until all elements, dignitaries and attendees were in place, and after quite a long wait, things had finally gotten underway. Graveside, two hundred of the county's finest were there to honor one of their fallen. Dana sat a few rows behind José's family: his elderly mother and stepfather, four-year-old Gracie, and seven-year-old Teyo, who sat stoically next to his grandmother, lower lip trembling. Dana wondered if he remembered his mother's funeral. He'd only been three when she'd had a stroke and died shortly after giving birth to Gracie.

She felt so bad for the kids. What would they do without him? What would *she* do without him? The thought had always been there, in the back of her mind, but she'd managed to shove it out of the way anytime it surfaced. Even more importantly, what would happen to Teyo and Gracie, now that their father was gone?

She watched as the Honor Guard folded the flag that had been draped across José's coffin and presented it to his mother, who sobbed quietly. Dana reached underneath her sunglasses and did her best to stem her own tears. But when the bagpipes started playing, she totally lost it.

Fishing in her purse for a tissue, a candy bar wrapper, a Post-it note, anything to wipe her nose with, she was startled when a shadow fell across her lap. She looked up to see a man hiding behind huge aviator sunglasses with a baseball cap pulled down low on his head, and used the sleeve of her uniform instead. Screw it. That's what dry cleaning was for.

"Officer Sinclair?" he said. "Officer Dana Sinclair?"

"Yes?" Dana tried to get up but the man stood so close that it was impossible. He was definitely in her personal space bubble and she shifted a little and rested her hand on her knee to stop its bouncing up and down like a kangaroo on speed.

"Here." A bunch of pink flowers was thrust in her face, and she dropped her purse as she bobbled them.

"Who..." She reached down to get her purse off the ground. When she looked up again, the service was over and people were leaving. Frowning, she hurried out of the row of chairs, trying to get past the other mourners without shoving them out of her way, but by the time she got into the aisle, there was no sign of the strange man. She made her way out to the parking lot as quickly as the crowd would allow, but it was too late. She'd lost him.

That was really weird. Why would someone bring me flowers, especially here? She shook her head. No time to dwell on it now. She wanted to say goodbye to the kids, who were just about to climb into the limo. But before she could reach them, someone grabbed her arm and whirled her around.

"Hey!" That was totally uncalled for and she meant to give whoever it was a piece of her mind. Instead, she took one look and crumpled into the man's arms.

"It's okay," he told her. "I'm here." Michael Finnegan MacDermott, her childhood friend and the person who knew all her childhood secrets, wrapped his arms around her, crushing the flowers between them.

"I can't believe he's gone."

"I know. I'm so sorry." Finn gave her a crumpled linen handkerchief and she blew her nose with it.

"What are you doing here?"

"I told you I'd be here if I could."

"You also said you were really busy and probably wouldn't make it."

He shrugged. "Had to be here for my BFF, right?"

Dana cringed. Not only did she hate that expression, but she really didn't think of him that way. Not anymore. Granted, he'd been a good friend when they were kids, one she'd known forever, but as fond of him as she was, he could never be the friend and confidante that José had been.

"Come on," she said, shaking it off and slinging her arm across his shoulders. "I know a little spitfire who's just dying to see you again." Charlie, her nine-pound Miniature Pincher, loved everybody but seemed to have a special affection for Finn. She'd sit in his lap and demand he rub her belly for hours.

"How is the little mongrel?"

"She's good." They walked to her car. "Why don't you follow me?"

"You kidding?" He leaned on her door as she climbed behind the wheel. "I'll race you."

He pushed the door closed, ran over to his car,

jumped in, and sped off. Dana shook her head and wondered if he'd ever grow up. Good thing he didn't peel out.
She would have had to kill him if he did that.

erses

   On the drive home, she blasted her favorite oldies
station and tried not to think about things, but it was a
losing battle. After José was shot, she'd given her statement about it to Internal Affairs, and it had stirred up all
kinds of emotions in her: sorrow, anger, guilt. To top it
off, she'd been placed on administrative leave. Routine.
Perfectly normal under the circumstances, but being re-
lieved of her service weapon and badge—even temporarily—left her feeling powerless. As if all that wasn't bad
enough, today was her twenty-seventh birthday.
   She entered the lobby of her building, grabbed her
mail from the box, and considered taking the stairs. But
as drained as she was, she decided to give herself a break
and ride the elevator for a change. She stepped inside,
pushed the button for her floor, and leaned against the
mirrored wall while the elevator climbed slowly upward.
When it finally got to the fourth floor, the car made its
usual bumpy landing and the doors contemplated opening. She squeezed through them and headed slowly down
the hall.
   As she fished in her purse for her keys, she realized
that Finn had, indeed, beaten her home. He was sitting
against her front door. She hoped to be able to convince
him to leave so she could go to the wake and surround
herself with her fellow officers to commiserate and tell
stories. Maybe have a drink or three. It wasn't that she
didn't appreciate his being here—she did. She couldn't
really explain it, she just wanted to wallow in her sadness

a little longer, be with others who *really* understood what she was going through. "Hey, Finn."

"Hey."

She unlocked the door and couldn't help but laugh as Charlie leaped past her and jumped on Finn. He knelt down and let her lick his face.

"Okay, little girl, okay." He tried to push her gently away but she was too excited and kept coming back for more. He looked up at Dana. "Little help here?"

"Sorry pal, you're on your own." She set her purse and the flowers down on the kitchen table and searched for something to put them in. She no longer had an actual vase, thanks to Teyo and José, who'd broken the only one she'd had during a Father's Day free-for-all involving a Nerf football. She rummaged around and found an old plastic Circle K soda cup.

José must be laughing his ass off. The warm and fuzzy feelings that sprang up caught her off-guard, and she smiled. It felt good.

Charlie's toenails clicked on the linoleum. "How about some dinner?"

The little fireball woofed her agreement and trotted over to her food dish. Dana took the hint and dumped a cup of kibble into her bowl. Charlie practically inhaled it.

Dana's cell rang, jangling her already sensitive nerves. She tripped over the kitchen table leg in her rush to answer it. It might be the department calling her back to active duty.

"Hello?" she asked without taking the time to look at the caller ID.

"What, no 'Dana Sinclair'?" Finn said quietly. She'd nearly forgotten he was there with her. "What would the goon squad say if they found out? You'd be kicked out of the club."

"Stop it," she mouthed, but he wasn't looking at her.

He pulled back the kitchen blind a few inches and peered out the window. She frowned and turned her attention back to the phone. "Hello?"

When no one answered, she clicked off and put her phone down.

"Wrong number?"

"Guess so."

"Hey, I know things are pretty crappy right now, but I just wanted you to know that I'm here for you." He turned and glanced into the living room, almost as though he expected someone else to show up.

"You looking for someone?"

He turned back to her and smiled. "Nope."

She pulled out a chair and sat down. It was another sticky autumn day, and she blew her regulation-length bangs off her forehead and fanned the back of her neck.

"So," Finn began as he sat down across from her, and Dana chuckled. She knew what was coming. "How many times you clean your six-shooter today?"

"This isn't the wild, wild west, you know," she told him. "Besides, it's not my service weapon. Had to turn that in when they put me on administrative leave. That there's just an itty bitty little thirty-eight caliber Smith & Wesson."

"Answer the question, girlie."

"Only twice."

"How many?"

"Twice."

"How many?"

"All right, four. Four times. But my boots only once. Hardly thought about it at all. Seriously."

In reality, she'd thought about nothing but justice as she sat in front of the television while she cleaned her revolver and polished her heavy black service boots until she was afraid she might rub a hole in them if she didn't stop. It had comforted her and helped her pass the time.

She'd made sure her superiors noticed the resemblance between the shooter and the composite sketch of the home invasion suspects, and was glad when it turned out he was one of the perps. But it hadn't explained what he was doing at McDonald's or why he'd shot José. Had it been some sort of gang initiation? They were hoping to get a confession out of the boy, but until they did, the best she could do was take small comfort in the fact that they had caught the shooter.

"Yeah, that's what I thought," Finn said. He plucked a petal off one of the daisies. "What else did you do? Oh, wait. Let me guess. Umm, haul your carcass out of bed, drag yourself into the living room, and stare at the walls for hours before finally deciding to watch some grainy old film noir on TV."

He knew her so well. On a typical day, after grabbing a Pop-Tart and taking a six-mile run around the neighborhood, she'd slip into her uniform, shove her feet into her freshly polished service boots and give her badge a final spit-shine before she raced out the door. Today, she'd barely been able to pull herself together in time for the afternoon funeral.

Finn plucked another petal and frowned. "Where'd you get these?"

"Some guy at the funeral gave them to me."

"What guy?"

"Dunno. Just some guy I've never seen before."

"Well, who're they from?"

"Beats me. He just shoved them at me and took off. No card or anything."

"You know what they are, don't you?"

"They're pink English daisies. You know—" She hesitated. "—Fairy Fire." It was what her father had called them. She hadn't seen any English daisies in the

last twenty years, not since the night her father was murdered.

Strangely, Finn just sat there a moment, stone-faced
and silent, even though he knew exactly what they were
and what they meant to her. Then he got up and wandered
into the living room. Dana pushed back her chair and
watched him. Was he pacing? Why? What was going on
with him?

"Finn?"

"Hmm?"

"You hear what I said?"

"Yeah, I heard you."

"Don't you think it's weird?" she asked. "Who
would have sent them to me? It's not like I've met any-
body new."

Normally, he would have teased her unmercifully
about getting flowers. But his silence was starting to
freak her out.

"I never even met anyone who knew what English
daisies were," she told him. "Except Dad, of course." She
paused. "Think he's come back from the dead? Sent them
to me from beyond the grave?"

"That's ridiculous." He sounded angry. His back was
to her, and she wondered again what was wrong.

"Geez, Louise," she said. She walked over to him.
Touched his arm. "I was only kidding. Lighten up, will
ya?"

More silence. Not even the usual "don't call me
Louise."

"How do you explain it, then?" she pressed. This cat
and mouse shit was really starting to piss her off. She
smacked his bicep. "Hey. Will you just turn around and
look at me? What's the matter with you?"

He turned to glare at her, his voice hard. "I think you
should just forget about them. Toss them in the trash and

be done with it." He brushed past her, his voice softening a bit. "You don't need some anonymous asshole sending you flowers."

She followed him back into the kitchen. "I'm not going to throw them away just because I don't know who sent them." She'd never have chosen them herself, but since they were here now, she might as well enjoy them. She turned the cup a quarter of a turn. "They're kind of pretty, don't you think?"

"No, I don't think."

"Maybe I have a secret admirer." Even though the very thought made her uneasy.

"You should be worried about a stalker," Finn said, reinforcing how well he knew her. "Not wondering about a secret admirer."

"I'm not." Where was his anger coming from? "It's just—if it were any other flower—I don't—"

"Leave it alone, Dana."

"Leave what alone? What're you talking about?"

"I have to go now."

"Wait!" Dana followed him to the front door. "Where you going?"

"Do yourself a favor, Dana. Throw the damn things out and forget you ever got them."

"Will you just stop and tell me what your problem is?"

"Take care of yourself," he said. "And for God's sake, be careful."

"Finn, wait."

"Oh, and by the way, happy birthday." He charged out the door and fled down the hall, leaving Dana wondering what the hell that was all about.

CHAPTER 3

Back at the kitchen table, Dana fingered the delicate petals. She'd thought the flowers were a gift, but in light of Finn's bizarre reaction to them, she had to wonder if they were meant as a warning of some kind. But a warning about what?

Finn had definitely been trying to get her to back off, but she had no clue why. Was her old friend hiding something? If so, what could it be?

He claimed he didn't know who sent the flowers, but the way he looked when she mentioned her father made her wonder if he knew something about his murder that she didn't. All she knew was that he'd been killed in the line of duty. Could there be something more to it?

It had to be something else. Whoever sent them had to know what they meant to her. Could whoever it was want her to believe her father was still alive? Could he be? She shook her head. It was absurd. He was long dead. Wasn't he?

Too many questions and no answers. There was one thing she was certain of, though. No way had her mother sent them to her. She barely acknowledged Dana these

days, never mind sending her flowers, even for her birthday. And she didn't even know about José.

Restless, Dana got up and roamed the apartment. She
tried without success not to think about José, not to picture his face, not to remember how cold he'd felt when
she held him in her arms that last day. Or how it had tak-
en him barely two minutes to bleed out.

She checked her watch. She had about an hour to kill
before it was time to meet her fellow officers to commiserate over José's death, so she flopped down on the couch
and flipped on the television.

As she stared at the screen, a commercial of a mother
and adult daughter strolling arm in arm down the beach
appeared.

Dana dreaded telling her own mother about the mess
that was her life these days. Her constant barrage of "I
told you so's" would only make matters worse.

"Screw it," she said. "This is ridiculous." She turned
off the TV, slammed down the remote, and grabbed her
keys. Time to put on her big girl panties and quit avoiding things. Quit avoiding her mother. She wasn't a child
so she should stop acting like one. As she drove to her
mother's house, she blasted the radio and did her best to
avoid thinking.

When she arrived, she pulled into the driveway—
something her mother hated, claiming Dana's car leaked,
which it didn't. It was just one more thing to gripe
about—and marched up the walk. With only a slight hesitation, she rapped sharply on the door.

"Hello, Mother," Dana said when the door opened.

"Oh. Hello, Dana."

"How are you?"

"I'm fine. You?"

"Not so good. Can I come in?"

"Why? What's wrong? You arrest someone for

sleeping in their car? Oh, no, let me guess. Somebody failed to get a permit for their pet rhinoceros."

Dana bit her tongue. It was always the same. Her mother just couldn't accept the fact that she'd chosen to follow in her father's footsteps. Hell, she'd *needed* to. "You know that's a Norco law. I patrol Orange County, Mother, not Riverside. I've told you that a hundred times."

"Oh, well, excuse me. I meant to ask if you'd caught someone peeing with the bathroom window open again."

It was no use. Her mother's anger and disappointment would never diminish. Dana'd been on the force seven years, and her mother was as bitter about it today as the day Dana joined the Academy. She suspected her mother spent quite a few hours looking up strange city ordinances just to annoy her. "That's Dana Point law, Mother. South County. I patrol North County, remember?"

"Then you must have—"

"Mother."

"—arrested someone for—"

"Mother!"

"—failing to give the right of way to a duck."

"Mother. For God's sake. Are you going to let me in or what?"

Her mother simply stood there and glared at her.

So that's how it's going to be. Dana sighed. "Have it your way. I just thought you might want to know that José's dead. Shot by some punk while we were on duty. His funeral was today."

"Oh."

"Oh? Is that all you can say? Oh?" Anger and confusion welled up inside her.

"What is it you want me to say, Dana?"

Whatever, Mother. I know we've never had a good

relationship, but can't you put aside your resentment just this once and think about me *for a change? I am your daughter, after all.* "How about you're sorry, to start with. How about that?"

"I am sorry."

"Well, it sure doesn't sound like it." Dana knew she was being petulant, but she couldn't help it. Talking to her mother always seemed to bring out the worst in her.

Her mother's voice softened. "Truly, I am." She opened the door wider and motioned for Dana to come inside. "Didn't he have two little children?"

"Teyo and Gracie, yeah." Tears welled up and Dana struggled to keep them in check.

"How are they doing?"

"As well as can be expected, I guess." Dana took a deep breath and prepared to discuss the real reason she was here. "Listen, Mother. The reason I'm here...well, two, actually..." Her mother remained expressionless. "First off, did you send me some flowers today?"

Not unexpectedly, Mother snorted but said nothing.

"Yeah, that's what I thought. I also wanted you to know that I haven't forgotten what tomorrow is." *Or today.*

"Tomorrow?" Her mother sat down in her favorite chair. Dana took a seat on the couch.

"October sixth. The anniversary of Daddy's death."

"I know what October sixth is. What do you want me to do about it?"

"What do I—" Dana shook her head. "I don't want you to do anything about it. I just wanted to talk to you, let you know that I remembered."

"Two Brownie points to you."

Dana closed her eyes and counted to five. *Ignore her. Whatever you do, just don't take the bait.* "Mother, I know you're still angry Daddy's job took him from us, even after all these years. But I miss him. You know, you always said I was just like him." She paused and looked her mother directly in the eye. "Do you think you'll ever forgive me for becoming a cop?"

"Don't hold your breath."

"Is it because seeing me in uniform reminds you of Daddy?"

"I'm sorry about your partner, Dana. He was a good man, and I know you loved him." Mother stood. "You can see yourself out." She left the room.

Dana shouldn't have been stunned at her mother's abruptness, but even after all these years, it still stung.

CHAPTER 4

Dana sat up suddenly, heart pounding, not sure what had awakened her. She'd gone to bed half-drunk, having partaken of too many shots of Glenfiddich, not only toasting her dead partner but also in hopes of putting the afternoon's dismal outing to her mother's behind her. Her hand went automatically to her hip in search of her weapon before she realized where she was. Home. In bed. Alone. As usual.

A dream. It was just a bad dream. She tossed back the covers and swung her legs off the bed. Her toes grazed the tops of the slippers Teyo and Gracie had given her for Christmas. They had overstuffed piggy heads on them, and she could almost hear the kids' giggles. It was the second time she'd been caught by surprise with a happy memory in as many days. José and the kids had definitely brightened her life.

As she slid her feet into the fuzzy slippers, her cell phone squawked loudly. She ground the heels of her palms into her eyes and swore under her breath. Who the hell was calling her at…she squinted and looked at her watch…one o'clock in the morning?

She stretched across the bed and grabbed the phone.

Its green screen light glowed in the dark like some alien homing beacon.

"Dana Sinclair," she announced. "Hello?" Silence. "Hello." She ran her hand through her tangles. Another crank call? Seriously?

"Dana?" It was faint, but she recognized the voice immediately.

"Mother? Is that you?"

"I'm so sorry." Mother sounded exhausted, and Dana wondered if she was ill.

"What's wrong?"

"I only—did it—" her mother wheezed, "—because I—love you." There was a dull clunk, then silence.

"Mother?" Dana shouted. "Mother!"

Still nothing.

"Hang on, Mother," she said, ripped off the slippers, and reached for her hoodie. "I'm on my way."

She tugged the sweatshirt on over her tank top and quickly pulled on a pair of jeans. After yanking the charger cord off the phone and jamming the phone into her pocket, she snagged her pristine white sneakers out of their box in the closet and rammed her bare feet into them.

Stopping only long enough to snatch her personal sidearm from the nightstand, she grabbed her bag, locked her door, and sprinted down the hall. She burst into the stairwell and bolted down all four flights.

Her heart thundered against her chest, and her breath came in short, harsh bursts. She erupted out the building's side entrance and into the parking lot. There were more than a hundred parking spaces, and she silently thanked the gods that be for favoring her enough to have scored a spot in the closest carport.

She unlocked the car door, climbed into her late model Buick, and jammed the keys into the ignition. The car started, and she revved the engine. The tires squealed as she backed out.

Her mother still lived in the same house where Dana and her brother had grown up. She could drive there in her sleep and, in fact, had driven by many times when she'd first joined the Department, hoping to find her mother gardening or otherwise puttering around outside the house. Back when she still allowed herself to hope for a better relationship with her. Or any relationship.

Normally, the drive took about twenty-five minutes. That night she made it in twelve.

CHAPTER 5

Her mother's front door stood wide open, beckoning to the night like a portal to Hell. Goosebumps rose all over Dana's body, and she approached her childhood home with a growing sense of dread. The house was dark. Silent. Only the occasional chirp of a cricket stuck somewhere within its walls punctuated the silence, and Dana was comforted by the weight of her revolver. She swallowed the lump in her throat, took a deep breath, drew her firearm, and crept inside.

Crouched just beyond the door with her gun ready, she listened intently for any sound from a hidden intruder. Sweat beaded up on her forehead and trickled down between her breasts.

Someone was hiding inside. She could feel it.

Her breathing was rapid and shallow. Her heart hammered inside her chest. She would have to rush the room.

"One," she mouthed silently, willing her heartbeat to slow. "Two." She closed her eyes, took a deep breath, let it out slowly, and then opened her eyes. "Three."

She exploded away from the wall. Scanned the room. The gun moved in concert with her eyes. Nothing seemed out of place. No one huddled behind the couch or next to the bookcase. She crossed the living room and started down the hall. Cocking her head, she squinted into the gloom.

Something flew out of the dark.

An indistinguishable figure, clothed in darkness and silhouetted by the moonlight, knocked her backward and ran past her. Dana gathered herself quickly and raced after the intruder.

"Help."

The voice was barely more than a whisper, yet she heard it clearly and stopped short.

"Mother?" she called, turning back inside the house. "Mother, it's Dana. Where are you?"

"Here."

Dana sprinted down the hall, pausing only long enough to flick on the light switch before rushing into her mother's bedroom.

A pungent coppery smell assaulted her, and she nearly gagged when she saw the blood splatter on the mirror and the overturned perfume bottles on top of her mother's vanity. Her years on the force couldn't prepare Dana for the sight of so much blood and gore in her mother's bedroom. Nausea filled her stomach, and she struggled against it.

Someone had flung the elegant stool her mother always sat on while she brushed her hair at night across the room, and it now rested up against the dresser. Throw pillows, normally decorating the bed, had been strewn haphazardly across the floor.

"Mother?"

The only response was a thick gurgle. Careful not to brush against the blood-streaked doorjamb, Dana sidestepped a bloody footprint and entered the bathroom.

The once-beautiful tile floor was bathed in blood. A

rivulet of it spread onto the eggshell-colored bedroom carpeting. Her mother lay face down on the cold tile, her normally perfectly coiffed silver-gray hair dark and matted. An open cell phone lay beside her.

Dana stuck the gun into her waistband at the small of her back and knelt down next to her mother, avoiding the blood that pooled around her body.

"Oh, Mother."

Her skin was ashen and sallow, her pulse thready and weak. Dana's hands shook. Her instinct was to turn her mother over, but her training told her not to. Instead, she fished her cell out of her pocket and dialed 911. While she waited for the call to connect, she leaned down and whispered into her mother's ear.

"I'm here, Mother. Hang on. Help's on the way. Yes, hello."

"This is the nine-one-one operator. What is your emergency?"

"This is Deputy Dana Sinclair. Badge three-two-four-seven-nine. I need backup and a bus immediately." She gave the operator the address. Her mother's eyelids flickered as if she might have heard the call.

"Dana," Mother croaked.

"Shh." Dana gently brushed a sticky lock of hair off her mother's pale forehead. "Don't try to talk. Save your energy."

Mother shook her head slightly. Her eyes blazed with that familiar fire Dana knew so well. She wouldn't have been able to look away even if she'd wanted to. "I'm—sorry—honey." Her mother struggled to get the words out. "It was—for—your own—good."

"My own...What are you talking about?"

As quickly as they had blazed, her mother's eyes lost their fire. Her breathing slowed then stopped. No fanfare, no battle, no fighting against the inevitable. Just gone. Like José. Except this was even worse.

"No," Dana whispered. Then she punched the wall. "No!"

She leaned heavily against the bathtub, rubbed her bruised knuckles, and waited for help. At some point, she couldn't say when, she used the inside collar of her sweatshirt to wipe the tears from her eyes.

When she heard the paramedics arrive, she stood up and called to them. "In here." Then she looked down at her mother's body. "Mother, I swear to you, I'll find whoever did this." She crossed her arms and walked out of the bathroom. "And then I'm going to find out what you've been hiding from me all these years."

CHAPTER 6

Five thirty a.m. Her mother had been taken to the morgue. Dana collapsed into her mother's favorite chair and tried to concentrate on the crime scene techs as they cataloged the scene. She couldn't believe it. Her mother's house was now "the scene." Bright yellow triangles littered the house, the numbered tabs indicating spots where the CSIs found trace evidence.

Uniforms milled about and spoke in hushed tones. She gave up trying to listen in on their conversations and wished someone would bring her a cold compress to lie across her burning eyes. The first officer on the scene had briefly questioned her then informed her that the detective in charge would arrive shortly, and she should stay where she was. Dana leaned back in the chair and tried to get comfortable. Damn thing had huge immovable wings that served no purpose other than to look stupid and make comfort impossible. She shifted first to one side, then the other before she finally gave up and rested her head in her hands. Memories of her mother burrowed into her thoughts and crowded out everything else. Tears welled up and she angrily brushed them away. Even though they'd hardly spoken for the past seven years, she couldn't bear the thought of her mother being taken from her so suddenly, so violently. So soon after José.

No use. There was just no getting comfortable in this stupid chair, so she got up to get some fresh air.

"Hey, Frank," she said to the uniform nearest her. "I'll be out front."

Frank nodded. "Right."

She went out on the front porch, stretched, and looked up at the pink and orange stripes that stained the early morning sky. What she wouldn't give for a cup of coffee. She sat down on the top step and wrapped her arms around her knees to ward off the chill in the air. Her eyelids began to droop, and she laid her head on her arms.

"Excuse me, miss?" Dana lifted her head and rubbed her eyes with the heels of her palms. All the color had gone out of the sky. How long had she slept? A man with thick black hair that accentuated the greenest eyes she'd ever seen stood before her. "Miss?"

"Yes?" She stood up too quickly and immediately regretted it. Her head was pounding, and her knees threatened to buckle. She groaned.

"Are you all right?" The man reached out to steady her. "Can I get you a glass of water or something?"

"I'm fine. Really," she assured him. Dana drew her hand through her hair then grabbed a strand and twisted it absently around her fingers. "I'm sorry. Who are you?"

"Steve." He flashed a smile. "Steve Campbell."

"Dana," she responded. "Sinclair."

She grasped his outstretched hand, glad his handshake was firm and dry. Too many men went all fish-handed when they shook hands with a woman. She hated that.

"I live next door." Steve aimed his thumb over his shoulder. "Is everything okay?" He stood on his toes and looked past Dana into her mother's living room.

"No, Mr. Campbell, everything is not okay. My mother is dead."

"Oh, shit." He stood back on his heels and ran his fingers through his hair. "I'm so sorry. Your mother was a real nice lady."

"Thanks." A real nice lady? Had he ever met her mother? Nice was the last thing Dana thought anyone would have called her.

"She was a little gruff at first, you know?" he continued.

Dana nodded. Now that was definitely Mother.

"Do you mind?" He gestured at the step and when she shook her head, they both sat down. "But she always spoke to me whenever we were both doing yard work. She made me chicken soup when I had a cold—or thought I might be getting one." Steve scratched his cheek absently. "Once she even baked me a cherry pie. From scratch."

"Sounds like you knew her pretty well." She was amazed at the fondness in his voice. She'd never even caught a glimpse of the soft side of her mother that this stranger seemed to know so well.

"Not really. I mean, we never really socialized or anything."

"Oh." Dana glanced at her watch. What was taking that detective so long? She was beat. All she wanted to do was to go home and take a long shower, followed by an even longer nap. Her clothes were soaked with her mother's blood, and she hated the feel of her now-stiff sweatshirt against her skin. Her head pounded and her ears had a slight ringing in them. *Too many shots last night.*

Steve stood up and glanced into the house. "Well, I guess I'd better be going."

"Maybe you should hang out here for a while," Dana

suggested and looked again at her watch. "The detective in charge should be here any minute."

"No, I don't really have time." He raised one hand and waved to emphasize his point. "I don't know anything anyway. I just came over because I saw all the cop cars."

Something about the way he kept looking over her shoulder made her wonder if that was really the reason he was here. Seemed more like he was looking for something. "You really should give a statement. I'm sure it won't take long."

"When I saw you sitting outside, I just wanted to come over and introduce myself." He patted his front pocket. "Offer my condolences. That's all."

Dana watched as he took his wallet out of his back pocket. Although none of the officers milling about seemed to pay him any mind, something about this guy put her senses on high alert. Maybe it was because he hadn't even asked what happened. She made a mental note to check him out as soon as possible.

He took out a card and handed it to her. "Stephen M. Campbell," it read, and listed a phone number. She flipped it over but there was nothing on the back. It was a strange business card, and she wondered what he did for a living.

"That's where you can contact me," he said. "I'm just next door, so you can come over any time." He cleared his throat. "Talk about your mom. Or whatever."

After he returned the wallet to his back pocket, he patted his front pocket again and seemed to be waiting for a response.

"Right." She tapped the card against her hand. "I'll give this to the detective when he shows up. I'm sure he'll be contacting you."

"Well." He hesitated and looked past her into the

house again. "Let me know if there's anything you need." Then he stepped off the porch and was gone.

There was that look again. *Was he looking for something in particular?* What was it about him? Could he know more than he was saying? Or was it nothing more than morbid curiosity? After all, civilians weren't used to crime scenes. And what was with his odd habit of tapping his pocket? She'd never seen that one before. She'd have to mention it to the detective in charge.

And maybe look into this Stephen Campbell character herself.

ᏉᎧᏉᎧ

Right after the neighbor left, Lieutenant Brian Jackson appeared on the scene. Relief flooded through her as she realized that her long-time friend and mentor was the investigator she'd been waiting for. There was an air of authority about him that she'd always respected. She'd been a young teen when they first met and had become more comfortable with him over the years than anyone else. Except José.

She sat up straight and tried to adjust her bloody clothing in anticipation of his interview. As he strode up the driveway toward her, his face dissolved into a study of emotional pain and sorrow for just an instant before his game face returned. She stood and stuffed her soggy tissues into her pocket.

"Dana. Sweetie. I'm so sorry about Agnes." He enfolded her into a warm hug. She closed her eyes and allowed him to stroke her hair. He smelled like Old Spice and Tootsie Rolls. She wondered how long it would be before he pulled a miniature candy out of his pocket and offered her one. "How are you doing?" He pushed her gently away and searched her eyes. "You okay?"

Dana nodded. "I'm good."

Brian narrowed his eyes, studying her, but said nothing.

"Had better days," she admitted. "But I'm okay."

They went inside and sat down on the couch. Brian immediately went into cop mode. "I understand you found the body." He took out his notebook and pen. "Can you tell me what happened?"

"Sure," she said. The cop in her kicked in, and she looked Brian directly in the eye as though she had just come off patrol and was reporting on an incident that wasn't so personal. "Mother called me a little after one last night."

Brian frowned. "She called you? Since when did she start speaking to you again?"

"She hadn't. But for some reason, she called me instead of nine-one-one."

"Why didn't you call nine-one-one after you talked to her?"

"Because I didn't realize she'd been hurt. I just thought she was sick or something."

"Okay. So what did she say?"

Dana shrugged. "All she said was that she was sorry, that she only did it because she loved me. She couldn't seem to say anything else, so I told her I'd be right there. And then when I got here..." Her voice faltered, and she cleared her throat. "She was lying on the floor in the bathroom, barely conscious."

"Did she say anything else? Like who attacked her?"

She shook her head. "All she said was that she was sorry, and that she'd done it for my own good." She looked over his shoulder and tried to maintain her composure. Wiped her nose on the cuff of her sweatshirt. "Then she died."

"Dana, I know this is painful." Brian patted her knee.

"But we're almost done. Any idea what she meant by that?"

"Not a clue. Do you?"

He shook his head. "She have any enemies?"

Dana shrugged. "Not that I know of. But you know we weren't very close. Especially since…you know."

Brian nodded. Of course, he knew what their relationship had been like. She'd used him as a sounding board for her anger and resentment almost since the day they'd met. He'd listen patiently to her teen tirades and tried to help her understand her mother. Why she was the way she was, who she was, what made her tick. He'd been the father she desperately wanted.

Wait a minute. She squinted as she leaned forward. Needing a closer look at the front door, she got up to examine it. Her legs wobbled slightly before they gave out completely. Brian grabbed her elbow to steady her as he guided her back onto the couch.

"Take it easy, Dana." He turned to the closest patrolman. "Gibbs," he barked. "Water. Now."

"Right away, Lieutenant." He hustled toward the kitchen.

Brian gently shook her.

She brought her hand to her forehead and rubbed. "What happened?" She felt groggy, like she'd been in bad need of a two-hour siesta but had only managed a ten-minute cat nap.

"You fainted," Brian told her.

"I did not." She had never fainted in her life.

He smiled. "Okay, Sinclair. If you say so. You're right. You're Wonder Woman."

"That's right," she agreed. "I am. Want to see my golden bracelets?"

He shook his head and handed her the glass of water Gibbs gave him. "Here, drink this, smart ass."

"Thanks." She gulped down half the glass and felt better.

"I'm going to stand up again," he informed her. "You okay now, or should I have Gibbs bring the smelling salts?"

"Ha ha. Very funny," she replied. "I'm fine, see?" She got up and moved toward the front door. "Look." She motioned Brian over and pointed at the doorknob. "No scratches or marks. No sign of forced entry."

"Right. That should narrow down the suspects." Brian closed his notebook, returned it to his uniform shirt pocket, and buttoned up the flap. "Who had a key?"

"Other than me, you mean? No idea."

"Okay. I'll have Gibbs drive you home."

She wasn't about to let that happen. The guys in the department would never let her live it down, having to be driven home like a "mere" woman. "I told you, I'm fine." She'd drive herself home, thank you very much.

☙❧☙

When she got home, Charlie met her at the door, barking an enthusiastic hello the second Dana put the key in the lock.

"Okay, okay," she said wearily once she had the door open. Charlie accepted a pat on the head and raced off. Dana went into the bathroom, turned on the shower, and leaned on the sink. After a moment, she peered into the mirror. Blood was smeared across one cheek. Her hair was a tangled mess. She leaned a little closer and rubbed a dark spot of blood off her bottom lip. It was all just too much, and she finally lost the battle against her emotions.

She allowed herself a good long cry, something she had rarely done since her father died. When she'd cried herself out, she stripped off the sweatshirt and pants she'd

been given by one of the lab techs when they took her
bloody clothes to examine for trace evidence and tossed
them on the floor. She stepped inside the shower and
leaned into the hot water, enjoying the force of the spray
as it cleaned off the blood. She wondered if she would
ever feel clean again.

CHAPTER 7

The mid-afternoon sun was streaming in through the window when Dana awoke. Dust motes floated in the air above her head. She stretched her arms and legs leisurely and listened to her wrists and ankles crackle, then ran her fingers through her hair and looked over at Charlie, who blinked sleepily.

"Come on, lazy bones." Dana scratched her between the ears. "Time to get up."

Charlie responded with a yawn.

Dana climbed out of bed and pulled on a clean pair of jeans. She padded barefoot down the hall and into the bathroom. After brushing her teeth, she filled her hands with cool water and splashed her face. When she looked in the mirror, she was shocked at the dark purple bruises that had formed underneath her eyes while she slept. She still couldn't believe that the two people she loved most of all—for she did love her mother, in spite of everything—were gone. Would she always feel this alone?

Sighing, she decided to grab a quick cup of coffee, and maybe a Pop Tart, and then get started on her day. Pick up a few things at the market and then head back over to her mother's, see if the CSI team was done yet.

The urge to be at her mother's house nagged at her. If she hurried, she could take Charlie out, straighten up the apartment, pack an overnight bag, and still have plenty of time to get over there and look for clues. It wasn't until she was actually in the car and almost to the market near her mother's house that it occurred to her that the yellow crime scene tape would likely still be plastered across the front door. To cross the police line would not only be career suicide, it could contaminate the area and destroy any evidence that hadn't yet been collected, resulting in whoever slaughtered her mother to get off scot-free.

Dana pulled into the market's parking lot, found an anonymous spot somewhere in the middle, and contemplated her options. It went against her nature, but she supposed she could pretend she wasn't a deputy, just this once, and hope for the best. That thought lasted about a second and a half. She shook her head. No way. Once a cop, always a cop.

Her only other option, she realized as she chewed on a hang nail, was to try and wheedle Brian into giving her the go-ahead to enter the crime scene, and risk disobeying a direct order when he told her to keep out of it. She had a right to know who killed her mother, and why, and wasn't about to just sit on her thumb and spin while others handled the investigation. It might cost her her beloved job, but she'd just have to risk it.

A knock on her window startled her. That strange next-door neighbor of Mother's hovered beside her car, flashing a toothy grin, and made a winding motion with his finger, indicating that she should roll down her window. When she did, he looked inside the car. Charlie growled on the seat beside her.

"Hi, Dana," he said. "It's me. Steve." He patted his chest as if to prove his sincerity.

"Steve." She tried not to show her concern but couldn't help wondering how he'd found her here. He wasn't carrying any grocery bags. "What are you doing here?"

"I saw you drive in and thought you'd want to know that the cops left Agnes's."

"They have?" She glanced at her watch. Three thirty-five p.m.

"Left about twenty minutes ago, I'd say."

"Okay, thanks."

"Glad I could help."

She grabbed her purse off the passenger seat, patted Charlie on the head and told her to stay, and opened the door.

"Hey, how'd you know I was here?" she asked Steve, but he had disappeared. Dana frowned as she scanned the parking lot. She couldn't help but wonder if he was following her.

And if so, why?

c/ɔc/ɔ

After picking up a few groceries, she decided to go talk to Brian in person rather than call him. It would be harder for him to turn her down if they were face to face. Or so she hoped.

When she got to the station, she marched through the bullpen and headed directly to Brian's office.

"Hey, Sinclair," Bill Moore, a fellow patrol officer, greeted her.

So close. She turned around slowly. "Hey, Bill."

"Sorry to hear about your mother."

"Yeah, thanks. Is the lieutenant in?"

"As far as I know."

"Great. Thanks." She didn't miss the puzzled look on

Moore's face as she quickly turned away and headed toward Brian's office. When she reached his door, she stood silently in front of it. Eyes closed, she took a deep breath and let it out slowly. After smoothing the front of her T-shirt, she knocked.

"Come."

"You busy?" she asked as she stuck her head in the doorway.

"If I said I was, would you go away?"

"Probably not." She gave him her best fake smile. It usually worked on him, but not so much this time. She took another deep breath and plunged ahead. "I don't suppose—"

"No." His refusal came even quicker than she had expected.

"But—"

He held up his palm to cut her off. "Dana, you know I can't let just anyone enter an active crime scene, especially when there's a personal relationship with the victim."

"I know, but I thought—"

"You thought you could take advantage of our friendship, that I'd just look the other way while you fumble your way through the crime scene?"

She sighed. "Something like that."

"Any particular reason you can't wait a few days?"

Admit that she just needed to be near her mother's things? *Rather stick a fork in my eye.* Plus, she wanted to look for clues, but she certainly couldn't tell him that. She scrambled to think of something plausible, but nothing came to mind.

"Dana?"

She bit down on her lip. Might as well be honest. At least partially. "You know how things were between my mother and me. Can you imagine how it felt, growing up in that house and then not feeling welcome for more than seven years?" She took a couple steps forward, put her hands on the edge of Brian's desk and closed her eyes. "I just need to be in there. Near her things." She cleared her throat and looked at her mentor. "Does that make any sense at all?"

In response, Brian got up and left the room without saying a word. Not knowing if he'd left the station, went to the vending machine for a cup of nasty coffee, or just what was going on, she figured she might as well hang out for a while and sat in one of the two chairs on this side of the desk. She crossed and uncrossed her legs. Her feet danced rapidly up and down. She checked her watch. Twisted her hair around her fingers in intricate patterns. Checked her watch again. And again. *Hope Charlie's okay this long in the car. Did I remember to leave the windows down a little for her?* She sighed and blew her bangs off her forehead. *What the hell's taking him so long?*

As if on cue, the office door opened and Brian strode in without looking at her. He settled himself once again behind the desk. "Okay." He straightened a stack of files that looked like a Jenga game. "Here's what we're going to do." He looked her in the eye. "You listening?"

Dana pushed herself off the chair and stood in the middle of the room. "I'm listening." Although it was hard to hear anything over the pounding of her heart.

"You don't go into the master bath. You don't even go into the master bedroom. Not to clean, not to poke around. Not until I tell you otherwise. Treat it like the crime scene it is. Got that?"

"Got it." She flashed her fake smile again.

"You know, Sinclair, I shouldn't even be on this case, being as how I've known you and your mother since you were a snot-nosed kid."

"Unlike the perfect picture of femininity I am now."

Brian didn't even crack a smile, but his eyes twinkled and his nostrils flared a little. "Look, smart ass, I'm out on a limb here."

"I know," she said. "I appreciate it. Really." She turned to leave then stopped with her hand on the doorknob. "Thanks, Brian. I won't let you down."

"Make sure you don't."

Dana left quickly in case he changed his mind.

ফেওফে

Twenty-five minutes later, Dana pulled into her mother's driveway and shut off the engine. She sat in the car and stared at the garage door. Memories from when she was a child in Nebraska were pretty vague, but one thing she did remember was her father bursting through the door at the end of his shift and booming a hello to them.

He looked so handsome in his uniform. Like every other little girl, she supposed, she'd had a crush on her father. She couldn't wait for him to come home at night. He'd throw open the front door, stand with one hand on top of his holster and the other on his waist. "Hey," he'd shout. "Either of you little perps seen a big, hairy monster? Stands about this tall." Here he would always put his hand way over his head. "Ugly mug, eagle beak. Answers to the name of Tickle Monster."

He'd charge across the room. She and her brother would squeal and bolt away from him. He'd give chase, scoop them up, and plop them onto the couch. Then he'd tickle them until they screamed for him to stop. They all loved it.

How she had missed him when he died. Seven-year-old Dana had been afraid that moving to California meant they were supposed to forget all about Daddy. But she never did.

A loud bark reminded her that Charlie had needs, too. "Sorry, girl."

She unstrapped her and opened the door. The dog raced across her lap, jumped out of the car, and immediately squatted on the grass. Dana popped the trunk and picked up her purse, slung it over her shoulder, and walked around to the back of the car. She pulled out her overnight bag and a couple of grocery sacks.

Slamming the trunk shut, she turned and bumped into Steve. The bag and groceries flew out of her hands. Steve smiled and bent to pick up everything.

"Sorry." He handed her the groceries but held on to her overnight bag. "Didn't mean to scare you."

"That's okay." She held out her hand. "May I have my things, please?"

"Why don't I just walk you in?" Steve asked, and patted his pocket.

"No thank you. I can manage." She grabbed one of the straps of the overnight bag. When he didn't let go, Dana tugged until he did, and his smile quickly disappeared. She also noticed that his eyes narrowed slightly as she slung the bag over her shoulder.

"Whatever." He shrugged. "Just trying to be neighborly."

"Sorry." *Neighborly? How is it neighborly not to let go of my personal belongings? What's up with this guy, anyway?*

"Apology accepted." He casually brushed the hair out of his eyes and smiled again.

Charlie finished her business and romped back over to Dana. But when she saw Steve, the usually happy-to-see-anyone-who'll-rub-my-belly lover immediately planted her paws and snarled, head down, teeth bared.

"Charlie. Cool it." When the dog ignored her, Dana stomped her foot and clapped. "Now."

Steve took a step or two backward and wiped the corner of his mouth with his thumb.

"I'm so sorry. I don't understand it. She usually takes to just about everyone."

"Got to go."

He practically ran down the sidewalk. When he got to his doorstep, he turned and waved. Dana gave him a half-hearted wave back. She watched as he went inside and closed the door. Charlie's reaction to him told her to be wary of this guy. So did her own instincts.

And she always followed her instincts.

CHAPTER 8

Dana picked up her gear and walked slowly toward the house, dreading the fact that there was crime scene tape plastered across her mother's door. She'd been in such a hurry to get over here, but now that she was, she wasn't sure she could handle it. The sight of her mother's blood and the stain on the floor was something she knew would haunt her forever. *Oh, Mother, why couldn't you let me in, just a little bit? Why'd you wait until you were dying to call me?*

She ran her fingers through her hair, wrapped a strand of it around a finger, and chewed on her lip. This was the kind of thing she normally would have talked to José about. But she'd never be able to talk to him again. Not about this. Not about anything. She had to talk to someone, though, so she unclipped her phone from her belt, turned her back to Mother's door, and dialed.

"Michael Finnegan MacDermott here. Sorry to miss your call. I'll get back to you shortly."

"Dammit." So much for that idea. She waited impatiently for the beep. "Finny. Call me." She closed her eyes. "Mother's been killed. I'm staying at her place until after the funeral." Her voice caught a little. "I need you, buddy."

The key her mother had given her when she was a teen still worked. Once inside, she set the groceries down in the kitchen and wandered through the house. When she got to her old room, she tossed her things on the bed. The room was exactly the way it was the day she entered the Academy. The way she'd left it all those years ago.

There were many memories of the years spent in this house, both good and bad, but one jumped out at her. Seventh grade. After pestering her mother for months, Agnes finally agreed to let Dana have a sleep-over, as long as she only invited one girl. Out of the three class-mates she'd asked, Melissa had been the only one to agree to come over.

They'd had some chocolate chip cookies when they got home from school and were in her room. Melissa sat on the bed and applied bright red polish to her toenails while Dana parked herself at the desk and pretended to read a teen magazine. Her mother wouldn't allow her to wear nail polish of any color, and she'd always wondered what it would look like on her.

Melissa looked up from her toes and caught Dana watching her. "Wanna try some?" She held the bottle out to Dana, who shook her head.

"No, my mother won't let me."

"Aw, come on."

"No, really, I can't."

"Baby." Melissa turned back to her toes. "Don't know why I even agreed to come over, anyway."

"I'm not a baby." Dana's pride—and middle school fears—couldn't let Melissa show up at school on Monday and tell everyone that Dana was a baby. She knew she'd catch hell for it later, but she wasn't about to give the girls at school one more reason to tease her. "Give it here."

Melissa screwed the top onto the bottle and handed it over. Dana ignored her smug smile and pulled off her socks. She'd have to keep her toes hidden, but it was worth it. She opened the polish and meticulously applied it to her toenails.

"So," Melissa said, flipping through Dana's *Teen People*. "Is it true?"

"Is what true?"

"You know. About your dad."

"What about him?"

"That he's in prison."

"That's a lie!"

"They also say he went crazy and killed a bunch of kids."

"Liar! Take it back."

"Why should I?" Melissa sneered. "It's the truth. Your stupid brother told Justin, who told Lisa's brother Eddie, who told Lisa. Who told me."

"He did not," Dana yelled. Her own brother? "Phil would never say that."

"Shows how much you know."

Dana slapped Melissa across the face. Scratched her arm. Pulled her hair. Then pulled it again, so hard she yanked out a big hunk.

"Ow!" Melissa screamed. "You bitch! You crazy bitch!"

"Get out." Dana waved the strands of hair in her face. "Get out before I pull it all out."

Melissa ran for the door. Agnes opened it just as she reached for the knob. "What is going on in here?"

Melissa shoved Dana's mother out of the way and raced out. Dana hoped she'd get run over by a car on the way home.

"And just what was that all about?"

"Oh, Mother." Dana ran to her and wrapped her arms around her waist. Head buried in her bosom, she sobbed. For all of about ten seconds.

Then her mother grabbed her by the upper arms, pushed her away, and held her at arm's length. "Stop your sniveling and tell me what happened."

In big hitching sobs, Dana told her what Melissa had said.

"You know that isn't true. Your father died in the line of duty."

"I know."

"Let this be a lesson to you. People are not to be trusted. Now clean up your room. And get rid of that polish. You can take that horrid little girl the rest of her things on Monday." She paused with her hand on the doorknob and her back to her daughter. "I'm sorry this happened."

Her mother hadn't given her the comfort she'd wanted, and at the time, Dana was sure it meant she didn't love her, but now she thought maybe it was just that her mother had trouble showing her emotions. *Had to get it from somewhere.* She chuckled softly.

Now, years later, Dana sat on the same bed she'd slept in as a child. On it was the same comforter where the nail polish had spilled. She laid her head down and lightly ran her hand over the stain.

"Oh, Mother," she said. "We wasted so much time being angry when we could have just loved one another."

She closed her eyes and allowed all the old childhood feelings to come to the surface. Anger and frustration over her mother's lack of understanding and refusal to let Dana even speak about her father. Loneliness and depression over her father's death. Embarrassment at the way the kids in school had treated her after they heard about what she'd done to Melissa.

Her thoughts wandered back to that slumber party so long ago. She had only wanted to be accepted by her peers, but it had been a losing battle. Even with an incredibly popular older brother, she'd always been a bit of a social pariah. The way the other kids had treated her after that night followed her throughout high school. Sophomore year, she'd spent a lot of time thinking about what Melissa had told her about her father being in prison for killing someone. Was it true? Had Phil really known all about it but never even bothered to tell her the truth? *Why would he keep something like that a secret?* She'd had every intention of interrogating him, but always chickened out. *And all those times I tried to Google Daddy, to find out something about what happened, then couldn't. I was so afraid of the truth. Afraid that all was not as it seemed. That it was all a lie, somehow.*

There was a knock on the door, and Dana frowned. No one except Brian and Finn even knew she was here. God, please don't let it be some neighbor she'd have to make small talk with.

She put on her game face, walked down the hall, and opened the front door.

"Hey, girl."

"Maura?" She couldn't believe it. Maura worked miracles in the crime lab, analyzing and processing latent fingerprints for the Identification Bureau of the Forensics Unit. "What are you doing here? I thought you were on vacation." She reached out and hugged her friend, surprising them both.

"I was." Maura hugged her back. "But Lydia got sick so we came back a little early." Lydia was Maura's eight-year-old.

"Is she okay?"

"Oh, yeah." Maura laughed. "Just chicken pox. Great, huh? Jimmy and Rachel will probably get it, too. Johnny had it, but I never did, so I'm batching it up at my mom's. Can you imagine Johnny taking care of three sick kids? He who thinks he's dying of pneumonia every time he sneezes?"

"Lucky guy. Why don't you come in and sit down? Can I get you something to drink?"

Maura stepped inside and Dana closed the door behind her. "No, thanks," she said. "I can't stay long."

"What are you doing here?"

"Lieutenant Jackson told me you were here. Hey," Maura continued. "I heard about José. I'm so sorry. I liked him. He was one of the good ones."

"Thanks."

"I came as soon as I heard," Maura said quietly. "It must've been awful for you. Why didn't you call me?"

She and Maura had only known each other a few months, but they'd formed an instant bond. Not one to make friends easily, particularly with other women, Dana was grateful for Maura's companionship. She seemed to understand Dana. Most women tended to see her as aloof, when in fact she was actually a little on the shy side, and Maura, bless her, had realized it right away.

"I didn't want to spoil your time off." Actually, it hadn't even occurred to her, and she wondered why.

"Don't be stupid. I'm just sorry I wasn't there for you." Maura paused and Dana closed her eyes against what she knew was coming. "And then finding your mother dead on the floor like that. How awful that must have been. Is there anything I can do?"

"No, thanks," Dana said. "I appreciate it, though."

"I don't know what I'd do if it happened to me. Guess that's why I stay in the Lab while you're out there doing. Don't have the stomach for it."

"But you're great at what you do. I certainly couldn't."

"Okay, well, keep me posted on…you know." The Coroner hadn't performed the autopsy yet. "I've got to run. See you soon."

"I will. Bye, Maura. And thanks."

"Welcome," Maura responded. "Bye."

Dana locked up and headed back down the hall. Maura's visit was a pleasant surprise, and made her feel like she wasn't so all alone after all. When she got back to her room, she spotted the framed photograph she'd kept on her desk at her brother's insistence, and picked it up. He'd taken it the night of his high school graduation. Mother had splurged and taken them both out to an expensive restaurant in celebration. Phil had worn a suit, and she and Mother donned budget-conscious gowns. The next time she'd worn hers had been for her own graduation five years later.

Dana frowned as she looked at the photo, and peered at it closely. Around her mother's neck was a heart-shaped locket on a long Byzantine chain. She had completely forgotten about her mother's favorite piece of jewelry. How was that possible? For as long as she could remember, the woman had never taken it off. But Dana was pretty sure Mother hadn't been wearing it the night she died. At least not by the time she'd gotten there.

Things couldn't have changed so much in the last few years that her mother would simply stop wearing something she had cherished for so long. It wasn't an expensive item, just full of sentimental value. Pewter and sterling silver. Ugly as sin. To tell the truth, she had no idea why Mother liked it so much or what it really meant to her. She'd never bothered to tell them where it came from or even if there were any pictures in it.

Okay, so if Mother didn't stop wearing it on her own, where was it? Could something so worthless be the reason she was murdered? If Phil and I didn't even know where it came from or why it meant so much to her, how could anyone else think it was worth killing over?

Searching for it was as good a place as any to begin looking for her mother's killer.

CHAPTER 9

Dana spent the next few hours searching the house for the locket. Several times, she stopped in the doorway to her mother's bedroom, itching to rummage around. It had to be in there. If only she could figure out a way to get across the yellow tape crisscrossed through the doorway without breaking her word to Brian. After the fourth time, when she'd glanced at her watch and was surprised to find that it was well after midnight, she finally gave up and went to bed.

Hours later, something woke her. *Thump. Thump.* Slow and rhythmic. Disoriented, Dana's heart beat quickly and her breathing was shallow. Her watch showed her it was four-forty-five. In the morning. Charlie whined softly from the edge of the bed.

"Shh." Dana crept toward her.

The dog flashed her a look.

The sound came again from outside the house. She closed her eyes, held her breath, and stayed perfectly still. As she identified sounds, she dismissed them, until the only one she heard was the thumping that woke her. She pulled back the drapes. The glass was cool to the touch.

Still unable to determine exactly what was making the racket, Dana pulled on a hoodie and jeans, grabbed a flashlight and her gun out of the nightstand, and crept down the hall. She opened the front door a crack and peered outside. Nothing. Cautiously, she stepped onto the porch and inhaled the fragrant early morning air. Under different circumstances, she just might sit on the step for a while, have some coffee, and enjoy the sights and sounds of the old neighborhood as it began a new day.

Not today, though. The thumping turned out to be Steve shooting hoops in his driveway. *He's got to be kidding.* The man had absolutely no consideration at all. Nothing wrong with a little exercise—Dana had to admit that she'd noticed Steve's athletic build—but did he have to disturb the whole neighborhood in the middle of the night?

She sighed and snugged her gun into the waistband of her jeans. As she charged across the dewy lawn, blades of grass stuck to her bare feet. Even though the moon was almost completely down, the yard was aglow with a silvery light. But she barely noticed. She was too busy trying to keep her temper in check.

At the edge of his driveway, she stopped and watched as Steve executed a shoddy free throw. The ball ricocheted off the backboard. He rushed after it and plowed into her, knocking her flat on her back. At first, she blinked several times and noted that the few stars visible through the city streetlights were fuzzy. Then she wondered when she'd be able to breathe again. All she could do was to lie there, with her eyes closed, and hope it would be soon.

After what seemed like forever, she was able to take a tiny breath and cool morning air flooded her lungs. A coughing fit forced her onto her side.

Steve crouched beside her, backlit by the anti-theft lights over his driveway. "Are you all right?" His voice seemed to come from inside a tunnel.

She rose up on her elbow and tried to take in a deep breath. Even another tiny one would help.

"Hey," Steve continued. "You sure you want to get up?"

"Yes." She pushed herself into an upright position.

"I'm sorry, I didn't see you there." Steve placed his hand under her arm and helped her get up off the asphalt. "Sure you're okay?"

"I'm fine." Dana looked at her skinned elbow through the new hole in her sweatshirt. "Really."

"You'd better let me take care of that for you."

"It's just a scratch."

"What are you doing out here?"

"I could ask you the same thing." She shaded her eyes against the bright lights. "Do you realize it's not even five o'clock in the morning?"

"Really."

"Yes, really."

"So what's your point?"

His voice still sounded a little tinny to her. She stuck her fingers in her ears and yawned in an attempt to clear them.

As she did so, she noticed again how green his eyes were. Plus he had the blackest hair she had ever seen. It was straight with the tiniest curl at the very ends. He was really quite handsome. Too bad he annoyed her so much.

"Well?"

"Well, what?"

"Any particular reason you came over?" His smile was untroubled, and his tone seemed to mock her. "Other than to inform me of the time, I mean?"

"Are you aware that by playing basketball at this hour, you're actually disturbing the peace?"

"I was not aware of that." He bounced the ball a few times then smiled at her and shrugged. "Sorry. It helps me figure things out when I have a problem. And the exercise helps me sleep."

"That's all well and good, Steve, but I *was* asleep. Until you woke me up, that is."

"Gee, I'm really sorry." He seemed sincere, at least until he bent slightly at the waist and dribbled the ball. His eyes challenged her. "But now that you're here and awake and all, how about a short game?" He bounced the ball to her.

"Thank you, no." She bounced the ball back at him, just a little bit harder than she needed to.

He snugged the ball under his arm. "Aw, come on."

"I said no."

"What are you?" he asked. "Chicken?"

"I beg your pardon?"

He tucked his hands under his arms and began to cluck. Dana stared at him in disbelief.

"Come on," he insisted, a devilish grin on his face. "I dare you. In fact, I double-dog dare you."

Had he really dared her to shoot hoops? What was he, ten? Even though she realized he was being juvenile, and that he was manipulating her, she nevertheless took the bait. She couldn't help it. She never was able to back away from a challenge. Not when she was twelve, and not now.

"Tell you what," she said. "I'll make you a deal. We play to twenty-one. If you win, you can keep shooting hoops anytime you want to." That got his attention, so she continued. "But if I win, no more hoops between midnight and seven in the morning. Eight on the weekends. Deal?"

"Hmm," Steve mused. "Let me see if I've got this straight." He pointed at her. "If you win, you get what you want." He turned his finger around and tapped his chest. "But if I win, I get to do what I'm already doing now, even without beating you?" Then he clucked his tongue. "Hardly seems fair."

"Okay, so what do you want?"

"Have coffee with me."

"What?"

"Have coffee with me," he repeated. "In the morning."

"So." She had to admit Steve's offer intrigued her. "I win, no more midnight b-ball. You win, all you want is a cup of coffee?"

"Yep, that's right." He smiled and Dana found herself smiling back. "Deal?"

He extended his hand, and she shook it. Their eyes locked for a brief second before she broke away, grabbed the ball, and charged across the driveway, executing a sloppy but effective lay-up.

"That's two points for me." She shot the ball all the way across the driveway and into Steve's waiting hands. "Well?" She rolled her hands into loose fists and planted them on her hips. "We playing or not?"

❧❦❧

Dana wasn't quite sure how she felt about what happened next. They'd played to twenty-one. She lost, but not by much. In fact, the score had been so close she demanded a rematch. Best two out of three, she told him. Why did she do that? Especially since she'd lost the second game by so much more.

She came home sweaty and exhilarated. Now, as she soaked in a tub surrounded by lavender-scented candles,

Dana replayed the events of the past few hours. First, she'd cried until her eyes ached, which left her feeling tired and deflated. Then, she'd driven herself nuts trying to find her mother's missing locket before falling into a restless sleep, only to be interrupted by Steve's attempt to rid himself of insomnia. Her response had been to charge over there in a huff. And finally, and here was the crazy part, she had allowed herself to be goaded into a pre-dawn basketball game. *Which you lost*, she reminded herself irritably. *Now you have to have coffee with the guy.* But at least it might give her a chance to find out how well he really knew her mother. See if he was being truthful with her.

And really, it wouldn't be a terrible thing, having to have coffee with the guy.

As she stepped out of the tub, the doorbell rang.

"Just a second," she called, looking around for something to throw on before she realized that all her clean clothes were still in her overnight bag. In her bedroom. The bell rang again. She grimaced as she pulled on the still-damp tank top she'd played in and scrambled into her jeans. How she detested not wearing underwear—what José had laughingly called "going commando." She smiled at the memory.

The doorbell rang a third time and she zipped up her jeans as she rushed down the hall to answer it. "Hold on. I'll be right there." Who on earth could it be and what could be so important that they just had to ring someone's bell at the crack of dawn? Maybe it was Brian with some news.

When she reached the door, she threw it open. "This better be important."

"If you're anything like me, you need a jumpstart to your day." Steve, already cleaned and pressed, held the biggest, shiniest silver Thermos Dana had ever seen. "This a good time?"

Before Dana could stop her, Charlie charged out the door. She stood between her owner and this unwelcome stranger, hackles raised and growling low in her throat.

"Charlie, stop it!" The dog persisted. Dana tried to pick her up, but she was so agitated she nipped Dana's finger. "Ouch. What're you biting me for?"

She picked Charlie up by the scruff of her neck, grabbing her hind feet and holding her close. The dog's eyes went wide and she bared her teeth, but was unable to move. "Let me just put her in the back yard."

Dana returned from the yard to find Steve standing in the entryway. The door was closed behind him. Her eyes narrowed. "I'd invite you in, but I see you already are."

"Oh, sorry." He took a step back and put his hand on the doorknob. "Should I come back some other time?"

Between Charlie's tirade and the hard time she'd given him last night—not to mention their deal—she hated to begrudge him something as simple as a cup of coffee. And there was no question she needed the caffeine. Especially after being so rudely awakened at such an ungodly hour.

"No," she said, giving her damp hair a good shake in an attempt to tame it into submission. "Come on in. Please."

Steve headed into the kitchen, and she watched as he pulled two mugs out of a cupboard and opened the refrigerator door. Out came a brightly colored bottle that appeared to be some sort of flavored creamer. He set everything down on the table and poured steaming hot coffee into each mug.

"Creamer? Sugar? Black?" He handed one of the mugs to Dana.

"Black, thanks." *What the hell? For someone who claims not to have known Mother very well, he certainly seems to know his way around.* She took the mug he offered and watched over the top of it as he dumped half a bottle of Irish crème flavored creamer into his coffee. She narrowed her eyes as she watched him. *Just what is he up to?*

When he was settled in one of her mother's avocado green 1970s era kitchen chairs, she put her mug on the table but kept her hands wrapped around it.

"How is it that you seem to know your way around my mother's kitchen?" She tried not to let her anger show too much. She didn't want to spook him until she could get a better handle on his motives. "I thought you didn't know her very well."

"I didn't." He sipped his coffee. Dana noticed his eyes flash up and to the right before quickly returning to hers, and she wondered what he was hiding. "But she invited me in a couple of times for coffee. I think she was lonely."

That made no sense at all. Her mother wasn't the "I'm-so-lonely-I-could-cry" type. She couldn't picture her mother so forlorn that she sought out a neighbor to keep her company. It was hard enough to believe her mother brought Steve soup when he was sick.

"Maybe you're right. She could've been lonely. I really wouldn't know." She shifted in her chair, trying to find a comfortable position. Her jeans rubbed her in places she'd rather they didn't, and she wished again that she'd been able to throw on some panties before opening the door.

"Why is that?" Steve reached across the table to lay his hand on hers. "If you don't mind my asking."

Dana removed her hand from underneath his and picked up her coffee. "We weren't very close," she said simply.

"Yeah, I know what you mean."

"You do?"

"Sure." He took a sip from his mug. "When my sister, Maracella, got married, our father refused to give her away. Wouldn't even go to the wedding."

"Why not?"

"Jaleel's black," Steve said. "Well, actually, he's French Creole, but he's about as dark as midnight in the Bayou." He cleared his throat. "Don't know if Dad will ever forgive her."

"That's terrible," she pronounced then instantly regretted it. "I'm sorry. I don't mean to sound judgmental."

"It's okay. I agree with you. What makes it really bad is that Jay's the nicest guy in the world. Treats my sister really well."

"So what's the problem?" She shifted in her seat again and wished she could get rid of her own immediate problem.

"Exactly." He tilted his head and frowned. "Are you okay?"

"Sure. Why do you ask?"

"Because you keep squirming around, like...well, like you have to go to the bathroom or something."

"Actually, will you excuse me for a minute?" She bolted from the room, rushed down the hall, and into her bedroom.

Great. She tossed the contents of her overnight bag onto the bed then scooped up some clean clothes. *Just great. Nothing like making a fool of yourself in front of a total stranger.*

Once changed, she went back into the kitchen and was surprised to find Steve washing the mugs. "I think

I'd better go," he said, reaching for a dishtowel hanging off the stove handle.

"Yeah, maybe you'd better," she agreed. The aroma of the coffee was battling the caffeine to lull her to sleep. "I'm really beat."

"Rain check?" He put the mugs back in the cupboard, replaced the dishtowel, and twisted the lid back onto the Thermos. When he turned to look at her, he had a wide, toothy grin on his face. Dana couldn't help but notice how striking it was and how it lit up his entire face.

"Sure." She could see how it would be easy to fall under the man's charm, and it put her on guard. "I'll just walk you out."

"Don't bother," he told her. "I know the way."

She watched him as he walked out of the kitchen and noted with some amusement that as he walked across the living room, Charlie growled loudly. At least she didn't try to get at him by eating her way through the screen door. Dana also pretended that she didn't notice the way Steve's hips moved as he walked.

❧❦❧

Once Steve left, Dana opened the screen and Charlie charged across the room, barking angrily at the front door.

"All right, you ferocious beast." She scooped her up, carried her down the hall, and into her old bedroom.

She dropped the angry animal onto the bed and looked around the room. Her mother hadn't gone out of her way to lavish them with everything they wanted, but she had provided them with what they really needed. A bed, a dresser, a nice desk with a bright light by which to do her homework, and all the books she could read. They may not have had designer clothes, but what they did have was always clean and wrinkle-free. And they never went hungry.

She should have thanked her mother, told her that she understood how hard life had been for her, and how much she appreciated everything she'd done for them. But she'd never have a chance to say any of that. Now the only thing she could do was to find her killer.

It made her think about her brother's death. Over five hundred people had shown up for the funeral in the pouring rain. The church was so packed that it wasn't until she got to the cemetery that she'd found her mother. She waited for the limo to pull up grave-side, shivering from the wind-blown rain that soaked her no matter how she held the umbrella, and tried not to fume at not being invited to ride with her mother. Her only remaining family. The driver ran around to open her mother's door and held a huge black umbrella over her head. Agnes emerged shrouded in a heavy black veil. Dana hurried over.

"Mother," she began.

Her mother paused for a split second before silencing her daughter with her palm only inches from Dana's face. When she continued walking without saying a word, Dana knew, once and for all, that her mother blamed her for Phil's death. And she was right.

It was Dana's fault that her brother was dead.

CHAPTER 10

When the phone rang later that morning, she had no idea it would be the coroner's office. She'd only met Shelby, one of the morgue techs, a few times, so the courtesy call really surprised her.

"Hey, Officer Sinclair, it's Shelby Russo, from the morgue."

"Hi, Shelby."

"Just wanted to let you know that we've had to push the autopsy back a little. We're really swamped down here."

"Oh, I'm sorry to hear that."

"Yeah, me, too. But it'll happen in the next day or so."

"Okay. Well, thanks for calling."

As she hung up, her stomach rumbled, and Dana couldn't remember when she'd last eaten. There was a small diner a couple of miles from the house, and she decided to go there for lunch. She debated the merits of walking but ultimately decided that she needed to get back and get to work looking for Mother's papers. If she was lucky, they might contain a clue about who would have wanted her dead. And why.

As she drove into the diner's parking lot, she studied the storefront and almost opted for McDonald's. The restaurant had a sun-bleached pink awning shading the window that had definitely seen better days. Several people came and went, though, so she decided to suck it up, go inside, and hope for the best.

After finding a parking space, she strode across the asphalt and headed toward the diner. Just as she reached it, the door shot open and a man in a too-large jacket and a Dodgers cap practically flew out. Dana scurried to get out of his way then watched as the man disappeared around the corner of the building. It never ceased to amaze her how rude people could be. She stepped inside.

A fairly new pink and black doormat declared that this was "Sally's Coffee Shop." Despite the odors of fried hamburger and coffee, it was really cute. Pink and black counter stools matched the spacious booths. The linoleum, a 1950s black-and-white diamond pattern, looked new. The waitresses wore pink and black uniforms with skirts too short to be comfortable, fishnet stockings and little black hats set jauntily on their heads.

Dana stood just inside the door and watched the waitresses at work. She was surprised at how busy the place was for eleven o'clock on a weekday morning. As she looked around, she realized it was actually more a quaint neighborhood eatery than a greasy spoon. Most people would probably be quite comfortable here. Maybe even her mother.

"Sit anywhere you like," one of the waitresses told her.

Dana judged her to be about sixty, with bright pink lipstick that exactly matched her pink blush. It was a horrible color, but the woman somehow pulled it off. In fact, it complimented her complexion so well it made the plain woman look almost pretty.

Dana took the only empty booth.

Set for two, the table featured white plastic coffee mugs turned upside down and sitting atop scalloped paper placemats. Dana picked up a menu and instantly regretted it. Someone had plopped a big glob of catsup on it and, of course, it had gotten all over her hand. It looked like blood. Her mother's blood. Why had her mother died, and so violently? Who could have hated her so much that they'd go to such extremes to murder her?

"Coffee?" The old waitress popped her gum then turned her head and coughed like a barking seal.

"What?" Dana could barely pull her eyes away from the blood that covered her hand.

"I asked if you wanted some coffee." The waitress, whose embroidered name on her uniform announced that this was Sally herself, had an expression of concern on her time-worn face.

"Oh, sorry." Dana blinked a few times and when she looked back at her hand, it was covered with catsup again. She grabbed a napkin and wiped it off. "Yes, please."

Dana turned her mug over and watched as the steaming coffee flowed into it. The fragrance carried with it a hint of cinnamon, and something else, something nutty. She inhaled deeply, enjoying the aroma.

"Mmm," she murmured. "Smells heavenly."

Sally put the coffee pot down on the table. "Taste it. It's my own special blend."

Dana blew on it to cool the hot liquid before taking a small sip. It tasted even better than it smelled.

"It's fantastic."

"Good." Sally paused a second. "You're Dana, aren't you?"

Dana set down her coffee and scrutinized Sally's face. "Have we met?"

Sally coughed again and patted Dana's hand. "Sorry. Too many years smoking." She smiled. "I thought I recognized you from your pictures. Your mother was a good friend of mine. I still can't believe what happened to her."

"Thank you." Dana withdrew her hand from underneath Sally's. The woman's familiarity with her mother surprised her. How did they know each other? What kind of relationship had they had? Were they really friends? It was hard to believe—Sally didn't seem like the kind of person Agnes would have given the time of day to. "I'm sorry, where are my manners? Please, join me." She put her hand in her lap and discreetly wiped it on the bottom of her shirt.

"Thanks." Sally slid into the booth and watched as Dana took another sip of coffee. "Is there anything I can do for you?"

"Well…" Dana paused and looked at the older woman.

"What?" Sally asked.

"How did you and—" Dana was startled by the sound of a glass shattering somewhere behind her.

"Dorothy," Sally yelled at the other waitress. "Can you go tell that numb nuts that if he breaks one more dish, he's fired?"

Dorothy grumbled something under her breath.

"What was that, dear?"

"Nothing," Dorothy assured her. "I didn't say a thing." She headed into the kitchen as Sally shook her head.

"Just can't get good help these days," she told Dana. "Know what I mean?"

Dana, unsettled by the woman's rudeness to her employee, smiled weakly.

"You were saying?" the waitress asked.

Dana shook her head. "Nothing."

"Well, can I bring you something special for lunch? A nice salad, maybe?" Sally gave Dana the once-over and shook her head. "No, you look more like the meat-and-potatoes type. How about some homemade meat loaf?"

"Sure. That would be great."

Sally picked up the coffee pot and headed back toward the grill. Her huge sneakers made that annoying *sweek, sweek* sound shoes make when the floor is sticky and hasn't been mopped in a while. Dana tried to ignore it. While she waited for her lunch to arrive, she looked around the diner. There were Moo Cow creamers on the tables; a pink clock in the shape of an old Chevy Bel Air hung on the wall over the register; the famous diner picture whose customers were James Dean, Marilyn Monroe, and Elvis filled the wall behind the counter. A genuine Rock-Ola stood in the corner.

She fished several quarters out of her purse and strolled over to the jukebox. It had a lot of good songs. Golden Oldies: *Rock Around the Clock, That Old Black Magic, Chain Gang.* She flipped through the list until she finally found what she was looking for: *Earth Angel* and Doris Day's *Love Me or Leave Me.*

She dumped four quarters into the slot, punched H-12 and I-9, put both hands on the sides of the machine and watched as the record arm reached in, grabbed the first record, put it on the spindle and set the needle on the vinyl.

At first, the only sound that came from the Rock-Ola was static. Round and round the record went. Finally, when the song started, she went back to her seat and rested her head on the back of the booth. It felt good to relax a little and let someone else take care of things for a change.

"Dana?"

Her eyes fluttered open. A huge slab of meatloaf slathered in brown sugared tomato sauce, mashed potatoes drenched in margarine, green beans with real bacon and cling peaches swimming in heavy syrup sat in front of her.

Dana rubbed her eyes. "Must have dozed off." She turned the plate so that the peaches were directly in front of her. "Wow," she said. "This smells so good."

It reminded her of that long ago slumber party. After the catfight with Melissa, her mother had surprised her with this same meal. Ever since that night, this simple meal, this simple comfort, always made her feel better. *One woman's chocolate.*

"Dig in." Sally handed her a set of silverware rolled up in a paper napkin, then stood there and watched as Dana did exactly that.

"Oh, my God," she moaned with pleasure. "This is delicious." She forked another piece of meatloaf covered with mashed potatoes into her mouth, then stopped in mid-chew. "Wait a minute. Is this—"

Sally nodded. "You bet. Your momma gave me the recipe, right down to the peaches. Said it was your favorite meal when you were a little girl. Been my Monday night special for the past five years."

Dana dabbed at her eyes with the rough paper napkin. "Sorry. Dumb things seem to come and go as they please these days."

"Well, it's no wonder, what with everything that's going on."

"Maybe so," Dana agreed. "Even still, I don't normally cry at the drop of a hat."

"I know."

Dana paused, her fork in mid-air. "How do you know?"

Sally shrugged. "Agnes talked about you a lot."

"She did?" *Mother talked about me? When she wouldn't even talk* to *me? How crazy is that?*

"Dana," Sally said gently. "Your mother loved you very much. She used to show everyone your Academy graduation picture. Lord, how she'd go on about how beautiful you looked in your uniform."

Dana put down her fork, her appetite gone. They'd wasted so much time, she and her mother, time that they'd never be able to get back. She choked down the rest of her lunch, wiped off her mouth and gathered up her things.

She was scooting out of the booth when Sally appeared as if out of thin air. "How about some fresh apple pie?" she asked.

"Thanks, but I'm stuffed." Dana took a final swig of coffee, now cold, and felt around inside her purse, looking for her wallet. She didn't want to open it wide enough to let Sally see that she carried a concealed weapon. No sense alarming her.

"How about a piece to go?" Sally persisted.

Dana shook her head. "Just the check."

Sally waved her hand in Dana's general direction. "It's on me."

"Oh, no, you don't have to do that."

"But I want to," Sally told her. "Hell, it's the least I can do for Agnes's pride and joy."

"Thanks," Dana said quietly.

It was hard to believe the things Sally had said about her mother, especially since she'd always acted like she didn't give a rat's ass about her own daughter. To think that her mother might actually have been proud of her was mind-boggling.

"My pleasure." Sally stacked Dana's dirty dishes. "Come back anytime."

"I will," Dana agreed. "Have a good one."

She watched Sally disappear into the kitchen. *I don't understand any of this. This woman doesn't seem to have any reason to lie, but her claim to have been friends with Mother just doesn't ring true. How could she have been so totally different to me than she apparently was to the rest of the world?*

As she headed to her car, Dana noticed a dark blue sedan as it cruised the next row. The heavily tinted windows kept her from seeing the driver. It felt like she was being paced. She fished inside her purse for her notepad, intending to cross over to the same row and write down the license plate number, but before she could, the sedan accelerated and shot away.

What was that all about? Probably nothing, but just in case it was somehow connected to everything that was going on lately, to her feeling that things weren't quite right, she made a note of the incident, jotting down a description of the vehicle: dark blue Honda Accord, possibly 1999 or 2000, with illegally tinted windows. After she returned her notepad and pen to her purse, Dana studied the cars in the small parking lot servicing not only the restaurant, but also the bank, a hobby shop, a Mexican mercado, and a strip club. Three older men stood just outside the door to the club, smoking cigarettes and laughing. They glanced her way before they tossed their butts onto the sidewalk and went back inside.

Dana turned and looked down the street just as someone crossed at the end of the block. He was too far away for her to distinguish his features beyond medium height and slender build. Whoever it was wore dark clothing and a baseball cap. He might even have been the guy who nearly knocked her over coming out of the diner when she first arrived, but she couldn't be sure.

Since he was walking away from her, and the three pervs had disappeared back inside the club, she headed home, figuring there was no real reason to worry.

Except that her instincts told her otherwise.

CHAPTER 11

Eager to begin her investigation, but with no idea who could have killed her mother or why, the only place she felt she could conceivably start was to search for her mother's will. Perhaps it would establish a motive, but even if it didn't, she still needed to find it in order to discover what funeral arrangements her mother had made.

The obvious place to start was in her mother's office. She only hoped the keys to the filing cabinets weren't somewhere in Mother's bedroom. That would be just her luck, to be so close and yet so far. If that turned out to be the case, she'd have to hope Brian would release the crime scene sooner rather than later.

As she turned onto her mother's street, a little boy ran out in front of her car. She slammed on the brakes, yanking the wheel away from him as he shot past her front bumper, and hoped she wouldn't hit him.

The car skidded to a stop. She threw the gearshift into park, scrambled out the door, and ran to where the child stood, a red rubber ball tucked under his arm. He had a bewildered smile on his face, like he didn't fully understand what had just happened.

"Are you okay?" Dana crouched and took him by the arms to give him a quick once-over. He seemed okay.

"Hank?" someone called to the boy from behind them. Dana rose and turned to look. Steve walked across his lawn in long, efficient strides. "Hank, what're you doing over there?"

Dana led Hank across the street, her arm protectively around his shoulders. "He ran right out in front of me."

Steve bent down to look Hank in the eye. "You okay, buddy?"

"Sure, Uncle Steve." He stepped closer to Steve and smiled at him. Dana noticed the same lopsided grin that she'd seen on Steve during their pre-dawn b-ball game.

He put his hands on his hips and looked at Hank sternly. "Why'd you do that?" he asked. "You know better than to chase a ball into the street without looking first."

The little boy held out the ball as if for inspection and looked sheepishly down at the ground. "Sorry," he mumbled, shifting back and forth on his red and black Johnny Romano's. "I forgot."

Steve ruffled his hair, and Dana smiled. He reminded her of Teyo, who was a year or two older than Hank but had the same smattering of freckles and shock of black hair.

How she missed José and the kids. Remembering the promise she'd made, she vowed to have the kids over just as soon as things settled down.

Steve took Hank by the hand and the three of them stepped onto the curb. "Now tell Dana you're sorry," he directed.

"Sorry." Hank looked up at her with his head cocked and one eye shut. "Hey, are you the Dana my uncle thinks is hot?"

"Hank!" Steve's cheeks flushed the color of a grade

school eraser. He cleared his throat loudly. "Why don't you go get yourself a fudgy bar?"

"Okay." Hank smiled at Dana and ran across the grass to the gate that led to the back yard. As he stepped through it, he turned back to them and giggled. "He's gonna ask you out," he shouted. "On a date."

He giggled again and disappeared into the back yard, slamming the gate behind him.

Dana walked back to her car. She'd left the door open when she flew out to check on the boy, and now she stood behind it as if to shield herself from Steve and anything he might ask.

She didn't know if what the boy had shouted was true, but it was her experience that kids his age usually told the truth, at least when they didn't think they were about to get into trouble. "So, Hank's your nephew?"

Steve nodded. "Maracella's kid."

He turned and looked at the front of his house. Hank munched on a chocolate ice cream bar and watched them through the curtains.

When he realized Steve had seen him, he quickly disappeared.

"I'm helping my sister out," Steve said. "But I'd spend time with him even if she didn't need the help. Hank and I are tight. He's my little buddy."

"Really? Somehow I don't see you as the 'favorite uncle' type."

He cocked his head and smiled. "But then," he countered, "you don't really know me now, do you?"

He had a point. Dana shook her head and reached up for a strand of hair to twirl around her fingers. "No, I guess not."

"Well, we'll just have to remedy that situation, won't we?"

Oh, no. Here it comes.

"Look, I'm having a little get-together later and I was hoping you were free and could drop by."

"Here?"

"Yeah, here. In the back yard." He gestured over his shoulder. "On the patio. Bug spray optional."

She squinted up at him. "So, Hank was right. You were planning on asking me out."

"Okay, you caught me. I couldn't have done it without him. But it's not a date."

"No?" she asked. "Then what do you call it?"

"I call it asking my new neighbor to come over and have a beer, meet some people, take her mind off things. Maybe even relax a little. If you're able to relax at all, that is."

Oh, brother. Had he really challenged her again? "Thanks, but I don't think so."

"Aw, come on," he coaxed, leaning against the top of the car door. "Who knows? You might even enjoy yourself."

She doubted it, but he was right about one thing. She did need to relax. She felt all keyed up, and wasn't looking forward to an evening with Mother's files. Besides, she could ask around a little, maybe find someone who knew something about what was going on. It was worth a shot.

"What time?" she asked as she climbed into the car and shut the door.

"About five-thirty, six. Hank's going to teach me how to barbeque some burgers and dogs." He stepped back as Dana started up the car. "Could even throw on a steak or two, if you prefer."

"Sounds good," Dana said as she put the car into gear. "Maybe I'll see you later."

"Hope so."

As Dana steered her car into her mother's driveway,

she wondered who would be at the party, and what, if anything, she'd be able to learn about her mother's murder.

ᏋᎧᏋᎧ

Before she even got out of the car, she could hear Charlie barking shrilly. Dana reached across to the passenger-side floorboard and bent to gather her things. Her purse had flown off the seat when she'd slammed on the brakes to avoid hitting Hank, and the entire contents had dumped out onto the floor: her firearm, wallet, assorted paper clips, pens, note pad, even a long-forgotten roll of Tums. She shoved everything except her house keys back into her purse then got out of the car and hurried to the front door, hoping she'd make it before Charlie had an accident. By the time she got the door open, the dog was frantically bouncing around doing her pee-pee dance.

"Okay, okay," Dana told her. "I get it. You need to go out. Stop yelling at me."

She let the dog out and stood by the back door while Charlie went about her business. She should get started, work her way methodically through her mother's things, but she just couldn't face it yet.

"Want to go for a walk?" she asked when Charlie was ready to come back inside. Dana grabbed her leash and harness off the hook by the front door where she'd hung them when she first brought Charlie over. Growing up, it had been where her mother insisted they all hang their keys when they came home. Her way of keeping tabs on them. God, was it only yesterday that she'd come home? That she'd lost her mother and the last of her family? It was starting to hit her.

As they walked the four blocks to the park, Dana mused over the events of the past few days. She'd met Steve, who had seized upon her mother's death to...

what? Be a good neighbor and offer his help? Be her friend? Or was there something else? Something sinister? She wondered if he had some ulterior motive for his friendly "welcome to the neighborhood, so sorry about your mom" routine.

She tried to take her mind off things and just enjoy their walk. The old neighborhood hadn't changed much the whole time she lived here, or since she moved away, for that matter. The few leaves left on the oak trees lining the street were varying shades of red, orange, and umber. Charlie was having fun leaping on piles of leaves that had collected on the sidewalk and sniffing every blade of grass.

The tiny neighborhood park was filled with brightly colored playground equipment, a basketball half-court, and several picnic areas that included barbeques. Small children played and laughed in the early afternoon sun, their mothers gabbing on benches that bracketed the playground. A flash of color swooshed down the slide, and Dana caught a glimpse of bright green frogs. Men raced back and forth on the basketball court, shouting insults at each other. A gaggle of pre-teen girls sat on top of one of the picnic tables, chattering and giggling among themselves, presumably gossiping about the thundering herd of adolescent boys playing football while studiously ignoring the girls.

Dana was glad that the park had been cleaned up. It was a run-down mess when she'd left home. Now it was clean and well-maintained. The City had finally installed light standards and neighborhood families no longer fled the park before dark. Once again, it was a place where parents could let their children play safely in a clean environment.

They crossed the street and entered the park. The big wooden sign proudly proclaimed it *Premier Park* in bright blue letters. It was a testament to the neighborhood that it hadn't yet been tagged.

"Hey, Dana."

Steve walked toward her, a basketball tucked under his arm. Charlie growled, and Dana pulled on her leash and mumbled for her to knock it off.

"Hey, Steve. What are you doing here?" It seemed she always managed to say something stupid whenever this guy was around. He was playing basketball. Duh.

His hair glistened in the sun, perspiration plastering it to his head. The neck of his shirt was damp as well. Behind him, his friends stood on the basketball court, bent over with their hands on their knees, out of breath and trying not to keel over. Steve was barely even breathing hard.

He glanced warily at Charlie before he put his forearm up to his face and wiped off the sweat. Then he pointed over his shoulder with his thumb. "Shooting hoops."

"Oh." It was all she could think to say.

"Hank wanted to play on the slide, so I brought him over." He gestured to the court. "These guys begged me to teach them how to play."

"I heard that, you lying scumbag," one of the men cheerfully called out. Steve ignored him.

"What are you doing?" A smile slowly spread across his face. He was mocking her. Again.

"Me? I'm looking for Big Foot." If only he knew.

Steve chuckled. "Well," he said matter-of-factly as he made a production out of looking her over. "You seem to have lost your, your...hey, what do you hunt Sasquatch with, anyway?"

"Beats me." They looked at each other a second or two before they both burst out laughing. Dana had to admit it felt good.

"Hey, beautiful," one of the men on the court called out. "You want to toss the ball? Unless you plan on joining us any time this decade."

Steve lobbed the basketball to him. "You guys go ahead."

His friends grumbled but quickly resumed their game. Dana and Steve watched in silence for a few minutes. She was acutely aware of how close he stood. As much as she wanted to think of him as a possible suspect, she found it very difficult to do so. No use denying the attraction. It wasn't just that he was handsome in a rakish sort of way. There was something else about him, something she couldn't quite identify. Whatever it was, it put her on her guard. She didn't think he was capable of hurting anyone. Or was he?

Abruptly, she turned to face him. "I've got to go."

"See you tonight," he said.

On the walk home, she vacillated between looking forward to Steve's party and dreading it. It was too soon. She wasn't up to socializing, especially with people she didn't know. But she couldn't pass up an opportunity to find out more about the enigmatic Mr. Steve Campbell, and how well he really knew her mother.

At this point in time, he was merely a person of interest. In more ways than one. There was no way around it. She'd have to go to the party.

Only then would she know for sure.

CHAPTER 12

D
ana frowned as she approached Mother's front
porch. A large manila envelope leaned against
the door. Strange that someone would just leave
it like that. As she got closer, she could tell that there
were no delivery service markings on the envelope, so it
hadn't been delivered by any legitimate service. Maybe
the flower dude had left them. It wasn't a stretch to believe that since he'd hunted her down at the funeral, he
could know she was staying here. It was also possible
that he and the driver of the Honda at the diner were
somehow connected to the package, too. Which meant
that they could all be connected to her mother's murder.
Or not.

When she reached the steps, Dana's skin broke out in
goose bumps. Her name was scrawled across the front of
the envelope in large blue letters. She looked warily up
and down the street. Other than a few leaves blowing
along the gutters, though, nothing moved or appeared out
of the ordinary.

Only four people even knew she wasn't staying in
her own apartment: Brian, Maura, Finn, and Steve. Sally
might suspect she was staying at Agnes's place, although

she hadn't specifically mentioned it to her. And why would she have left anything for her, anyway? They'd never even met until a few hours ago.

Brian wouldn't have just left something sitting out in the open, not without at least a note or a call. Maura hadn't mentioned anything about having something delivered to her. Finn seemed angry about something, something he was obviously hiding from her, but she was pretty sure he would have given whatever it was to her in person, if for no other reason than to watch her face when she saw whatever it was.

But if it wasn't that guy from the funeral, the driver of the Honda, or any of her friends, then who?

The only one left was Steve.

Except he was still at the park. He couldn't have left it. So who did? And why?

The envelope looked innocent enough. She studied it closely before she bent to pick it up. No hidden wires. No powder or evidence that it was rigged to explode. She shook it gently and felt something slide around inside. After another quick glance up the street, where the faint sounds of children playing drifted over to her, Dana unlocked the door and headed inside. She set the deadbolt and considered the writing on the envelope. Plain block letters. She sniffed it. No unusual odor.

At the kitchen table, she carefully tore open the sealed flap, glanced inside, then turned the envelope over and dumped the contents onto the table. As she spread everything out, her stomach muscles clenched and the hair on her arms stood up. She had a sudden, almost overwhelming urge to get up and run back to the safety and comfort of her own apartment. Instead, she forced herself to look at the contents.

There were almost a dozen photographs, many faded and worn around the edges. A little girl of various ages, somewhere between two and seven, smiled back at her. The girl had thick, curly auburn hair. In several of the photographs, she was winding her hair around her fingers. Dana's stomach twisted in a fierce cramp.

They were all photographs of her.

ɛ∕ɔɛ∕ɔ

Dana's stomach continued to flip-flop as she examined each photo in turn. In one, she was sitting on a pony wearing a red felt cowboy hat. In another, she splashed around in a kiddie pool. You could see the end of a hose as it filled the pool with water, but you couldn't see who was holding it. Several photos were run-of-the-mill, we-have-nothing-better-to-do-so-let's-take-pictures-of-the-kids photos. Two were school pictures—kindergarten and second grade.

But the one that stood out the most, the one she actually remembered being taken, was the first time Mother let her bake cookies. She'd made a huge mess in the kitchen. Bowls, spoons, measuring cups and other assorted baking utensils all dirty and dripping on the counter. She was so little she had to stand on a small footstool so she could reach everything. Mother's Christmas apron was wrapped around her twice.

It looked like she'd dumped an entire bag of flour over her head. Cookie dough coated her face and hands. Since it smelled so good, she hadn't been able to resist sampling it, and had used a large wooden spoon. The picture had been snapped just as her jaws clamped down on it. She'd seen the camera at the last minute—her eyes were huge. The cat that swallowed the canary, her father had said. He was the one who'd taken the photo.

It was a mystery how they had gotten here, or who could've had them all these years. Or even why they'd been left at all. If there were any fingerprints or DNA on them, surely Maura could process them for her. Too late, she realized she shouldn't have touched anything without putting on some gloves, or at least held everything only by the corners.

Dana groaned and put her head in her hands. It just didn't make any sense. There were only three people in the world who would have cared enough to keep the photos all these years: her mother, her brother and her father. But they were all dead. Murdered. So who would have sent them to her?

Some people had genetic deformities or congenital weaknesses that ran in their family. She was beginning to think being a murder victim ran in hers.

The last thing she needed right now was for some freak to stalk her. She had enough on her mind. First the flowers, then the strange warning from Finn, now this. She needed answers. She reached for her cell phone and punched in the number for the crime lab.

"Forensics. Henderson."

"Maura? It's Dana."

"Hey, girl." Maura's voice changed from strictly business to sympathetic in a heartbeat. "How you holding up?"

"Okay, I guess." Dana ran her fingers through her hair, catching them in a small knot. "Listen, Maura," she said, working out the tangle with her fingertips. "Can you meet me for coffee?"

"When? Now?" The concern in Maura's voice touched her, and her burden eased just a bit.

"It'll take me about thirty minutes to get there," Dana told her.

"Well…"

"Please, Maura. I wouldn't ask if it weren't important."

"All right," Maura agreed. Then she lowered her voice. "Hold on a sec."

Dana could hear some muffled conversation through the phone before Maura came back on the line. "Sorry. That was close. Didn't know if you wanted Lieutenant Jackson to know I was talking to you."

"You're right. I don't. Particularly with what I need to talk to you about." Brian would be pissed that she was sticking her nose into an active investigation—his investigation—particularly when he'd specifically told her to butt out. Not to mention asking Maura to use department time and resources for personal business.

"Dana," Maura asked. "What's wrong?"

"Nothing. I'll see you in a half. The usual place. My treat." Dana stared at the photos spread out before her. She couldn't help but wonder again who had sent them. With the exception of the one of her in the kiddie pool, where all you could see of the person holding the hose was a bare foot and what she could only assume was her father's hairy leg, she was the only one in each of the pictures, and it made her very uncomfortable. After all, once upon a time they'd been a family of four. Mother, father, big brother, and little sister. So how come there weren't any snapshots of them?

She stacked the photos and dropped them back into the envelope, using the hem of her tee shirt to carefully tuck in the flap. Without a zippered storage bag big enough to put the envelope into, she'd have to make do, so she pulled out a plastic grocery sack and used it to protect the envelope from further contamination.

Dana grabbed her purse and hoodie, stuck the bag under her arm and opened the front door warily. No way was she going to leave herself vulnerable again. After a last look up and down the street, she walked out to her car and climbed inside, tossed everything onto the passenger seat and glanced at the envelope before starting the engine.

She was pretty sure the photographs were somehow tied to her mother's murder. But were they a warning of some kind? Could she be next?

⁂

Forty minutes later, Dana and Maura were sipping lattes in a small coffee house two blocks from the station.

"Okay, Sinclair," Maura said. "Fess up. Why all the cloak and dagger stuff?"

Dana took a big sip of coffee, then pulled the envelope out of her purse and laid it on the table between them. "I need your help."

"You got it."

Dana fiddled with a corner of the envelope before pushing it toward her friend. "I found this on Mother's front porch a little while ago."

Maura raised an eyebrow but didn't reach for it. Instead, she picked up her coffee and gestured with it. "What's in the envelope, Dana?"

Dana shifted uncomfortably and looked around the coffee house. One man, average height and weight, blond spiky hair, mid-twenties, sat behind a laptop in the WiFi section. A trio of middle-schoolers played on their iPhones at the only other occupied table. A young, harried-looking woman wrestled a stroller full of twins out the door. Nothing out of place. Dana leaned forward and spoke in hushed tones. "There's a dozen photographs in here." She patted the envelope.

"Photographs?" Maura asked. "Of what?"

"Of me. As a kid. I need you to lift any fingerprints there might be on these things."

"Why? Where'd they come from?"

"I'm not sure." She looked up at Maura and was re-lieved to see the concern on her face. "Can you do it?"

Maura took another sip of her coffee as she glanced around before scooping the envelope into her purse. "If whoever sent them to you licked the seal," she said, "then I might be able to test for DNA, too."

"I was hoping you'd say that," Dana said, smiling at her. "Thanks, Maura. Thanks a lot." She paused. "And let's keep this on the down low, okay? At least for a while."

"Understood." Maura paused. She seemed to be de-bating about whether or not she should say something. "This have anything to do with your mom's murder?"

"I'm not sure."

"Well," Maura said. "I'll process everything as soon as I can and let you know when I have the results. On the off chance I do find any DNA, I'll run it through CODIS for you." She hesitated. "But, Dana?"

"What?"

"You know CODIS is only a DNA indexing system, right? It'll only give us positive results if the DNA is al-ready in the system and we have a sample from a suspect to match it against."

"I know. Just see if there's a match. Then we'll wor-ry about a suspect."

Maura looked at Dana for a moment before she nod-ded at her friend. "Right."

"Thanks again. I owe you one."

"Eh," Maura said, waving her off. "What are friends for?" She pushed her chair back, took a final swig of her latte, and stood up. "I'd better be getting back. I'll call you when I know something. Thanks for the coffee."

Dana watched her friend as she headed back to work. With any luck, Dana would soon be back as well. And after the party tonight, maybe she'd be one step closer to finding her mother's killer.

CHAPTER 13

Having Maura process the photographs was a step toward finding out what was going on, and whether or not they were connected to her mother's murder. It helped her relax a little. While she waited for the results, she needed to start looking for her mother's will. It was already after two o'clock. In about three hours, she'd have to get ready for Steve's party, which didn't leave much time to search, but it would at least give her a decent start.

Standing in the doorway to her mother's office, she took a moment to look around. There was a battle-worn desk, scarred by years of abuse but still sturdy after all these years; an ancient VGA computer monitor; a wooden desk chair in only slightly better condition than the desk; two gunmetal gray filing cabinets; a small clock radio; and, surprisingly enough, a treadmill in the corner. Everything else reminded her of the woman who had raised her. Austere. No nonsense. But a treadmill? She tried to picture her mother working out, but it was no use. The image just wouldn't come. Sighing, she decided to start by looking through the desk, but as she headed toward it, she frowned.

"Wait," she said. "What happened to Mother's computer? Monitor's here, but where's the tower?" Had it gone on the fritz? Damn thing was about a hundred years old. Maybe she'd taken it in for repairs. If so, there'd be a work order. But where would she have kept it? A glance at the corkboard above the desk showed it hadn't been tacked up there, so she must have filed it somewhere.

"No time like the present," she said then smiled and shook her head sadly.

One of her mother's favorite sayings. Mother had frequently told her that, with her curiosity, astonishing blue eyes, and love of the force, she was just like her father, but Dana suspected there was more of her mother's practical side to her than either woman was willing to admit.

More than an hour later, Dana had finally finished the top drawer in the bigger file cabinet. *Only three more to go—in* this *cabinet.* Each drawer was packed solid with file folders, all neatly arranged and labeled. It seemed like Mother had saved every utility bill, bank statement, financial statement from the accounting firm, and credit card bill since they'd left Nebraska twenty years ago. There were insurance policies, cancelled checks, even birth certificates and childhood immunization records for both Dana and her brother.

Dana went through each folder carefully and reviewed every page before moving on to the next one. She was sweating heavily in the balmy autumn afternoon and slammed the drawer shut before crossing to the half-open window. There was no air conditioning—her mother wouldn't allow it. Too much pampering, she'd told them, led to lazy children, which in turn led to shiftless adults.

Dana leaned across the treadmill to push the window the rest of the way open and was standing in front of it enjoying the breeze when her cell phone rang.

"'Lo." She wiped the sweat off her forehead with the back of her arm. "Sinclair."

"Dana?" the tiny voice asked diminutively.

"Teyo?" Dana asked. "Honey, what's wrong?"

"Can I come over?"

Dana didn't like the way the little boy sounded. Tired beyond his years, but something else was there, too. Something she couldn't immediately identify. "What's the matter?"

"Nothing," he tried to assure her. "I just miss you."

"Teyo," Dana said patiently. "I know something's wrong. I can hear it in your voice."

The little boy was silent. He reminded her so much of José. She pictured him holding the phone up to his ear, lower lip stuck out sullenly, dark eyebrows knitted fiercely together, and smiled in spite of her concern. "Teyo?"

"Everyone's always crying over here," the boy blurted out. "Buela's sad all the time, Lolo never says a word. And Gracie keeps having bad dreams."

"Your sister's having nightmares?"

"Yeah," Teyo told her. "Keeps calling out for Papa." He paused, and Dana could hear his breath hitch. The boy was close to tears himself. "But he never comes."

"Oh, honey. I'm so sorry. I know you miss your dad."

"That's not it!" he said. "It's not."

"I miss him, too."

"So can I come over or not?"

How could she tell him no without hurting his feelings? But she couldn't very well tell him that her mother had been murdered just like his dad. Or that she was investigating Mother's murder but not José's.

"Now's really not a good time—" she tried to explain, but he cut her off.

"Fine."

"Let me finish, little man. I'm not at home right now, but I could get you and Gracie in a day or so. Hey," she said brightly. "I met a boy about your age the other day, name's Hank. You could come over to my mom's house and play ball or something with him. How's that sound?"

When Teyo didn't answer, Dana wanted to reach into the phone and grab him, pull him through, and hug him until he squirmed.

"Teyo?"

The little boy breathed heavily into the phone. His gloom nearly broke her heart. "Okay," he finally said in that same tiny voice with which he'd said hello.

"You know you can always call me, right?"

"Yeah."

"And you also know that I'll do anything for you, don't you?"

"Yeah."

"So I'll give your buela a call in a day or so and set it up, okay?"

"'Kay."

"Now, you call me if you need me before then," she told him. "I love you, sweetie pie."

"'Kay."

She looked at her watch and saw that it was almost five. Time to get ready to go next door. Hopefully, she'd done the right thing by putting Teyo off. It just wouldn't do for the kids to come over with her all distracted, unable to pay them the attention that they obviously needed. She had to focus on solving Mother's murder as quickly as possible and consequences be damned.

CHAPTER 14

Just after five-thirty, she made her way up the driveway past Steve's blue Honda Accord and his beat up white work truck and stood in front of his door. She'd cleaned up and donned a simple green sheath and sandals.

Butterflies flittered around in her stomach, and she placed her hand on it in an effort to soothe them. She'd rather face a hopped-up drug dealer protecting his stash than attend this party. At least then she'd have her service weapon to comfort her. She took a deep breath, knocked sharply on the door, and was taken aback when a beautiful woman with hair as dark as a raven's back opened it.

"Oh." It was all Dana could think to say.

"Yes?" The beauty smiled cautiously. With her jagged bangs swooping down across one exotic blue eye, Dana was reminded of Mary J. Blige, although as she recalled, the R&B singer actually had brown eyes and skin. But the hairstyle was the same, and both women shared the same guarded smile.

Before Dana had a chance to respond, a small freckled face with the same startling blue eyes framed by curly black hair poked its way around the woman at the door, followed by a pudgy finger pointing right at Dana's head.

"Mom, that's Uncle Steve's friend," Hank said as he stepped out from around the woman. "The one he thinks is so hot." He threw her a little wave. "Hiya."

"Hi." Dana blushed. "I'm Dana." She gestured back over her shoulder. "I'm staying next door, at my mom's."

The woman took her hand and shook it. "Maracella Duplanchier, Steve's sister."

Hank pushed past his mother and raced back into the house. "Five more minutes, young man," Maracella told him sternly then turned back to Dana and rolled her eyes. "Video games." She stepped back and held the door open. "Please, come in."

"Thanks." Dana went inside and Maracella closed the door behind her.

"I'm so sorry about your mother, Dana."

"Thank you."

Maracella led her past Hank and his very loud attack on some alien lizards and onto the patio.

Steve and another man were drinking Miller Genuine Draft and discussing the latest Robert Rodriguez movie. The other man was smoking a nasty-smelling cigar the size of a baseball bat, and Dana could barely contain the cough straining to get out.

"Boys, our company is here." As they turned in their seats to see who it was, Maracella introduced Dana. "Honey, this is Dana from next door. My husband, Jaleel." She turned to Dana. "I'm sorry, what's your last name?"

Before she could respond, Steve jumped up from his beach chair, nearly knocking it over in the process. Dana brought her hand up to her mouth to hide a giggle.

"Dana." He kissed her cheek. "I'm sure glad you came. I was just telling old Jay here that you've got the cutest little dog."

Right. She struggled to keep from frowning at the blatant lie and wouldn't have been surprised if Steve hated Charlie as much as Charlie hated him. Jaleel stood and offered his hand, which she took, grateful for the distraction. "Nice to meet you."

Maracella grabbed his arm. "Come on, honey. Help me make the salad."

"But I haven't finished my beer," he whined.

She tugged on his arm and practically dragged him as she called out to her son. "Wrap it up, tiger. Dinner will be ready soon."

"Aw, Mom," Hank whined, sounding just like his father.

"Now."

"Just don't expect me to tear the lettuce into nice little bite-sized pieces for you," Jaleel grumbled as they brushed past Dana and headed into the kitchen.

Steve gestured toward the patio. "Have a seat," he said.

"Thanks." She chose the patio chair that faced the huge gas barbeque. The redwood chair had a purple-and-green print cushion and was surprisingly comfortable. She settled back and felt her anxiety ease.

Steve sat down next to her and reached into the cooler beside his chair. "Beer?" He pulled out an ice-cold MGD, popped the cap and handed the bottle to her.

"Great." She reached for it and absently brushed away the water that dripped onto her knee. So far, only Steve's sister and her family were here. Not many people to question, but maybe they'd be able to help anyway. "So." She took a polite sip of beer. "Who all's coming to this shindig?"

"You mean besides you?"

"And your family." She waved her beer in the general direction of the kitchen.

"Well, let's see." Steve tilted his head and looked up at the sky. He counted on his fingers. "There's you, and me. Hank, Maracella, and Jay." He flashed his smile at her. "That's what, five?"

She nodded.

"Then I guess everyone's here."

Confused, she took a sip of beer then turned to him. "I thought you said this was a party."

"Don't believe I ever used the word 'party' in the invite. I think I called it a 'get-together.'"

Disappointed that there wouldn't be more opportunities to gather information, she nevertheless felt positive she could uncover something just by chatting with Maracella. She seemed friendly enough, and was obviously close to Steve. Maybe she'd seen or heard something useful.

She shrugged. "Whatever," she said. After setting the beer down, she stood and stretched. "Think I'll see if Maracella needs any help."

"Hey, don't be mad." Steve grabbed her wrist as she walked past. "I invited a couple other people from work, but they couldn't make it."

"Don't be silly," she told him, twisting her wrist out of his grasp. "Why would I be mad?" *Disappointed, yes, but not mad.*

"Tell that bum of a husband of hers to come out and help me with the barbeque," Steve called after her.

"I heard that," Jaleel yelled cheerily from inside. As Dana entered the kitchen, he passed her carrying a platter of burger patties and wienies. "Got to watch him, make sure he doesn't turn everything into charcoal briquettes," Jaleel told her on his way out.

Maracella sliced tomatoes at the counter. "Those two," she said to no one in particular, a faint smile on her face. She looked over at Dana and her smile widened. "Hey."

"Hey," Dana replied. "Need any help?"

"Well, since it seems I lost my first helper, can you check the potatoes?" Marcella nodded toward the oven. "They've been baking over an hour."

"Sure," Dana agreed. "Fork?"

"Third drawer over. Plate's on the counter there."

Dana grabbed a fork and stuck it into the potatoes. She pulled out the seven medium-sized foil wrapped potatoes that were done and left two to cook a little longer. "My God, you expecting an army?" Dana asked. "I thought we were the only ones coming tonight."

Maracella shrugged. "We're potato people, I guess."

Dana laughed. "Guess so. What else?"

Maracella waved a knife dripping with tomato seeds in the general direction of the refrigerator. "Can you pull out the sour cream and butter? And would you mind prepping the lettuce for the burgers?"

"No problem." They worked quietly for a few minutes. Dana was just about to start a conversation about Steve and her mother when Maracella bellowed unexpectedly.

"Hank! Turn off that damn game and come set the table. Now."

She turned to Dana. "Sorry about that. He'd sit there forever if I let him."

The sounds of alien destruction ended, and Hank wandered into the kitchen. After glaring at his mother, he disappeared into the pantry. When he came out, he was juggling bright blue plastic plates and matching cups. He set them down on the counter behind Maracella with a bang, yanked open a drawer and extracted the correct amount of plastic cutlery, then shut the drawer just as loudly. The little boy, who could barely see over the counter, juggled the dinnerware and stomped outside to set the patio table.

Once he was safely out the door, the women looked at each other and burst out laughing.

"Shh," Maracella hushed, then giggled some more. "He'll hear us."

"Sorry. But he's just so cute, I want to take him home and put him up on a shelf."

"I know. Everyone does," Maracella cooed. "Steve was the same way at that age."

"So," Dana asked casually. "Are you and Steve close?"

"Yep. Always have been, even when we were little." Maracella arranged the tomatoes on a plate where she'd also arranged red onion and bread and butter pickle slices. "What about you? Any siblings?"

"Just a brother."

"Are you close?"

Dana shook her head. "We were."

"Were?" Maracella asked. "You mean he's not around anymore?"

"No, he died a few years ago."

"Oh, Dana." Maracella wiped her hands off on a kitchen towel and turned to face her. "I'm sorry. I shouldn't have asked."

"That's okay. Really. But I was wondering," she continued. "Did you know my mother?"

Was that a slight hesitation before the other woman responded?

"No, I didn't. I mean, not really. I met her once or twice. She'd wave to us if she was gardening when we came to visit Steve. And of course, Hank adored her." She lowered her voice. "We haven't told him yet."

That blew Dana away. Hank adored her mother? How was that even possible? "They were close?"

"Oh, yeah. What with her right next door to Hank's favorite uncle, and the whole park thing, they couldn't help but be close."

"Park thing? What park thing?"

"You didn't know?"

Dana shook her head.

"Agnes headed up the committee to save the park from being sold to someone who wanted to build a restaurant or something on the land. Raised most of the money herself."

Dana wanted to question Maracella further, ask more about the park and about Steve's relationship with Agnes, but when she grabbed the condiments and toppings and nodded at the potatoes, Dana had no choice but to follow her out to the patio.

Any further questioning would have to wait until later. But, Dana assured herself, she would question her further. And hopefully get to the bottom of things.

CHAPTER 15

She'd had a surprisingly good time at Steve's house, in spite of the fact that she hadn't had a chance to question Maracella further, or Jaleel either. She'd fully intended to go through her mother's papers some more when she got home. But as soon as she walked in the door a little after midnight, she realized she was pooped—or pizzle-sprung, as her brother used to say. Little Hank had crapped out about ten and was snoring softly on the couch when she left. They seemed to be as close a family as they'd all claimed. Jaleel had told Maracella, as they were getting ready to leave, that they should just let Hank sleep and they could pick him up in the morning. Steve had seemed pleased to have the little dynamo.

Dana hung up her purse and keys, peeled off her sweater, and let it drop to the floor. Despite having a good time, she'd felt something in the air, almost as though she were being watched. But that was ridiculous. Who would have watched her at Steve's?

After Charlie went out, they both collapsed onto the couch. Charlie immediately fell asleep, but Dana wasn't so lucky. Her brain just wouldn't turn off, and she found herself looking back over her day. Somewhere around the conversation at dinner, she finally dozed off.

When she woke up the next morning, she was still on the couch, draped across Charlie with her cheek resting on the dog's hindquarters. Drool had puddled beneath her and she could feel the little black hairs Charlie shed winter and summer glued to the corner of her mouth. She wiped them off and sat up.

"Ow." There was an enormous crick in her neck. Hoping a long hot shower would help work out the kinks, she let Charlie out and headed down the hall to the bathroom. She started the shower, had just pulled off her clothes, and the doorbell rang.

"Oh, that's just great," she muttered as she pulled the sheath back over her head. "What moron rings someone's bell at..." She glanced at her watch and couldn't believe that it was already nine o'clock. She shut off the shower and walked quickly down the hall.

Brian, dressed in tan chinos and a tight blue golf shirt, was at the door. He nodded at Dana. "Morning."

"Morning." Dana felt exposed, and crossed her arms over her chest. She'd left her bra on the bathroom floor. "What are you doing here?"

"Don't you ever listen to your voice mail?"

"You left me a voice mail?" She hadn't even heard the phone ring. "Sorry. What's up? You find out who killed Mother already?"

"We going to play twenty questions right out here on the front porch, or do you plan on letting me in anytime soon?"

"Oh, right. Sorry." Dana stepped back and motioned him inside. "I was just about to put on some coffee," she lied. "Would you like a cup?"

"Sure, why not."

"Have a seat. I'll be back in a minute."

While she started the coffee, her mind went straight to the investigation. It was possible they had uncovered a serious lead into who killed her mother. They might have even arrested someone.

Before the coffee pot had a chance to finish brewing completely, Dana pulled two mugs out of the cupboard and filled them half-way. When she went back into the living room, Charlie was standing in Brian's lap, stretched out as long as she could make herself, giving him a multitude of kisses.

"Charlie!" Dana laughed at her strong display of doggie affection. "Get down from there."

Tail wagging and eyes sparkling, Charlie turned and eyed Dana for a second then went right back to licking his face. Brian laughed and tried unsuccessfully to push the dog away.

"Charlie," Dana repeated more sternly. "I said, get down." She put the mugs on the coffee table and grabbed her off Brian's lap. She set the dog down on the floor and ignored the fact that Charlie was giving her the stink eye.

"How did you get in here, anyway?" Dana asked her. "I thought you were outside."

Brian chuckled and wiped the dog slobber from his face with the back of his arm. "Oh, that was my fault. I let her in." He patted the couch. Charlie jumped up next to him and seemed quite pleased with herself. She rolled over and Brian immediately obliged by rubbing her belly.

"Such a cute little girl." He reached for the coffee Dana had set in front of him, took a sip and grimaced. "I see your culinary skills haven't improved. Got any sugar?"

"Yeah." Dana went into the kitchen, filled a small glass custard dish with some sugar from her mother's baking supply, took out a tablespoon from the drawer, and went back into the living room. When she handed the dish and spoon to him, Brian raised his eyebrow but took them without comment. She sat at the opposite end of the couch and blew on her coffee while she watched him sweeten his. He took a tentative sip, grimaced again, and dumped in three more spoonsful. Just when she felt she couldn't stand the silence any longer, he put his coffee down.

"Well," he began. "Since you didn't listen to your voicemail yet, you're probably wondering why I'm here." When she started to say something, he held up his hand and continued.

"Three reasons. First of all, I wanted to let you know that the coroner has released your mother's body. They need to know where to send her…"

He trailed off and shifted in his seat. It was obvious he was very uncomfortable. Dana had always found his compassion endearing. It was good to know that the job hadn't made him completely callous like it had so many others she'd come in contact with over the years. She hoped it never would.

"I think Mother might have had a particular mortuary in mind, but I have to find her will first."

He nodded. "Second, we have a lead on your mother's case. Seems she filed a report three days before she was killed."

"What kind of report?"

He pulled out his notebook, flipped through a few pages, then stopped and looked up at her. "A six-forty-seven."

Dana frowned. "Disorderly conduct?"

"Six-forty-seven, sections h and i. Apparently, she heard someone in the back yard, but didn't see anyone, then a little while later, she thought she saw a shadow move outside the bedroom slider. That's when she called us."

Every muscle in Dana's body tensed. That same feeling came over her again, the one she had when she got home from Steve's barbeque. That feeling of having been watched. "She had a peeping Tom? Why didn't anyone tell me about this?"

"Calm down, Dana." He pulled a tiny Tootsie Roll out of his pocket and popped it into his mouth.

"Don't tell me to calm down." She stood up and started to pace. "No disrespect intended, Brian, but what the hell? Six days ago, someone came onto my mother's property, and what? Peeked in a window at her?"

Brian nodded. "The uniform who responded looked around outside, but there was no sign of anyone." He inspected his notebook again. "Just a broken azalea or two."

"And it took three days after she was murdered for the incident to come to your attention? Has anyone followed up on it?"

Brian picked up Charlie, who had climbed into his lap and fallen asleep, and gently placed her on the couch next to him. He stood and brushed off as much of the dog hair she'd shed on his pants as he could. Dana paced up and down the room, twisting a thick strand of hair around her fingers. She tried to calm down and think before she blurted anything else out. She'd just questioned his ability to do his job, but dammit. How could something as potentially important as a prowler slip through the cracks? It made her wonder what else had been overlooked.

Brian reached out and took hold of her arm as she paced by him. His grasp was not gentle. "Better watch it, Dana. I'm not the enemy here."

"I know. I'm sorry," she mumbled. "It's just that something like that could turn into a useful lead." He released her arm, and even though it hurt like hell, she re-sisted rubbing it.

"I'm well aware of that. I know how to do my job. Look," Brian told her, his tone softening a little. "I know you're upset. It's no wonder, what with everything that's happened the past few weeks."

Damn straight I'm upset. I'll figure out who mur-dered Mother on my own, if I have to.

"I know what you're thinking, and I'd strongly ad-vise against it."

"What makes you think I'm thinking anything?"

"Because I know you."

Dana folded her arms tightly across her chest.

"Sit down for a second." Brian sat down, but when she made no move toward the couch, he frowned. "Sit."

She sat.

"There were no fingerprints at the scene other than the vic—uh, your mother's. We took samples of the blood from the mirror, the bathroom floor, the bedroom walls, and the carpet. Chances are it all belonged to your mother. But we're still waiting on the DNA match to be sure."

"What about the handprints on the bathroom door-jamb?"

"Your mother's."

"Any word on the bloody footprint?"

"The print itself was pretty smeared, but forensics thinks it's about twenty-six and a half centimeters long."

"That's what, about ten, ten and a half inches?" Dana sat upright again. Finally, something concrete. She looked at her size-six foot and made a quick guesstimate as to its length. A little over nine inches or thereabouts.

"Ten and a half. Size nine men's shoe. Approximate-ly."

"Well, that's good news. That's very good news."

"And, you'll be happy to know this is no longer a crime scene." He gestured toward the back of the house. "You're free to go back into the master bedroom." He rose, pulled his wallet out of his pants pocket, and took out a business card, which he handed to her.

"'Bio-Clean Specialties?'" Dana read. "'Crime Scene Remediators. Peace of Mind in Distressing Times.'"

Before she could comment, she felt Brian's hand wrap around her own, gently this time. She looked up and searched his cognac-colored eyes. They were full of sympathy. She looked away quickly and rubbed the back of her neck.

"Before you go back there, give these guys a call. Ask for Stewart. He's a good guy. Retired LAPD. He'll take good care of you."

"Thanks, Brian," she said and stuck the card in her back pocket. "I will."

He took a last swig of coffee and headed for the door. She followed him. "Remember what I said, Deputy," he told her. "Stay out of this and let me do my job."

She opened her mouth to tell him that she'd stay out of his way as best she could, but he cut her off.

"I mean it, Dana. Leave it alone."

The hell she would. She'd look at every pair of feet in the county if she had to, to find the man who murdered her mother.

And she'd start with Steve.

CHAPTER 16

The first thing on her agenda, Dana decided after Brian's announcement, was to get busy searching Mother's papers for her will. Now that the body had been released, it was imperative that she find the document as soon as she could.

She also had to figure out a reason—legitimate or not—to pay Steve another visit. Unless she could work shoe size into the conversation, which she seriously doubted, she'd need to sneak a peek at his shoes. All of them.

But how to do it? She supposed she could knock on his door and pretend she wanted to tell him about the funeral to make sure he came. Perps often went to the funerals of their victims. They got off on it. She could ask him to go with her on the pretext of her being so very upset. That way, she could watch him, see if he acted suspicious in any way.

Then, assuming Steve had not left the bloody footprint, she'd sort through her mother's papers to see if she could find any other clues.

Dana felt another twinge in her neck and winced. The quick shower she'd taken after Brian left hadn't done a thing to loosen her up. A vision of sitting on a beach, sipping a pastel-colored drink with an umbrella in it, delivered by a bare-chested hard body, flashed into her mind. She shook her head to clear it.

Before she did anything, though, she had to do something about José's kids. The promise she'd made to him as he lay dying nagged at her. What would José say if he knew she'd put his son off just because it was "inconvenient" to see him when he asked? Probably nothing. He'd likely be the first one to understand, but still, she couldn't help feeling like she was letting him down. Letting them both down.

She'd just have to make the time to see the kids. Teyo obviously needed her, and she could certainly use the distraction.

She'd call Mrs. Herrera to see if it would be okay for her to take the kids to Mickey D's. Not a fan of fast food and soda, their grandmother nevertheless might see the benefit of getting the kids out of the house to have a little fun, if only for an afternoon. It was the best Dana could do right now.

After she poured herself a second cup of coffee, she dialed Mrs. Herrera's number. It rang only once, and Dana wondered if she'd been expecting the phone to ring before she remembered that Mrs. Herrera spent a great deal of time in a worn easy chair, a small wooden table covered with a Mexican lace doily next to it. The phone sat on top of the table.

"Hola."

"Hi, Mrs. Herrera. It's Dana, Dana Sinclair."

"Oh, Dana," Mrs. Herrera said in her thick Castilian accent. "How are you, *cariña*?" Even after forty-five years in America, she still spoke English carefully, enunciating each word.

"I'm good." Dana rolled her neck and let out a little

grunt when she heard it pop. "How are things over your way?"

"Poor little Gracie, she is having the nightmares. And Teyo…" Mrs. Herrera trailed off, and Dana had the sinking feeling that there was a lot neither the grandmother nor the grandson were telling her.

"You know, Teyo called me yesterday."

"He did?"

"Yes, he asked if he could come to my house for a visit."

"I do not think—"

"I told him I didn't think that was a very good idea right now," Dana interrupted. Now that she'd thought about it, she was really looking forward to seeing the kids and hoped José's mother wouldn't deny her a visit. "But that maybe you'd let me take them to lunch? At McDonalds?"

She held her breath and waited for what seemed like an eternity before the kids' grandmother spoke again.

"That would be a nice thing for them."

Dana leaned back in her chair and exhaled. She looked at the wall clock and saw that it was already nearly eleven o'clock.

"You come get them today?"

"Yes, I'd like to, if that's okay."

"Good. My little nietos, they will be very happy to see you."

"And I can't wait to see them. I should be there in about a half hour or so."

"Okay."

Now that she'd made the arrangements, Dana felt much better about taking the time to see the kids. In her line of work, she was always going to be busy, and it would be good for her to make a regular habit out of seeing the kids now, while she really did have the time. She took a final sip of coffee and headed out.

℮✺℮✺

As she pulled up to a red light, a kid shot his skateboard off the curb and across the street directly in front of a battered old work truck. The driver slammed on his brakes, narrowly missing the kid, who flipped him the bird before zipping off up the street. As soon as the kid jumped the other curb, the driver put the truck in gear and sped off.

The vehicle looked vaguely familiar, but she couldn't immediately place it. The light turned. As she drove the last few blocks to Teyo's house, her mind turned back to her own mother. She'd learned so much about her the past few days, things she never would have imagined. Apparently, her mother had been proud of Dana. Proud that she was a sheriff's deputy. Proud that she'd done so well at the Academy. That was the biggest shock of all. Why did she never let on about how she felt to her own daughter? All this time, she'd assumed her mother couldn't forgive her. If only she'd known how her mother really felt, things could have been so different.

When Dana pulled into José's driveway, Teyo raced out to greet her, shouted hello and threw his arms around her in a bear hug before she'd even gotten all the way out of the car. His grandmother shuffled along, leaning heavily on her cane. Gracie clung to her as she walked. Mrs. Herrera's arm was wrapped protectively around the little girl.

Dana picked Teyo up and swung him around several times before she put him down and kissed the top of his head.

"Hey, there, little man," she said, smiling. She watched as he raced across the yard and tossed a baseball up into the air before she extended her hand to Mrs. Herrera, who took it warmly in hers.

"How are you, Mrs. Herrera?"

The older woman's salt and pepper hair, normally pulled into a tight bun, was coming loose and looked like it would fall completely out any minute. Dark circles under her eyes, which she'd tried to hide with thick makeup, only accentuated her weariness.

Mrs. Herrera patted her hair and smiled thinly before replacing her arm around Gracie's shoulders in such a natural motion that for a heartbeat, Dana was jealous. If only she'd been held like that once in a while by her own mother, maybe today things would be different. But if wishes were horses, as her mother liked to say, beggars would ride.

She bent down and looked Gracie in the eye. The little girl had her thumb stuck in her mouth, her forefinger draped over the bridge of her nose. She shifted uneasily and moved slightly behind her grandmother. Was she scared of Dana for some reason? Dana tried hard not to frown. Her eyes shifted up to the grandmother's face. Mrs. Herrera shrugged. "She been like this since…well, you know."

Dana nodded and turned back to Gracie. "Hi, there, Gracie," she said softly. Three pudgy fingers wriggled slowly at Dana. Her thumb remained firmly planted in her mouth. The girl's big brown eyes watched her intently.

"Would you like to go with me and Teyo? Have some lunch?"

Gracie looked up at her grandmother, who smiled down at her. The little girl looked back at Dana and nodded.

"Great," Dana said, trying to sound more cheerful than she felt. When she stood up, her knees crackled loudly, which made Gracie giggle. Dana turned her head and looked at her out of the corner of her eye. "Oh, you think that's funny, do you?"

Gracie smiled broadly around her thumb. *She has such a gorgeous smile. Going to be a real heartbreaker, that one.*

She reached out, poked Gracie in the side, and elicited the hoped-for squeal. Dana then tickled her in earnest and laughed when Gracie let go of her grandmother and pushed herself into Dana's arms. She swept the girl up and planted a big wet raspberry on her tummy. Gracie shrieked with laughter. Teyo, never one to miss out on the fun, ran over and tickled his sister. The three of them fell onto the lawn and rolled around in the grass. It reminded Dana of those long-ago days when her father would come home from work, never failing to bring the Tickle Monster with him.

After a few minutes, they lay sprawled out, breathless and happy. Dana couldn't remember when she'd had so much fun, but guessed it might have been when José brought the kids over to bake cookies. The memory didn't bum her out.

"Okay, enough," Dana said, panting. "I—gotta—catch—my breath." They lay there like that for a few minutes, Gracie with her hand on Dana's shoulder, Teyo's sneaker dirtying her shorts. She didn't even care.

Once they'd all caught their breath—which mostly meant that Dana had, seeing as how the kids recovered so much more quickly than their old "auntie"—they'd piled into the car and headed for McDonald's.

The kids ordered Happy Meals, Teyo's with a cheeseburger while Gracie wanted nuggets. They sat quietly in a booth near the PlayPlace. Teyo dug into his

Happy Meal box, looking for the toy, and Gracie munched on her French fries.

"Here," Dana said to her as she picked up the greasy bag. "Let me help you out." She put the fry bag on the tray and spread out a napkin in front of the little girl before dumping the fries back onto the napkin. "Want some catsup?" Dana waved a red packet and smiled. She was worried about the beautiful little girl, who had fallen back into silence as soon as they'd gotten settled in the car. Gracie just sat there, big brown eyes glistening. Was she about to cry? "It's okay, honey," Dana said quickly. "I'll just put some out for you and you can use it if you want." She tore open a couple of packets and dumped the contents onto a folded napkin.

"You can use some, too, Teyo." The little boy struggled to open the sealed plastic bag surrounding his toy. "Need some help?" she asked.

"Nope, got it," he said confidently, and Dana had to turn away so he wouldn't see her smile and think she was laughing at him.

Always a strong-willed boy, she was glad to see that part of his personality hadn't changed with his father's death. The bag finally ripped. He pulled out a figure from some recent Pixar movie and set it on the table. He methodically set his cheeseburger and fries in very specific places on the table. The toy sat in the upper left-hand corner and watched him benevolently.

Dana opened the small box that contained Gracie's chicken nuggets. "Do you want some catsup for your nuggets too, Gracie?"

With his mouth full of burger, Teyo stated matter-of-factly, "She likes 'em plain."

"Oh, okay. Hey," Dana said as a thought suddenly occurred to her. "You guys should eat some vegetables with your lunch. Buela will have my hide."

"Dana," Teyo said, and frowned. It was obvious from the way he sighed that he was struggling to contain his exasperation, and Dana had to turn away again. He sat up on his knees, turned to face her, and tapped her on her shoulder. "Dana."

"Mmm?" He continued to tap until she was able to look at him with a straight face.

"'Tatoes are a vegable, you know."

"Yes, I know."

"And French fries are made out of 'tatoes, right?"

"Uh huh."

"So we're having vegables!" He laughed and shoved a fry into his mouth. Dana laughed with him. Even Gracie laughed as she tilted her head back and jammed in a fry.

The little boy ate with one hand while he danced his toy across the table and back. Gracie ate silently, her smile quickly fading. When they were done, Dana gathered their trash together and set it on the tray in front of her. Teyo turned to her. "Can we go play now?" He looked over his shoulder at the other kids who played in the playground.

"Sure," Dana agreed. "But," she said as she grabbed his shirt when he tried to shoot out of the booth. "Dump the trash in the can then come back and take Gracie with you." She turned to the little girl. "You done, honey?" she asked. José's death hadn't seemed to dampen her appetite any.

Gracie nodded and watched her brother walk over to the trashcan. "My papa's dead," she said.

Startled, Dana turned to her and frowned. "I know. I'm sorry."

Teyo appeared at the edge of the table. "Now can I go?"

"Yes." Teyo ran for the playground and Dana called out to him. "Hey, come take your sister with you."

Teyo dragged his feet on the way back, waiting impatiently while Gracie slid out of the booth. "Come on!"

"Hold her hand, Teyo."

"Do I have to?" He said this as though he hated the very idea, but Dana noticed that he'd grabbed her hand even as he'd asked the question. She nodded, and managed to hold back another smile until he'd walked away. She watched while Teyo first took off his own shoes, then bent to untie his sister's before stowing them all in a shoe cubby. Like a good big brother should, he took Gracie's hand and led her to the first tube.

While the kids played, Dana looked around the restaurant. As a teenager, she'd loved to people-watch and had used it to sharpen her observation skills. She'd spend hours at the mall and various fast food joints, watching people and making up stories about them. Then she'd go home and write down everything she could remember in her journal.

An older couple sat as far away from the play area as possible. A businessman surfed the internet on his smartphone, his greasy fry container and hamburger paper wadded up and shoved as far away from him as possible.

A young couple, barely into their twenties, sat with their two children in a booth next to hers. They were all pale and fat, with what her mother would have called stringy dishwater-blonde hair. The parents and the boy wore faded sweats. The boy's pants had a big hole in one of the knees. It was obvious that the girl was the apple of the family's eye, because she wore what looked like designer jeans and a skimpy sequined tank top even Honey Boo Boo would have thought twice about wearing. Someone had attempted to curl the girl's hair. Dana squinted. Was that blue eye shadow? The girl couldn't be more than four, and they'd slapped make-up on her?

Granted, she was pretty, with a sweet if somewhat vacuous face. Dana wondered at the type of parents who would put makeup on a preschooler.

The couple started arguing about entering their daughter in the next beauty contest, and then Dana understood. Mom complained about the cost, what with entry fees, price of the dress, hair, and makeup. Not to mention the time they'd both have to take off work. Dad was all for it.

Dana shook her head. Sometimes, people made no sense to her. This was exactly the kind of thing she would have written about in her journal, if she still kept one. Instead, she got up to refill her Diet Coke, glad for a respite from the ridiculous family sitting next to her, then wandered outside to sit at a table in the PlayPlace, where she could watch the kids play.

That was when she realized Teyo was gone.

ᐁᓚᐁᓚ

Dana knocked her soda off the table as she ran over to where Gracie was sitting in a bright red and yellow McDonald's car. She grabbed the child by the shoulders. "Where is your brother? Where's Teyo?"

Gracie just stared at her with those wide eyes of hers.

Frustrated and scared, Dana sprinted around the PlayPlace tubes, hoping against hope that Teyo was simply hiding. "Teyo?" she called. "Teyo!"

There were a few other parents in the playground. After she collected herself, Dana spoke to each of them. "Have you seen a little boy, black hair, brown eyes, about seven, wearing a blue Transformers tee-shirt and jeans?"

"No."

"He was here a little while ago, but I haven't seen him lately."

"I haven't seen him. Sorry."

When she was sure he wasn't in the playground, she grabbed Gracie's hand and headed for the door back into the restaurant. Just as she reached for the handle, the door flew open and narrowly missed Gracie's forehead.

"Hey, watch what you're doing. There's children out here."

"Sorry, Dana." There stood Teyo, a big grin plastered across his face.

"Where have you been?" It was all she could do to keep from shaking him silly. "Your sister and I were worried sick about you. Come here."

With the two kids in tow, Dana went inside and sat down at the table recently vacated by the future beauty queen and her family. There were deep gouges in the tabletop where the little girl had dug with a pencil. "Sit down," she told Teyo, "and tell me where you went."

Teyo mumbled something, all signs of a smile gone now.

"What?"

"I said I'm sorry."

He looked so cute that Dana stifled another smile, in spite of her anger. The desire to laugh grew exponentially when he looked up at her, so serious and straight-faced. She wondered if he knew how his looks affected people, Dana most of all.

"Where did you go?"

He gestured vaguely, and Dana looked where he pointed. The boy had had to go to the bathroom, that's all. Could he have been too embarrassed to ask?

"Why didn't you tell me you had to go?"

Teyo blushed, but said nothing.

"Honey," she explained. "Everyone has to go to the bathroom, even me. It's nothing to be embarrassed about."

Teyo shrugged.

"Next time, just tell me, so I know where you are. Okay?" She leaned across the table and lifted his chin so he could look her in the eye, hoping her smile would put him at ease. "Okay?"

His eyes searched hers, for what she couldn't say. But he apparently saw something he liked, because he flashed his wide open grin back at her. "'Kay. Now can we go play some more?"

Dana looked at her watch. She'd promised to have them home by three o'clock. It was just shy of that now. Well, maybe a few more minutes wouldn't hurt. Holding up five fingers, she laughed. "Five more minutes. Got it?"

The kids ran out the door and into the PlayPlace. "Five minutes," she called after them, following them outside. *This was such a good idea. I really needed this.* She was already looking forward to the next time.

CHAPTER 17

After dropping the kids off, Dana headed back to Mother's and felt more relaxed than she had since this whole fiasco began. She sang along with whatever tune came on the radio. Pictures of the kids playing with her at McDonald's flashed into her mind. She sighed contentedly and vowed to see them as often as her work schedule would allow. Maybe even work up to an entire weekend spent together. Take them camping or something.

An unfamiliar car sat in her mother's driveway. Annoyed, she parked at the curb and got out of the car. Sally came running down the steps toward her.

"Hey, there you are," she said, her face a little flushed. She appeared to be stuffing something into her purse.

Dana exhaled softly. Really? Now? "Hi, Sally. Listen, I really don't feel like talking right now." Her shoulders started to tense up again. So much for staying relaxed.

"Have you heard anything about when your mother's coming home?"

It was as though the woman hadn't even heard her.

"They released her body this morning. I'll be going to the funeral home today or tomorrow to take care of things." *As soon as I can find that damn will.*

"You poor thing." Sally sniffed, and Dana wondered if the woman was about to cry. "Would you like some company?"

Dana didn't know Sally very well, and even if she really was friends with her mother—Dana had more than a few reservations about that—there was no way she wanted Sally's help with the funeral arrangements. "That's okay. My friend Maura's going to help me."

"Oh. I see."

Sally's frosty tone concerned Dana, but before she had a chance to comment, the warmth flooded back into her voice. "Well, you know where to find me if you change your mind."

Strange. She sure is pushing hard to be my friend. First, she quizzes me about the autopsy, then she makes a point of fixing my favorite meal, and now she wants to go to the funeral home with me. What's that all about?

Sally climbed into her car and waved as she quickly backed out of the driveway, nearly plowing over the mailbox, and honked the horn as she sped off.

There was something a little off about the woman, even if Dana couldn't quite put her finger on it. Not yet, anyway. But she'd definitely look into Sally. Find out just what kind of relationship she had really had with Dana's mother. After all, Dana was a cop. It was what she did.

And the relationship had better be what Sally claimed.

芝芝芝

The first thing Dana did when she walked in the door

was check everything out to see if Sally had somehow gotten inside the house. The door was locked, but she'd looked frazzled, like she'd been caught pouring salt into the sugar bowl. Or inside someone's house without permission. Things seemed okay, and since Charlie wasn't particularly disturbed, she'd have to try and let it go.

Upset that her sense of calm had been demolished so soon after such a pleasant afternoon spent with the kids, even if she had lost sight of Teyo for a few worrisome minutes, she thought it might be a good idea to jog through the neighborhood, see how much—or little—it had changed during her years away. She knew she was procrastinating, but Sally's nosiness had pissed her off, and Dana was back to needing to blow off some steam. After changing into running shorts and a tank top, she sat on the porch steps and grunted as she double-knotted her laces. Mother always used to say that the best way to get it done was to begin. But then again, José always told her that endorphins were Mother Nature's antidepressant, and half an hour of serious running would go a long way toward getting her good mood back.

Laces knotted, she'd spent several minutes stretching when she remembered her mother's iPod, retrieved it from the treadmill, turned it on, and searched through the play list. Mother's taste in music definitely wasn't hers— she'd never understood the woman's love of show tunes—but she chose something she could run to and headed out the door.

As she jogged down the driveway, Steve came out his front door. She almost pretended she hadn't seen him, but at the last minute gave him a little wave and waited for him to cut across the lawn toward her.

"Hey, how you doing today?"

She ran her hand through her tangled hair. "Good. You?"

"Good. Sure had fun last night."

"So did I," she told him. It was even true. "I had a lot of fun. Your family's nice."

"Thanks," he said. "I'll keep 'em."

Too bad she couldn't say the same about her own family. Or at least her mother.

"Listen." Steve paused and pulled on his ear lobe a couple of times. "I wanted to ask you something."

"Yes?" Was he nervous about something?

"You got any plans after your run?"

"Well, sort of."

"But you have to eat, right?"

"I can't. After my run, I have to go to the funeral home." It was the first excuse that popped into her head.

"Oh, hey, listen," Steve stammered. "I'm sorry. Do you need some company?"

"That's very sweet of you," she told him. "But I've already made other arrangements." Another little white lie, but she just didn't feel like having him tag along on such a personal errand. She was even second-guessing having mentioned it to Maura.

"Damn." He chuckled. "And here I thought I was so quick on the draw."

"Nope. Sorry."

"So, who was it beat me to the punch?"

"Well, my friend Maura, for one."

"For one? Who else?"

"Sally."

"Sally?"

"The woman who runs Sally's Diner."

"Oh." Steve's voice turned icy. "Her."

"What's the matter? Don't you like her?"

His answer was simple and immediate. "No."

"Why not? She seems very…helpful."

"Yeah, a little too helpful."

"What do you mean?"

"Let's just say she's not what she seems and leave it at that."

"No, really," she pressed. "I'm interested in your thoughts. Tell me."

"Maybe some other time. So," he added quickly. "Is there anything else I can do to help?"

"No. Thanks." She figured she'd ask him to go with her to the funeral later, and hoped it would somehow lead to the discovery of his shoe size.

"How about I fix you dinner when you get back?" Steve asked. "We could throw a couple of steaks on, toss a salad, and open a little wine. How does that sound?"

Sound's great, actually. "I'm afraid I couldn't possibly—"

"Aw, come on," he cajoled. "Can you believe it? No one wanted steak last night, so if I don't use it up today, I'll just have to toss it out." He chuckled again, a twinkle in his eyes. "You don't want to be responsible for that poor little cow dying in vain, now, do you?"

Dana laughed in spite of herself, and looked at her watch. Actually, a nice, medium rare steak sounded pretty darn good right about now. She glanced down the street and decided she knew when she was defeated. And if she did eat dinner with him, she'd definitely have a chance to sneak a peek at his shoes. "All right, you win. Throw in a great big baked sweet potato dripping in butter and loaded with brown sugar, and you've got yourself a deal."

"Did I hear you right?" He made a face like he was smelling fish left out in the sun for a week. "You expect me to ruin my grill by baking a nasty sweet potato on it?"

"That's the deal."

He sighed heavily. "Sweet potato it is," he said. "Lady, you drive a hard bargain, you know that?"

"So I've been told."

"Six okay?"

She looked at her watch again and mentally calculated what she still needed to do: finish her run, go back to the apartment and grab something interesting to wear, walk Charlie, find Mother's will. And she'd have to take another shower if she was going out tonight. "How about six-thirty-ish?"

"Ish it is. See you then."

"See you."

Dana headed down the street at a slow jog and rolled her eyes. This guy was a real character, and she normally didn't have too much patience for characters. But she suspected he was smarter than he let on. She'd have to be careful and figure out a reasonable explanation for inspecting his shoes.

CHAPTER 18

Thirty-five minutes later, her run over and shower taken, Dana headed to her apartment to pick up some more clothes. When she got there, she pulled into a parking space in front of her building and got out of the car. She leaned against the top of the Buick and allowed herself a few moments to admire the fading tie-dyed sky, the pinks swirling into the oranges like food coloring into fresh cake frosting. When she leaned into the car for her purse, she noticed another dark sedan with heavily tinted windows parked at the far end of the parking lot.

Okay, that was enough. It had to stop. She locked the car door, took a deep breath, and sprinted across the asphalt. The Honda shot out of the parking lot and roared off down the road. Although she was fairly quick—third fastest in her class at the Academy—she wasn't quick enough to catch up to the car or even get close enough to see the license plate.

Just who was driving that car, and what did they want? This feeling like she was being watched was really starting to piss her off.

Dana shrugged off her annoyance and dashed up the

stairs to her apartment. Once inside, she tossed her keys and purse onto the couch and went into the bedroom, pausing long enough to look at her bed. Flawlessly made, it was Spartan in appearance. The plain blue bedspread was smooth, not a wrinkle in it. Her father had insisted on hospital corners, military tautness, and no excuses. He was adamant that the covers had to be pulled so tight you could bounce a coin on the bed. As a child, Dana never mastered the technique, but once her teenage obsession about her father took hold, she'd worked and practiced until her bed-making skill would have pleased him.

Thinking about her father and how much she missed even his perfectionism caused her throat to close, and she swallowed angrily to clear it.

"Dammit," she said aloud. If he really was alive, she'd be damned if she'd waste any more tears on the man. After two decades, he'd have a lot of explaining to do.

She turned from the bed and opened the closet door. Up on her tiptoes, she managed to walk her large suitcase off the top shelf without dumping it on her head. After flinging it angrily at the bed, she turned back to the clothes in her closet.

Before last night, she couldn't remember the last time she'd worn a dress, and she pawed through nearly all her hangers before she found something flattering yet comfortable. After all, she told herself, her main purpose for heading over to Steve's was the shoe-hunting expedition. She pulled out a green and white Hawaiian print shift. *Perfect.* If only she had time to run it through the wash and freshen it up. But it was already after five, so that was out of the question. Maybe if she drove with the windows rolled down she could air out the mustiness.

She packed the suitcase with everything she thought she might need and checked the time. Five-twenty. She closed the suitcase, hoisted it off the bed, and wheeled it down the hall. The blinds were open and she crossed to the window to close them.

Someone was standing on the grass below, staring up into her window, their face obscured by shadows. When whoever it was saw her, he turned and walked quickly away, disappearing between her building and the next.

What the hell was going on? Mentally, she made a list of all the strange things that had happened recently, beginning with the stranger and the flowers at José's funeral. Now someone was watching her window. Were they all the same guy? Everything seemed to be connected somehow. But how?

She took another look out the window. The man was gone. She gathered her things and headed out to her car. If she hurried, she could still make it to Steve's on time.

ভদেভদ

Her mind continued to churn through her mother's dying words as she drove back to the house. *Could Daddy still be alive? We'd always just accepted it when Mother told Phil and me that he'd been killed on the job that night, but what if that wasn't true? What if that's what she meant when she said it was for my own good?*

Try as she might, Dana simply could not remember anyone visiting them in the days immediately following her father's death. *If he had died a hero, wouldn't the house have been flooded with officers coming to pay their respects to the widow and offer their condolences? I might have only been seven, but surely that's old enough to form a lasting memory of one of the most traumatic events of my life.*

And what about Mother? Could Daddy have hated her that much? Could anyone? She couldn't possibly

have been involved in anything that would be so danger-
ous. Mother didn't gamble or brook with those who did.
She didn't borrow or lend money, take illicit drugs, or
commit crimes. Hell, she hadn't even had a speeding
ticket in over twenty years. So why had she been mur-
dered?

Dana heard the whine of the truck just before she felt
the impact. Her head whipped back as her car was thrust
forward, then she slammed into the steering wheel. The
car began to spin. *Remain calm.* She relaxed her hands,
took her foot off the gas, and turned the wheel into the
spin.

She was rammed again. The spin accelerated. She
pumped the brakes. *Okay, steady. Light pressure. Don't*
slam on the brakes. Her heart raced. She began to feel
lightheaded.

Just a few more seconds and it'll be over. Just hold
on a little longer.

When the car came to rest up against the curb, Dana
put it into park and rested her head on the steering wheel.
Deep, slow breaths. In through the nose. Out through the
mouth. She just needed a few minutes to collect herself.

There was a thud on the window, and she looked up
sharply. "Hey, lady, you okay?"

A young woman stood beside her car, a look of curiosity on her face. She knocked again. "Lady? Lady, want
me to call nine-one-one?"

Dazed but otherwise unhurt, Dana opened the door,
forcing the woman to take a couple of steps back, and got
slowly out of the car. She raked her fingers through her
hair, shaking it a few times as she thought about what to
do. Brian. She should call Brian and tell him what happened.

"Did you see the truck?" she asked the woman. "Did
you see who was driving?"

"Truck?" the woman asked. "What truck?"

"The one that hit me."

"Sorry, lady, I didn't see any truck. Or who hit you. When I got here, you were already spinning around, then you slammed into the curb."

"Shit," Dana muttered. She rubbed the goose egg that was forming on her forehead. "What the hell just happened?"

"What?"

Dana looked at the woman. Assessed her. Plain-looking. Jeans and a pink hoodie. Blonde hair, hazel eyes, five foot six, one hundred thirty pounds. Early twenties. "What's your name?" They'd need her name and contact information for the police report.

"Look, I've got to get going." The woman backed up a couple more steps. Dana took a step toward her. The woman held up her hands, palms toward Dana, and shook them. "I don't want to get involved."

"Miss," Dana said. "You are involved. I'm an off-duty deputy sheriff, and I'll need your name for my report."

"Janey." She sighed. "Janey Smith."

Dana looked at her and wished she were one of those annoying people who could raise one eyebrow.

"I know, I know. It sounds fake, right? Parents had no imagination. Can you believe my brother's name is John?" She shook her head. "Seriously." She reached into her purse and pulled out a small black wallet. Showed her license to Dana. Her name really was Janey Smith.

"Hold on a sec." Dana grabbed a pen and pad of paper out of her glove compartment and wrote the information down, including the woman's phone number. "Thank you, Janey. We'll be in touch."

Janey grumbled and walked across the street to her blue VW bug, climbed inside, and drove off. Dana reached back into the car, pulled out her phone, and called Brian.

"Dana," he said warmly. "I wasn't expecting to hear from you today."

"I've had a bit of an accident."

"Are you okay?"

"Yeah, I'm fine."

"What happened?"

"I…I'm not sure. I think someone tried to run me off the road."

"Where are you?"

"About three blocks from the house." She gave him the address.

"I'm on my way." He hung up, and Dana was left to sit on the curb and wonder if someone had just tried to kill her.

❦❦❦

Brian arrived less than ten minutes after she'd called him—he must have flown out the door the second he'd hung up—and uniforms a minute or two after that. She'd given her statement, including Janey's contact information and as complete a description of the truck that rammed her as possible.

Not much damage to her car, just a blown tire and a bumper with twin dents and a couple of scratches. Brian offered to drive her home, but she declined. It was kind of like getting back on the horse after being bucked off. You either did it right away or ran the risk of being afraid of horses for the rest of your life. She couldn't afford to be afraid every time she got behind the wheel, not in her job.

So she'd had the tow truck driver change her tire and then driven home alone. A quick glance at her watch told her she had less than twenty minutes. She'd have to hurry if she was going to get to Steve's even close to on time. But before she did anything else, she needed to get someone in here to clean up Mother's bathroom. She dug around in her purse but couldn't find the card Brian gave her with the contact information for the cleaning service.

"Where the hell did I put that stupid thing?"

Charlie, lolling on the couch with her belly exposed, ignored her.

Dana was underwhelmed by her enthusiasm. "Fat lot of help you are, you little porker."

When her cell phone rang, she grabbed it out of her purse. "Sinclair."

There was no response from the caller. "Hello?" Not again. Not now. A glance at the phone's display screen showed that the caller's number was blocked. "Hello. Is anyone there?"

The only reply was breathing. Shallow and ragged. She trudged to the kitchen, peered inside the freezer, and pulled out a bag of frozen peas.

"Listen, who is this? Is there something you need to tell me?" She held the peas to her tender forehead, wincing quietly.

The uneven breathing continued.

"It's okay." Her mind raced, trying to think of a way to get the caller to talk to her. "You can trust me. Talk to me. Tell me what you need me to know."

The silence continued. It was either the killer, or someone who knew who the killer was. Or maybe it was her father.

"Daddy?" She held her breath. "Is that you?"

There was a sharp intake of air, followed by a faint groan. Then the call was disconnected.

Her fingers had begun to ache, so Dana loosened her grip on the phone. *Who the hell was that? Could it have been Daddy?* She was going to have to bite the bullet and see what she could find out about what really happened.

When the phone rang again almost immediately, she glared at the display screen and sighed in relief. "You find anything yet?"

"I know we just saw each other, but don't I even get a hello?" Brian asked.

"Hello," Dana said. "You find anything yet? Or did you call just to bust my chops?"

Brian sighed. "Nothing yet. Listen, I spoke to my friend Stewart," he said. "Says you haven't called him yet."

"You're right. I haven't. But I will. I was just looking for the card you gave me."

"Good. Because he can send a crew tonight, if you want."

Good old Brian. Always looking out for her. "Thanks. I appreciate it."

"I know you do. Give Stew a call." He gave her Stewart's number again. "You'll feel better after...once everything's cleaned up."

"I know," Dana agreed. "I will. Promise."

"Speaking of feeling better, how's that hard head of yours?"

Dana put the peas back in the freezer. "Little sore. But I'll live."

"Good thing it was only your head you hit. Anything else and you could have been killed."

"Gee, I'm touched by your concern."

"Seriously, though, you call me if you need anything."

"I will." He was right. She would feel better once all traces of Mother's...crime scene...were gone. She dialed the number and arranged for a crew to come over. As Brian promised, one would be dispatched immediately.

She cleaned up quickly, threw on her dress, and twisted her hair into a ponytail. Dissatisfied with the look, she yanked out the elastic band and arranged her hair around her shoulders. After turning from side to side and looking critically in the mirror, she shook her head and smoothed her hair back into a ponytail, making sure her bangs covered her goose egg. She applied a little mascara. As she stepped away from the mirror, she was surprised and pleased by what she saw—a woman ready for the first date she'd had in years. Even if it wasn't really a date.

CHAPTER 19

At six-forty, Dana hurried down the hall to answer the doorbell. Two men in white hazmat suits stood on her porch, proboscis-like masks dangling from their necks.

"Ms. Sinclair?" The taller of the two held a clipboard, while the shorter man set what looked like a large white tackle box on the ground next to him.

"Yes?"

"My name is Stewart Clauson with Bio-Clean Specialties. We spoke earlier."

"Yes. Thank you for being so prompt." Dana stepped aside and allowed both men inside. She gestured down the hall. "This way."

She led them to her mother's bedroom, but stopped a few feet from the door. Her stomach rolled and she just couldn't go any farther. Instead, she pointed. "In there."

Clauson put a hand on her shoulder. "Let's take a look." He nodded to his partner, who scooted past them and into the room.

"I have an appointment that I'm already late for," Dana said. "You have my cell number, right?"

Clauson nodded.

"Well, I'm going to go." Dana twirled a strand of hair from her ponytail around a finger. More than a little hesitant to leave strangers alone in her mother's house, she'd struggled with whether or not to cancel the evening at Steve's. Ultimately, she knew that if Brian had vouched for Clauson, she had nothing to worry about. "Call me if you have any questions."

"Will do." He was already heading into the bathroom.

Dana started down the hall, then turned and said, "Oh, and please lock the door when you leave, okay?"

"No problem."

"Thanks. I'll just be next door if you need me." Dana hurried out the door, ran her hand along her ponytail, and crossed her neighbor's lawn. She hoped Steve knew how to grill a steak because she was starving.

ᔕᔕᔕ

At ten minutes before seven—a little later than she liked, but it couldn't be helped—Dana stood outside Steve's front door. Too bad she hadn't taken the time to at least pass an iron across her dress. After smoothing out the wrinkles as best she could, she took a deep breath and rang the doorbell.

The door flew open before she'd even taken her finger off the bell, and she wondered if Steve had been waiting just inside, watching for her. He was wearing a blue and green Hawaiian shirt, tan shorts, and flip-flops. They looked at each other for a second before they both cracked up.

"I see you got my memo on going Hawaiian," Steve quipped.

Dana nodded. "Sure hope there's teriyaki chicken or at least some pineapple on the menu."

"Sure thing." He gestured for her to come in. "I think there's a can of rings in the back of the pantry somewhere. Can't vouch for their freshness, though." He pointed at her forehead. "Are you okay? That looks like it hurts."

She rubbed her forehead and winced. "No, not really."

"What happened?"

"Just a little fender bender. Hey, I wanted to bring some wine or something, but I'm afraid I just didn't have time to stop and get any."

"That's okay. I know how busy you must be. I've got some merlot breathing in the kitchen." He took her purse and set it on the ornate antique hall tree that stood sentry next to the front door. "Would you like a glass?"

"Thank you."

"Why don't you go on out to the patio? It's still warm, and I thought we could chat out there before dinner."

Native manzanita lined the cedar fencing that enclosed the yard. Interspersed with the manzanita, some sort of flowering vine grew up and over the top of the fence. There were many others she couldn't name. It was an explosion of pinks, purples, and blues with a little orange and white for contrast. Several hummingbirds flitted back and forth, sipping nectar and chattering to one another.

If the yard was this beautiful as summer wound down, she wondered what it must look like in the full bloom of springtime. She hadn't even noticed it last night. Someone had obviously taken a lot of time with the landscaping. Had Steve done it all himself?

Indian summer made the days hot and the nights brisk, but tonight was fairly mild. Tiny white lights twinkled among the trees and gave the garden a soft, romantic feel. She half expected tiny fairies to appear, darting between the trees and frolicking with each other. The temperature was nearly perfect, there was a slight breeze, and the shadows of a few puffy white clouds dotted the sky.

"Fall is the best time of year, don't you think?" Steve handed her a glass of wine before he opened his arms to take it all in. "Warm days, cool nights, and beautiful blue skies."

He headed toward the barbeque without waiting for an answer. She took a sip of her wine and refused to look at his sexy rear end, which she'd noticed on the way in and was accentuated quite well by his form-fitting shorts. Instead, she looked across the garden. The sun had just gone down, spreading shadows throughout the yard.

"It is beautiful, isn't it?" she said.

"Sure is."

He wasn't looking at the sky, and heat flooded up Dana's face. Steve blushed, too, and quickly turned back to the grill. She watched the muscles in his arms ripple as he jabbed at the steaks with the barbeque tongs.

"Can I do anything to help?"

"Would you grab the plates and silverware for me?" He concentrated on the grill, his back to her. "I already pulled them out. They're on the counter in the kitchen."

"Sure." As she went into the house, she could feel his eyes on her back. What was he thinking? She paused in the doorway. "Mind if I use your bathroom?"

"Down the hall." He waved the tongs in her direction. "Second door on the right."

If she hurried, maybe she could find his bedroom and hunt up his shoes. As much as she wanted to find Mother's killer, she prayed that it wouldn't turn out to be the first man she'd been remotely interested in for more years than she cared to remember.

The first door she came to was obviously his office. His desk faced the window and was fairly organized, something she wouldn't have suspected about him. Beautiful oak file cabinets lined two walls. She was about to move on when she noticed a door on the far side of the wall next to the window. With a quick glance over her shoulder, she peeked inside the closet on the off chance Steve kept some shoes in there. Nothing.

The next door led into the bathroom. Steve had told her the other day that he had an office and a gym in the house. Maybe she'd have time to check the gym as well as his bedroom, as long as she could find them quickly. She went around the corner and saw three more doors, all closed. There was no way she could check all three right now without arousing suspicion.

Oh, well, she was a master at driving herself crazy with "what ifs." She went into the bathroom, closed the door, and turned on the faucet. As the water ran, she flipped down the lid, sat on the toilet, and tried to figure out what to do next. She was so deep in thought that when there was a knock on the door, it startled her.

"Everything all right in there?" Steve asked through the door, and she wondered briefly if he'd been standing on the other side, listening.

She splashed water on her hands before she turned off the faucet, grabbed a towel off the rack, and dried her hands as she opened the door.

"Everything's great." She pushed the towel in his direction and brushed by him. "Dinner ready? I'm starving."

�െᎧᏋᎧ

"Tell me a little about yourself," Steve said. In addition to the steaks, he served a Caesar salad, garlic toast, and, as promised, the biggest baked sweet potatoes Dana had ever seen. She was pleased and a bit flattered that he'd actually chosen sweet potatoes and not yams. Not many people knew the difference. They'd finished eating and were relaxing with a second glass of merlot.

"Well," Dana said. "Let's see. I've been a sheriff's deputy for seven years, my roommate is a very tiny Miniature Pinscher with a very large attitude, and my favorite color is green."

"Sounds like a shopping list." Steve put his elbow on the table. "Tell me something interesting."

"Like what?"

"Like, do you have a boyfriend?"

Dana grinned. "None of your beeswax."

"Oh, really?"

"Yeah. Really." Her grin broadened. "Do you have a girlfriend?"

"Nope. My turn. Tell me what it was like growing up with Agnes as your mother."

She felt her smile flatten out. "Difficult."

"Can you be more specific?"

"What's there to tell? Mother was an unemotional, unsupportive, harsh, austere woman who lacked a sense of humor and never let me breathe. The end." What she didn't tell him was that, in spite of her unhappy childhood, she'd loved her mother and missed her very much.

"Whoa." Steve sat back in his chair and took a long sip. "I had no idea. She always seemed so sweet to me, if just a little shy."

He thought her mother was shy? Reserved, maybe, but definitely not shy. That woman could hold her own in any situation. But Dana didn't want to talk about her mother right now, particularly the difference between the woman she grew up with and the one who'd apparently lived next door to Steve.

"I have a question about your yard," she said in an effort to change the subject.

She just wanted to relax and enjoy his company. Maybe it was the wine. Or maybe just the circumstances, but she was beginning to feel at ease with him.

She was also fairly certain he didn't murder anyone.

He raised his eyebrow but didn't question the shift in conversation. "Okay, shoot."

"Who did it?"

"Who did what?"

"This." She waved her hand around. "It's gorgeous."

"Thank you." He downed the last of his wine. "Actually, I did it myself."

"You?"

He laughed. "Why is that so hard to believe?"

"I'm sorry. You just don't seem the type."

"Again with the type," he said. "Are you always so judgmental?"

"Sorry," she said. "I just never pictured you as a gardener."

"Landscape artist, if you please."

Now it was her turn to raise an eyebrow, if only she could. Instead, she raised both and looked at him over the top of her glass. "A rose by any other name, Figaro."

He laughed, and as she joined in, she noticed how musical they sounded together.

Steve picked up his wine glass and pointed it at hers. "More?"

"I'd better not." She hadn't been aware she'd even finished.

"Oh, that's right. You have such a long drive ahead of you." He grinned. "Wouldn't want you to get pulled over or anything."

"It's not just the drive." She tried to keep a straight

face, but in spite of everything that had happened lately, she was having a great time.

"Then what?"

"I don't want you to get the wrong idea about me."

"Oh," he said, and chuckled. "And what idea is that, pray tell?"

"That I'm...well, you know. Loose."

"You're not? Damn. In that case, I think you'd better leave."

"All right, already. Sheesh. Twist my arm, why don't you?" She handed him her glass. "One more. For the road."

She was buzzed. In her mind, she heard her mother's voice telling her she shouldn't be doing this, that she should go home right now. She ignored it.

"So when did you become a gardener? Sorry. Landscape *arteest*."

"My uncle was a gardener. I used to help him out during summer vacations when I was a kid. He taught me to love nature. To appreciate beauty." Steve took a sip of wine and waved his glass at his garden. "It was so much fun. I majored in Landscape Design in college. Started my own company while I was still in high school. Did well enough back then to be able to put in a few days a week now and still have plenty of time to enjoy all this."

"You planted some really beautiful things. How did you decide what you wanted?"

He pointed to a tree in the far corner. "See that tree over there? The one with the little pink flowers and red stems?"

Dana nodded.

"That's a manzanita. Hummingbirds love it, along with..." He pointed out various plants and flowers, and Dana found herself enthralled. "...golden currant, the blue island sage, the purplish honeysuckle, and the mountain lilac growing on the wall over there."

"They're all so beautiful, they take my breath away."

"I wanted to create a hummingbird garden that would be draught tolerant and would also attract butterflies."

"I love hummingbirds."

"So do I. Wait till you see the place in the spring." Steve smiled warmly at her. "So tell me why a hottie like you doesn't have a boyfriend."

She gulped some merlot. "Just never found the right guy, I guess."

"I find that hard to believe."

"It's true." Another gulp. Even though she could feel the wine loosening her tongue, she found she didn't even want to stop. "I'm a happily-ever-after, love-is-forever, romance and flowers kind of girl." She flashed on the English daisies. *At least when I know where they come from.* "It's hard to find someone who believes in love and monogamy like I do."

"Love is great," he agreed. "It makes the world go round. I love being in love."

"I'll bet you say that to all the girls."

"On the contrary." She'd meant it as a joke, but he sounded almost offended. "I've only been in love once. And even though it didn't end in happily-ever-after, I still believe in it. My parents were married to each other for almost forty years, until Mom died. That's what I want, too."

Dana couldn't help but think that he was very charming and especially good at flirtatious banter. He seemed to know just when to throw in something serious to make it all real. She wondered if he'd told her the truth about only having been in love once. But even if it was true, that didn't preclude his having a lot of less serious relationships. And she had no intention of being another one. Still, she had to admit there was something about him, something that made her think he might be telling the truth.

They talked far into the night, about love, life, and what they each wanted out of both. Turned out they weren't so different after all, the two of them. They shared stories about their pasts, dreams for the future, mistakes they'd rectify if they could.

At one point, after a particularly poignant story about his childhood, Steve got up and disappeared inside. Moments later, he brought out two heaping bowls of ice cream and set one in front of her, then dug into the other, scooping out a huge spoonful.

"I've tried all thirty-one flavors so now I'm working my way through Ben & Jerry's. This one's called Dublin Mudslide. What do you think?"

"It's delicious." She let the ice cream melt on her tongue and savored the creamy sweetness and the icy cold. They munched in companionable silence. By the time they'd finished, stars dotted the night sky. She watched Steve as he watched the stars.

"That's one thing I miss, living in the city," he remarked.

"What's that?"

"Stars. Where I grew up, in the desert, there were so many, you couldn't count them all. Here, only a handful are visible." He stacked the bowls and stood.

"Can I help you clean up?" Dana grabbed the plates and her glass. "It's getting a little chilly out here."

"No, that's okay. I'll just rinse everything off, then maybe we can sit inside and talk some more."

While Steve went into the kitchen to rinse off the dishes, Dana looked around his living room. It was designed for comfort. The couch Hank had napped on was well-worn and looked like the boy had picked a hole or two in the seams. Framed prints by famous artists—Van Gogh, Renoir, Monet, even a Picasso and a Dalí—lined the walls, but the centerpiece of the entire collection, in an oversized, gilt-edged frame, was a picture of a blue cat jumping over a green moon, with a yellow-and-pink spotted cow munching on purple grass watching from the ground. Dana leaned forward to look at the name of the artist, and smiled. Of course. Hank. As much as she tried to fight it, she felt a growing affection for Steve. Even though she knew it was probably wrong, she couldn't help herself. Besides, how could a man who made such a big deal out of a child's drawing possibly be a murderer?

☞☜☞☜

As she waited for Steve to finish up in the kitchen, Dana's sensible side won out and she knew she had to make good use of whatever time she had before he came back into the room. It was paramount that she continue her search for size nine shoes with tread that resembled ocean waves. She wouldn't allow her desires to cloud her judgment, so she hurried down the hall, past his office, around the corner and into the gym. Some sort of all-in-one total gym system sat in the center of the room. Floor to ceiling mirrors enveloped the room, even the back of the door. There was a small closet in the same corner as the one in the office. Dana opened it and immediately grimaced. The sweaty odor common to gyms assaulted her nose. The plastic laundry hamper was full of dirty socks and towels, but there were no shoes in sight, not even gym shoes. That left only the bedroom to search. She felt like she had as a kid on an Easter egg hunt. Her father would hide the eggs, and she and her brother would search for hours until they found every last plastic egg, each hoping to find the one filled with quarters. Only this time, the reward would be finding a pair of size nine shoes. Or not.

When she reached Steve's bedroom, she was surprised by what she found. The queen-size bed was neatly made, and she could see tracks in the carpeting where he'd recently run the vacuum. There were three floor-to-ceiling oak bookcases, filled not only with books but also with what appeared to be family pictures, assorted trinkets, and even a few plants. Not at all what she expected. And yet, it suited him, somehow. She liked it, felt comfortable here.

"Quit wasting time," she muttered. "Just get on with it." She stood in front of the closet, took a deep breath, and slid one of the double doors open. Not surprisingly, Steve's shoes were hung neatly on a wooden shoe tree. Even though it had a smooth sole, she grabbed the closest one—a penny loafer—and checked inside for the size. Nothing. She replaced the loafer and grabbed its mate, stretching the leather as wide as it would go. There was some worn lettering on the side and she backed out of the closet to see if she could read it with better lighting. When she bumped into something, she froze. A pair of flip-flops appeared beside her. She shook her head and looked up.

Steve stood there, his hands on his hips. He did not look happy.

CHAPTER 20

L ooking for something in particular or do you always go through people's closets without their permission?"

A tingle swept across the back of Dana's neck and across her face. Her ears felt as though they'd been seared in a nuclear blast. *Caught red-handed with a penny loafer in your hand. Way to go, Sinclair.*

"Um, well, ah," she stammered. Steve said nothing to make it easier on her, just stood there, that one eyebrow raised, and continued to glare at her. He'd probably throw her out. Nothing more than what she deserved.

If she told him what she was really doing, and he was the murderer, she could be in danger. Her eyes darted to the bedroom door and back to his face, then went just as quickly to his feet. He followed her gaze and looked quizzically at his own feet. There was such a comical look on his face that, under different circumstances, she probably would have laughed. Instead, she got up off her hands and knees and attempted a smile.

"Okay." She took a deep breath and let it out slowly. "You caught me. I was looking for your shoe size."

"My shoe si...any particular reason you need to know that?" Steve Groucho Marxed his eyebrows.

She ignored the innuendo. "Whoever killed my mother left a bloody footprint in the carpeting."

"And you thought I—" A kaleidoscope of emotion flashed across his face. Confusion. Anger. Frustration. Puzzlement. Concern. And finally, amusement. "Please tell me you're joking."

Despite the heat that made the skin on her face practically sizzle, Dana gathered her senses and peered inside the penny loafer. Nine and a half. Damn. The forensic scientists had determined the footprint to be about a size nine, give or take. Nine and a half didn't completely exonerate him.

"I don't know whether to be amused or insulted," Steve said, not quite able to stifle his smirk.

"Glad to tickle your funny bone." She stood in front of the closet, mimicked his Popeye stance, and tried to glare him into seriousness. It didn't work.

Steve grabbed her wrist and pulled her down on the bed next to him. She sat stiffly, arms crossed securely over her chest. He nudged her with his shoulder, and she turned to look at him.

"Hey, really." He'd finally stopped smirking. "I had nothing to do with your mother's murder. She was a fine old gal, and I could never hurt her. I could never hurt anyone." His eyes searched hers intently, and she felt herself warm toward him again. "That's exactly what I told that cop that grilled me this morning. Johnson. Jensen. Something like that."

"Jackson?" She should have known Brian would get here first.

"Yeah, that's it. Jackson." He inched slowly over toward her until his leg rested against hers. She dropped her arms and folded her hands in her lap. Her heart thumped against her ribs. When he leaned over and gently lifted her chin, their eyes met and held for a few seconds. His hand lightly touched her leg, and he leaned in even closer. She pulled away just a bit. He hesitated then continued toward her until their lips touched. He kissed her, softly at first and then with growing intensity. She told herself she shouldn't be here, doing this. Instead, her arms went around him, and when his lips parted, she tasted the sweetness of his tongue as it wrapped around hers.

Passion flowed through her only to be stifled by dismay. What was she doing? She should be trying to solve her mother's murder, not becoming emotionally attached to a possible suspect. But she'd been alone for so long, and her gut told her Steve wasn't a killer.

Steve's hand gently cupped her breast, and she moaned and pushed herself into him. When he flicked his thumb across her nipple, she shuddered and put up no resistance as he laid her down on the bed, his lips never leaving hers. His hand moved up her thigh, and she moaned again. She wrapped her leg around his and pulled him close.

His hard-on throbbed against her. Her hands went underneath his shirt and she stroked his back, running her fingers up and down his spine.

"I've wanted you ever since Agnes first showed me your picture," he whispered. He pulled away slightly and looked into her eyes. "Even when you were yelling at me that night we shot hoops, I wanted you."

She smiled and brushed his hair off his forehead. Gazing into his sparkling green eyes, she cupped the back of his neck and pulled him down to her. Just before their lips met, she froze.

"Did you hear that?" She sat up and pushed him away. Something scratched at the window.

"I don't hear anything," he murmured and pushed

her back down. And when he kissed her again, all sounds disappeared but the booming of her own heart.

Common sense eventually prevailed and she pushed him away again.

"Stop." She sat up and wiped her mouth on her forearm.

"What's wrong?"

"I can't do this. I'm sorry. I've got to go."

"But—"

"I need to feed Charlie. If I don't get home and take care of her, there'll be hell to pay later."

"Pre-empted by a mutt." Steve grinned. "This is very hard on my ego, you know."

"I'm thinking you'll survive." She smiled stiffly and backed slowly through the doorway.

"At least let me walk you home." He sat up and swung his legs over the edge of the bed. One of his flip-flops had come off, and he wriggled his toes when his bare foot touched the carpet.

"That's okay. I have to go. Thanks for dinner."

She walked quickly down the hall and out the front door, leaving Steve with a very confused look on his face. Somewhere down the block, she heard a car start up, and wondered briefly if one of the neighbors had had a more successful night. Or at least a little less dramatic.

CHAPTER 21

The next morning, as she drank her coffee and watched Charlie chow down on the scrambled eggs she'd made but hadn't had the appetite to actually eat, Dana did her best not to think about what had happened. She liked to think of herself as a good person, a decent person. Tried to follow the rules. So why had she let him kiss her?

Here she was, getting ready to bury her mother, and she'd let her loneliness, frustrations, and, frankly, her hormones, override her common sense. Other than a middle-schooler struggling through puberty, no one in their right mind did something like that. She never should have agreed to the steaks in the first place. If only she'd been honest with herself, she could have prevented the whole thing from happening. What had she been thinking?

Dana shrugged. It wouldn't do any good to dwell on it. No use crying over spilt milk, her mother would have said. Every time she thought about her mother, a thunderhead raged across her heart and filled her with regret.

She struggled to concentrate on where her mother's will and other important papers might be. Would she have hidden them somewhere, or would they be hiding in plain sight? She had to find them today. The sooner she found the will, the sooner the funeral could be scheduled. Mother was always a big planner who believed in being prepared for every contingency. She'd probably already paid for her funeral, and Dana didn't want to spin her wheels making superfluous arrangements. Mother might even have wanted to be cremated and left specific instructions for her ashes. It was hard to say.

She paused in front of her mother's room and looked around. The clean-up guys had done the impossible. Not only had they removed every last spot of blood from the carpet and the doorframe, they also straightened up the vanity, replaced the stool underneath it, and repaired the hole the stool had made in the wall when it was thrown across the room. It was likely that her mother had tried to defend herself by hurling it at her killer.

The bathroom was just as neat. Gone were the puddles of blood on the floor and the splatters on the walls. Both rooms smelled of disinfectant almost to the point of being overpowering, but it was certainly much easier to breathe than the metallic smell of her mother's blood. The image of her mother lying in a bloody pool with the back of her head bashed in jumped out at her, and Dana tried to block it out. She'd have to remember to thank Clauson for doing such a bang-up job.

And, of course, Brian. He was always there for her. Always had been—ever since he'd arrested her brother for tagging.

Phil had fallen in with the wrong crowd as a high-school freshman and, on a dare, had tagged the side of the school gym with the school mascot screwing the mascot of the cross-town rivals. It was really quite a piece of art, even if you didn't care for the subject matter. The school administration had not seen the value of it, however, and Phil ended up with two hundred hours of community service. Brian was the arresting officer and had quickly recognized his potential and taken the youngster under his wing. Tag-along Dana easily won a place in Brian's heart as well, and the three had remained close all these years, her particular relationship with him surviving Phil's death.

The doorbell chimed, jarring her back into the real world. She shook her head to clear her thoughts and strode down the hall. When she opened the door, she was dismayed at the person standing on the front porch.

"Hon, does it always take so long for you to come to the door?" Sally asked, snapping her gum. "I must have rung the bell a half a dozen times."

Are you always so nosy? "Sorry," Dana said. "What are you doing here?"

"Are you going to invite me in?"

Dana struggled to keep from rolling her eyes. "I'm sorry, but I'm busy and don't have time to chat right now."

"Oh, I'll come right to the point then." Sally peered around Dana as if she were looking for something. Dana shifted to block her view.

"What is it, Sally?" Dana tried not to sound impatient, but she had better things to do than stand here while Sally worked up the courage to ask her whatever it was she wanted to know.

Sally turned her attention back to Dana. "Have you planned your after-service event?"

"After service—" Dana frowned. "You mean like a wake?"

"Yeah."

"Hmm. No, I hadn't really thought about it."

"Well, first of all," Sally began, "do you know yet when the funeral will be?"

"Not yet but I'm sure I'll be able to finalize the arrangements in the next day or so. I'll get back to you when I know for sure."

"Okay. In the meantime, how does this sound?" Her take-charge tone reminded Dana of her mother, and she fought against the annoyance that flared up. After all, the woman was just trying to be nice. But something didn't feel right. It was almost as if Sally were enjoying the whole thing a little too much. "I'll make some calls and get the word out. How about I make a big sandwich plat-ter, some deli rolls, pickles, potato salad, that sort of thing, so you have plenty to feed folks?"

"That's very sweet, Sally, but—"

"It's settled then." She patted Dana's arm, and Dana tried hard not to draw it back. "As soon as you let me know the details, we'll figure out when to bring every-thing over, so we'll have it when people arrive. Just make sure there's room in the fridge."

It was no use. She'd never win this battle, so, re-signed, Dana nodded. "Okay, Sally. Thanks."

"My pleasure. Well, I guess I'll be going now." There was an uncomfortable pause as Sally appeared to be about to say something else. Dana raised her eyebrows but remained silent. Sally glanced over Dana's shoulder. "Okay, then."

"Thanks again. I really appreciate it." Dana did, too. But even so, she tried to convince herself that Sally had made the offer out of the goodness of her heart. Damn. Why couldn't the woman be completely despicable, in-stead of having these little rays of sunshine and good in-tentions periodically shining through?

Sally nodded. "No prob, Bob."

As she closed the door, Dana wondered how many people would show up to a wake for her mother. A wom-an she apparently knew less and less as the days went by. Maybe she was wrong. Maybe Sally really was just trying to be nice. But Dana couldn't shake the feeling that she'd had something else in mind, that there was another reason she'd come over and that she'd actually been looking for something. There was no way she wanted Sally pawing through her mother's things.

Over her dead body.

ℰↃℰↃ

Dana's stomach rumbled, and she was surprised to find that it was already after one o'clock. She was on a roll, and didn't want to end her search through Mother's files, so she stopped just long enough to order a small, thick crust pizza with everything. And to hell with the calories.

Forty-five minutes later, she stood in front of the file cabinet, licked the sauce off her fingers, and closed the lid to the pizza box. She wiped her hands on her jeans and pulled the last file folder—the only unlabeled one in the entire cabinet—out of the bottom drawer. She didn't hold out much hope that the will would be in there.

When she opened it, several scraps of paper fell out onto the floor. As she stooped to gather them, she realized they were once a photograph of some sort. Some-one—*Mother?*—had ripped it into quarters. She reassembled the pieces on top of the file cabinet, and recognized the photo as one Phil had taken of her and Finn at their high school graduation. There they were, arms flung across each other's shoulders, grins as large as the foot-ball stadium they stood in front of, their mortarboard hats perched precariously on their heads. The yellow tassels hung in front of their faces.

So that was the missing picture, the one that used to sit in the empty space on her mother's bookshelf. She'd taken it out of the frame and then ripped it to shreds. But if she'd been that angry at Dana, why had she saved it? Why not toss the whole thing into the garbage? And why that particular picture?

Dana put the pieces back in the folder and shook her head. Just one more thing she'd never understand about her mother.

As she pulled out the document that shared the folder with the torn picture, a smile spread slowly across her face. It was "The Last Will and Testament of Agnes Evelyn Sinclair," along with a Durable Power of Attorney, an Advanced Health Care Directive, and several insurance policies. Dana leaned against the workbench. It hit her that this was her mother's will. Her *dead* mother's will.

Before the waterworks started again, Dana slapped the folder closed, grabbed the pizza box, and headed into the living room. Typical of the fickle Southern California weather, the breeze had quickly turned autumn chilly, so she pulled a light cotton blanket down off a shelf in the hall closet and headed for the couch. Charlie settled in the middle. Dana curled up next to the lamp, switched it on, and pulled the blanket up over her legs. The will was several pages long, the font small, and it wasn't something she looked forward to, but she took a deep breath, turned to the first page, and started to read.

It took almost an hour to go through the whole thing. When she finished, Dana slowly shook her head in disbelief. Her heart pounded, and she felt lightheaded. She put her head between her knees and took several deep breaths. *What did it all mean?* Over the years, beginning when they'd first left Nebraska, Agnes had quietly bought stock in several companies, most notably Google, Apple, and BlackBerry. The woman, who rarely spent money on extras or anything frivolous, had bought hundreds of shares of stock, sold everything off several years ago and was worth millions when she died. It was all so mind-boggling.

After Dana read the will, there were only three things she knew for sure: her mother wanted to be buried, Dana was the executor of her estate and its sole beneficiary, and her estate was worth almost four million dollars. Four million dollars. It was all so incredible, way too much to digest. She wasn't sure it would ever sink in, not entirely.

She should be ecstatic at being a wealthy woman. Who wouldn't be? And under any other circumstances she would have been. After all, it was a dream come true.

But at what price?

CHAPTER 22

Dana's head still reeled as she went to the front door to see who was ringing the bell.

"Hey, there," Steve said from between two pints of Ben & Jerry's. "How's about some creamy goodness?" He extended the ice cream out to her. "Thought we could keep working our way through."

He held up the one in his left hand. "We got Cherry Garcia here, and…" He looked at the other carton. "…something called Imagine Whirled Peace." He read from the carton. "It's got 'caramel and sweet crème swirled with fudge peace signs and toffee cookie pieces.' So, pick your poison."

Dana couldn't help but laugh as she reached for the cherry ice cream and stepped aside so Steve could come in. Some of the tension in her body drained away.

"Ah," he said. "I see you're not into experimenting much. So noted."

She smiled as she closed the door and accepted his kiss on the cheek. "Not with my ice cream, anyway. Let me grab us some spoons," she said over her shoulder as she headed into the kitchen.

"No need." He put the ice cream down on Agnes's

coffee table, which made Dana wince internally—her mother would have shot him if he left a ring on her heavily-polished wood—and whipped a couple of tablespoons out of his back pocket, holding them up for inspection.

She cocked her head and frowned. "Tablespoons, Steve? You insinuating I have a big mouth?"

"Hell, no." He paused. "Overly opinionated, maybe. Stubborn, definitely. But as far as I'm concerned, your mouth is just the right size."

"We'd better dive in before this stuff melts." She put a growling Charlie outside and plopped down on her end of the couch. She reached out for a spoon at the same time Steve went to give her one, and her hand closed over his. *And before I melt as well.* Nothing would happen this time, she promised herself. Not if she had anything to say about it. And of course she did.

She enjoyed the smooth comfort of the cherry chocolate treat while he plowed through his so quickly she wondered how he wasn't getting a blinding brain freeze. She glanced over at him and was surprised to see him looking back at her. "What?"

He pointed his pinkie at her. "Um, you've got some…" He scratched his nose with the same pinkie and grinned.

"Oh." She wiped the end of her nose on the back of her hand and wiped the ice cream off on her jeans. "Sorry."

"No problem." He scraped his spoon against the bottom of the carton a few times then licked off the last of the ice cream.

"How do you do that?"

"Do what?"

"Eat something that cold that fast and not have your head explode."

"Practice." He aimed his spoon at her Cherry Garcia,

but she shielded it with her body and managed to keep it out of his reach. Temporarily, at any rate. A tanned hand, strong and masculine, snaked across the top of her shoulder just as she tried to take a bite. The fingers curled around hers, the hand completely engulfing her own.

"Hey, no fair!" She lunged forward and tried to reach the spoon with her mouth, but every time she was just about to close her lips around it, he jerked it away. They laughed so hard that on the third pass, the ice cream flung itself off the spoon and onto his lap.

"Oh, no." Steve's chuckles accelerated into hilarity as his hand flew to his mouth in a vain attempt to stifle himself. "I'm sorry."

Dana looked down at the sticky mess that dripped off his pant leg and flashed back to that day, so long ago, when she'd dumped ice cream on her father's lap.

They'd spent her whole birthday together, just Dana and Daddy. Went to the park, tossed a ball back and forth, flew a couple of kites, and played on the monkey bars. It had been a wonderful day. Right up until she'd accidentally dumped the ice cream cone. They were sitting outside Thrifty's Drug Store where he'd splurged on a three-scoop cone for his little birthday girl. It was a hot, muggy day, and she hadn't realized her ice cream was melting. She'd meant to give her father a hug, but instead had dumped the ice cream onto her father's pants. That was the end of that. Daddy wouldn't speak to her all the way home. Once they got there, he'd sent her to her room. She'd cried herself to sleep, but not before she threw the flowers he'd given her into the trash.

When she looked back up at Steve, hand covering his mouth, eyes crinkled almost shut with amusement, she thought he was laughing at her. Would his humor end as quickly as it had begun, like Daddy's had? Her stomach actually flip-flopped when, still chuckling, he grabbed the blob of ice cream off his lap and tossed it into his empty container. He wiped the few remaining drops off the couch and rubbed his hands across his shorts.

"Oh, hey," he said. Concern replaced his delight when he looked up at her. "I'm sorry, really. I didn't mean for it to spill."

Her eyes searched his. There was nothing but honest concern there. She relaxed and took his hand in hers. "It's okay," she told him. "It's stupid, really."

"What?"

"It's nothing, just some leftover baggage from childhood."

He took her hand in both of his and brought it up to his lips, kissing it softly. His eyes never left hers. "I wish you'd tell me about it, whatever it is."

Gently withdrawing her hand, she shook her head and brushed her bangs out of her eyes. "Maybe someday." She turned back to the carton of ice cream. "In the meantime, I really should give the rest of this back to you." She carved out a huge spoonful and jammed the entire thing into her mouth. What didn't fit inside oozed out the corners, and she took the end of her finger and tried to delicately push it all back inside.

"Here, let me help." Steve leaned forward until his face was mere inches from hers. His eyes twinkled. The richness of the green was like an enchanted field of shamrocks that dragged her deeper and deeper into their softness. She wanted him. Imagined him touching her, his calloused hands gliding softly over her skin, sliding across her belly, up over her breasts. When he wiped the ice cream from her lips with his thumb, she closed her eyes and relished the warmth of his skin on hers. His tongue explored the corners of her mouth, and her lips parted of their own accord. When his tongue found hers, she tasted the sweetness of the ice cream, and as their tongues swirled together, passion churned through her, filling her until she thought she might explode.

He cupped the back of her head to bring her closer still, and she wanted to lose herself in him, to just forget everything and revel in his body, the tautness of his stomach, the feel of his strong arms wrapped around her, protecting her. And when he ran his hand across her cheek and down her throat, she gasped. Stretching so he could feel the pulse in her neck, taste the soft flesh, her breath caught, a shocking little jolt with the first sharp nibble. She trembled with each new sensation as it slid through her. Clutched at him, nails biting into his flesh as his teeth nipped, unleashing wild new cravings until she thought she would go mad.

"I want you," he murmured. He gently pushed her down onto the couch, distracting her with soft kisses while he pushed up her bra and released her breasts. "You're so beautiful," he whispered as he bent to take her into his mouth.

Then the phone rang.

ℯↄℯↄ

Her lips felt hot and puffy as she wiped them off on the back of her hand. She avoided Steve's eyes and checked the display screen of her cell phone for the caller ID. Restricted. She cleared her throat, adjusted her bra back into place and answered the phone.

"Sinclair."

Someone breathed lightly on the other end of the line, but didn't say anything. It was starting to piss her off. Time for this phantom caller to shit or get off the pot.

"Hello?" Trying to keep her voice level, she snuck a peek at Steve, who was casually looking around the room.

"Did you enjoy the flowers?" the voice croaked.

"What? Who is this?"

Steve looked at her questioningly when he heard the tone of her voice. "Everything okay?" he mouthed.

She nodded and put an index finger to her lips. "I said, 'Who is this?'"

"Special flowers for a special girl."

"How did you know I like English daisies?"

"Fairy Fire always was your favorite."

"Daddy?" Dana's heart thumped irregularly against her ribs and she could feel sweat beading up underneath her hairline.

"Pink still your best color?" Not since she was a child. Not since the last time she'd enjoyed Fairy Fire. Until the other day, that was.

"Dad? Is that you?"

"Gotta go."

"No, wait."

"See you, Dana."

There was a faint click, then nothing. If she didn't know better, she'd swear it was her father's voice, although after so many years, she couldn't be sure. Memories faded quickly. But how could it be her father? A suspect fleeing arrest stabbed him. She'd only been seven, and most of her memories from back then were pretty fuzzy, but she remembered everything she'd been told about her father's death. He'd chased the man on foot for several blocks, through traffic, over fences, across neighborhood yards, until he'd finally cornered him in a blind alley.

Once the man realized he was trapped, he'd pulled a knife out of his pocket and thrust it deep into her father's side, puncturing his kidney. He'd bled out on the way to the hospital.

Hadn't he?

༄༅༄

Steve scootched over next to Dana, put his arm across her shoulders, and squeezed. "What was that all about?"

"Huh? What?"

"Are you okay?" He cupped the back of her head in his hand, gently stroking her cheek with his thumb.

She removed his hand from her face and put it in his lap. Although she was strongly attracted to him, she couldn't let herself get all caught up in him, not right now. "I'm fine, thanks."

"So," he asked, in a tone that seemed just a tad too casual. "Who was that, anyway?"

"Oh, no one important."

"Judging from the look on your face, I'd say that wasn't the case at all."

"Well," she began, against her better judgment. "See, I got these flowers the other day. The same kind my father used to give me. It was my birthday, and—"

"It was? Damn, I'm sorry I missed it." He flashed his world-famous smile. "Happy birthday."

"Thanks." *Don't get distracted by his eyes.* "Anyway, this guy came up to me and gave me some flowers." She didn't feel it was necessary to tell him exactly where he'd given them to her. She wasn't in the mood to talk about José, not with him. "There was no card, and I have no idea who he was. Or who the flowers were from."

"So the guy on the phone?" Steve asked. "Could it have been your father?"

"I don't see how," she replied. "He died when I was seven."

"Yeah, I thought I remembered your mom telling me that."

Once again, Dana wondered just how close her

mother had really been to her charming next-door neighbor. She couldn't imagine her sharing such intimate details with him when she wouldn't even allow Dana to mention her father the whole time she was growing up.

"Dana?" Steve touched her hand. "You okay?"

She stood, shoved her hands in her back pockets, and began to pace. "I don't understand it. It couldn't have been my father. But…"

As she paced from one end of the living room to the other, she could see Steve watching her out of the corner of her eye. When she got to the bookshelves, she picked up a tiny little trinket, some sort of glass animal, a seal, maybe? She turned it over, puzzled, and put it back on the shelf.

"But?" Steve prompted.

"They were English daisies, Steve." She turned to look at him. Continued to pace. "The flowers my father used to give me on my birthday."

"Those are the ones that look like pom-poms, aren't they?" he said.

"Yeah." She shrugged. "When I was a kid, I thought they looked like fire a fairy would use, so that's what I called them. Fairy fire." She nodded at the cell phone on the coffee table. "That's what the voice on the phone called them, too." Dana stopped pacing and stood directly in front of Steve. "It's so weird. Not many people in this country know about English daisies." *Interesting that you do. But then again, you are a landscaper. Sorry. Landscape arteest.*

"Yeah, and I'll bet even fewer call them Fairy Fire."

"Seriously."

"But if it wasn't your father, who was it?"

Dana shrugged. "No idea." She thought for a second. "The only other person who knows about my calling them Fairy Fire is my friend Finn, and I just talked to him the other day. Claimed he knew nothing about them."

"Finn?" Steve shrugged and looked away. "Who's this guy, Finn?"

"Just an old friend from childhood. Took me under his wing when we moved here from Nebraska. Taught me how to shoot hoops."

"From the way you play, he didn't do such a great job, did he?"

She grinned. "He's just a friend, Steve."

"Oh," he replied, visibly relaxing, and flashed that easy smile of his. "Good." He leaned in for a kiss.

Well, maybe just a little one. She closed her eyes.

Then the phone rang again.

෧෨෧

"God, it's like Grand Central Station around here." Steve pulled back. "Does your phone always ring this much?"

"Almost never." She picked up her phone and looked at the display. Restricted again. She unlocked it and walked away from Steve. "Listen, whoever you are, I've had just about enough of your games. If that's you, Dad, you need to tell me it's you. And if you're not my father, then you need to identify yourself immediately or I'll—"

"Whoa, slow down. It's me, Sinclair."

"Oh, Brian. Hi." Both his office and cell phone numbers were listed in her contacts so why was he calling from a restricted number? "Sorry, I was expecting someone else."

"You think?" he asked. "What's up with you, anyway? That's the second time you've answered like that."

"I—"

"Are you getting crank calls? Do we need to launch an investigation?"

"No, not really," she said. "I mean, yes."

"Well, that explains everything."

She lowered her voice a notch. "Yeah, I've gotten a couple...unusual...calls lately. But no, it's not something worth investigating." He hadn't mentioned her asking if it was her father calling, so maybe, if she was really lucky, what she'd said hadn't sunk in. She couldn't bear it if he thought she was ready for the rubber room.

"Define 'unusual.'"

Dana rolled her eyes and snuck a peek at Steve, who now stood in front of the bookshelves, turning the glass seal over in his hands. He looked at her with a puzzled expression and held it out to her. She shrugged and paced across the room and into the kitchen.

"Right before the last time you called," she told Brian, "I got a hang-up. Then I got another hang-up just now." She hesitated. The timing was just too weird. First, an unknown caller, then Brian would ring just moments later. Not once but twice. She shook her head. It was ridiculous. She'd known Brian forever. Why would her friend and mentor be trying to freak her out? It didn't make any sense.

"I think it might have been my father." She closed her eyes tightly and waited for the questions she was sure would come.

"Kind of an interesting timing issue, wouldn't you say?"

Had he read her mind? She took the phone off her shoulder and stood in the middle of the kitchen. "What do you mean?"

"Think about it, Dana," he said simply. "I've called you three times since Agnes died. The first time, I left you a voice mail, remember?"

"When you told me about the peeping Tom."

"Right. The second time, I just happened to phone you right after a hang up. And the third was after your conversation with a dead man. Sounds suspicious to me."

"No," she lied. "Not really."

"Oh, come on," Brian said. "I thought you were a better cop than that."

"Fine," she said, relenting. "You're right. But I only thought that for a second. Honest."

"Liar." He chuckled. Then his tone turned serious again. "So what do you want to do about it?"

"Nothing. No crime was committed, no foul language, no threats. Nothing to do," she repeated, although she wondered if there'd be any more calls, and if so, if they would be as creepy.

"If you say so. But you let me know if you get another one. In the meantime," he added, "let's get back to the reason I called."

She pulled out one of her mother's dinged up kitchen chairs and sat down. She put her elbow on the table and rested her head in her hand. "Shoot."

A shadow moved in her peripheral vision, and she turned quickly, startled. Steve stuck his head in the doorway and tapped lightly on the doorjamb.

"I'm going to take off," he mouthed, pointing over his shoulder toward his house.

Dana covered the phone. "Hold on," she told him.

He shook his head and turned to go. She didn't want him to, but she had to hear what Brian had to say. She flinched when she heard the front door close, not exactly a slam, but it was obvious he had some sort of problem with her taking so long on the phone. *Grow up, little boy.*

"I'm sorry," she said. "What did you say?"

"God, Dana, pay attention. This is important," Brian scolded her. "I said I'm on my way over, so tell whoever's there with you to go home."

"He just left," she replied. "What's up? Why are you coming over?"

"There's been another development."

CHAPTER 23

Brian knocked on her door minutes later. As soon as she opened it, he grabbed her in a fatherly embrace.

"How you doing?"

"I'm fine." She wriggled out from within his arms and brushed her hair away from her face.

"Really?"

"Really."

"Hmm." He frowned, but after a few seconds, he nodded and patted her arm. "If you say so. Mind if I sit down?"

"Be my guest." As she gestured at the couch, she noticed that he was carrying a large manila envelope. *Uh, oh.*

"Thanks." He tossed the envelope onto the couch and ran his fingers down the front crease of first one leg, then the other before he sat down. He always fidgeted with his clothes when he was either nervous about something, or so pissed off he needed a few minutes to calm himself so he wouldn't explode. It was a sucker bet what he was feeling right now. Finally, he looked over at her. "Anything you want to tell me, little missy? Anything at all?"

Little missy? Uh oh, she was in *big* trouble. That was even worse than his calling her "Deputy." She feigned innocence. "Like what?"

"Oh, I don't know. Like, maybe, possible evidence you received?"

Damn. Maura must have ratted her out.

"And before you go off all half-cocked and blame your little friend, she didn't come to me with the pictures. I just happened to walk into the lab when she was dusting them for prints."

"I was going to tell you when I first got them," Dana admitted, "but I wasn't sure they were connected to Mother's death, and I wanted to follow up on a hunch I had first."

"And what was that?"

"That my father is still alive." She watched his face closely but got no reaction. She came clean about everything, about the flowers, the feelings that someone was watching her, the hang-ups, and the weird visit from Finn.

She tried to remain calm, her voice steady, but when she got to the phone call she suspected was from her father, she couldn't help it. Her voice broke.

Brian reached out and patted her hands, which were twisting in her lap. "It's okay, Dana."

Her eyes welled up. "How could that have been him? If he's still alive, how could my mother lie to me all those years? Why would she tell me he was dead?"

"I think I know the answer to that question."

Frowning, she searched his eyes, so warm and full of compassion. "What do you mean?"

Brian reached for her face. When she flinched and pulled back, he hesitated a moment then used his thumb to wipe away a tear from beneath her eye. "If I were the parent of a wide-eyed little girl who loved her daddy more than anything," he explained, "I'd probably do the same thing. To protect her."

"To protect me?" Dana was confused. "What are you talking about?"

"The photos you received," he continued, picking up the envelope. "The ones of you as a child?"

Dana nodded, unsure if she really wanted to hear this.

"Seems there were two sets of fingerprints," Brian said. "One set belonged to you."

"I know, I know. I should have worn gloves. But if you're going to go all Gil Grissom on me about contaminating evidence, fine. I accept that." She took a deep breath. "But would you mind doing it after you tell me what in the hell's going on?"

"The second set belongs to your father."

So there it was. Out in the open, once and for all. She wanted to throw up. Bile burned the back of her throat, and she covered her mouth with her hand and tried to calm the tidal wave in her stomach. *How dare he keep something like that from me?*

"Dana?" Brian asked. "Dana, are you all right?"

"How could you keep that from me? You of all people." She pushed him roughly and walked away. *I cannot believe this shit.* She crossed her arms, closed her eyes, and counted to ten in a vain attempt to get her temper under control. When she turned back around, she struggled to keep from biting his head off, especially when she looked closer at him. His eyes searched her face, worry scoring his features. "I'm okay," she told him. "But how could you?"

"I can explain," he assured her. "But first, do you have anything to drink? Wine? Bourbon? Anything?"

"What do you think?" He knew Mother didn't approve of alcohol. And this was her mother's house, after all. "Besides, I don't need a drink." *That's a lie. But I'm not going to let him know that.* "How about some coffee?"

"I've had your coffee," he said with a grimace. "You stay here. I'll get it."

She started to protest, but one look at his face and she knew it was futile. She'd always had trouble accepting help, even with something as simple as making coffee. Phil always used to call her a control freak, and he was probably right. Brian hummed as he rummaged in the kitchen, preparing the coffee. She paced.

When the coffee was done, Brian handed her a mug and sat down. He gestured for her to do the same and blew on the hot liquid. He didn't look at her. "It must come as quite a shock, learning that your father is alive, after believing he was dead for the past twenty years."

Sipping the coffee, which was much better than any she'd ever made, she wondered again why her mother had lied to her. Dana didn't understand what could possibly have happened that would have made her father abandon them, or why her mother would keep it a secret for over twenty years.

☙◊❧

"Not as good as a margarita." Dana had finished her coffee and Brian poured her a second cup. "But it seems to have done the trick." She settled back on the couch, her arms wrapped around her legs. "So."

"So," Brian repeated. He took a deep breath and held it. "When we lifted the second set of prints off the photographs, naturally we ran them through IAFIS."

"Naturally."

"When they came back, and I realized who they belonged to, I knew I had to break my promise."

"What promise?"

"The one I made to your mother. She made me swear I'd never tell you that your father was alive."

"What? How?"

"He's been incarcerated in the Nebraska State Penitentiary for the past twenty years."

"My God," Dana whispered. It was even worse than she'd imagined. Had her father murdered someone? That would account for the length of the sentence. "What was he convicted of?"

"Brace yourself." He leaned toward her, his eyes downcast, elbows on his knees, and steepled his index fingers. "He beat a man to death."

"Always did have a temper," she murmured. Now that she'd heard the truth, she somehow wasn't surprised. "Who did he kill?"

"His name was Quadrees Rashard. No one was ever able to figure out exactly who he was in relationship to your father. Or what made your father kill him. Apparently, all he would say was that he lost his temper and killed the man. Other than that, he gave no reason." Brian took his time unwrapping one of his candies. "He pled guilty to second-degree murder." He placed the sweet in his mouth and chewed slowly. "And because he was a cop, they threw the book at him. But he was lucky, in a way. If he'd been convicted of first degree, it would have been life without parole."

Dana twirled a lock of hair around her finger and thought about her father. She was more confused now than ever. Her father wasn't the decorated hero she'd grown up believing in. The man she'd modeled her entire life after. So who did that make her?

Mother had apparently been this incredible woman who saved the neighborhood park, volunteered at the library, secretly squirreled away money for the daughter she was so proud of but couldn't bring herself to talk to. Someone Dana knew less and less.

Her father, the hero, was in reality a cold-blooded killer. Nothing was the way she'd thought it was, the way it was supposed to be.

And what about her brother? All these years she'd felt responsible for his tragic death. Now she wondered if he really was dead. He could be alive and well and living a secret life as someone else. Or hiding in plain sight. It seemed like anything was possible.

"How long has he been out?"

"Couple of weeks."

"That would explain a lot," she mumbled.

"What'd you say?"

"Hmm?" She took her finger out of her hair and unfolded herself. "Oh, nothing." After she stood up and stretched, she picked up her coffee mug and motioned to Brian's. "Done?"

He nodded, but when she reached for the cup, he took hold of her hand. "You okay?"

"I'm fine." She pulled her hand away and headed into the kitchen. "Why do you ask?"

Brian snorted. "Because you just got some extremely upsetting news and you look like shit."

"Wow, you kiss your mama with a potty mouth like that?" She set the cups in the sink and turned on the water.

"Such a comedian." He watched her from the doorway. "You sure you're okay?"

She picked up the sponge and shoved it into one of the mugs. "Yeah, I told you, I'm fine." She rinsed out the mug, inspected it, and, dissatisfied, started all over again.

Brian leaned against the counter, watching her with his arms folded across his chest and his legs crossed at the ankles. "It might work better," he commented, "if you used a little soap."

She pursed her lips and glared at him before she bent down and opened the cabinet under the sink to pull out the dish soap. Squirting a drop or two into each cup, she put it back in the cabinet and slammed the door.

"You know," he said as she rinsed and then handed him a cup, gesturing at the dish rag on the counter behind him. "I could stay for a while, if you'd like."

He dried the second cup and set it on the counter next to the first one.

Dana took the rag from him and hung it over the oven door handle to dry. "No, that's okay." She ran a damp hand through her mass of tangles before she steered him toward the living room. "Don't forget your jacket."

"Oh, right." He gave it a little tug. Charlie woke up and growled at him. She'd curled up on the edge of it and fallen asleep. He laughed and scratched her behind the ear. "Sorry, girl."

Charlie accepted his apology by licking the inside of his wrist then closed her eyes again and immediately began snoring softly.

"Must be nice to be able to fall asleep like that," he remarked. "How does she do it? Not a result of over-exertion, I suspect."

Dana snorted and shook her head. "Years of practice." Another tear had worked its way into the corner of her eye, and she stabbed it away with her pinkie. When she brought her hand down, she rested it on the doorknob.

Brian walked over and stood directly in front of her. "We good?"

"Yeah," she said. "We're good."

"Call me if you need anything." He pointed at her. "I mean it."

Dana pushed the door shut behind him and turned the deadbolt.

It was going to be a long night.

CHAPTER 24

She'd been right—it was a long night. She'd lain there, in her childhood bed, and heard every cricket chirp, every haunting, ethereal note of the neighborhood whippoorwill, every creak of the house as it settled, every dog barking in a four-block radius.

After what seemed like an eternity, she'd fallen into a restless sleep. When sunlight streamed through the window a few short hours later, she forced open her eyes and then immediately squinted. "Oooh, bright," she moaned, shading her eyes and rolling out of the sunlight. Whatever she rolled over on crinkled slightly. She blinked a couple of times and tried to focus her eyes.

The envelope Brian had brought with him last night lie next to her, its contents spread out across the bed. The pictures. Or rather, he'd given her scanned copies of the originals. After spending half the night tossing and turning, she'd given up trying to fall asleep and retrieved them from the couch. She'd spent hours studying each photograph. Every single one was taken when they still lived in Nebraska. When they were still a happy family. Okay, maybe happy wasn't the most accurate word to describe what they'd been, but at least they'd all been together. Before her father went to prison and the lies started. Before her mother had packed them up bag and baggage and high-tailed it all the way across the country.

She intended to get to the bottom of it. She was going to find out what had caused her father to murder a man, seemingly without provocation, and why her mother had taken her kids and run. Why she never wanted the kids to have any contact with him was beginning to make sense, she supposed, but nothing else did. Not yet, anyway. One of the things her father had drilled into her as a youngster was that there was always an explanation for everything. You just had to dig hard enough to find the truth. And she wouldn't stop until she uncovered it.

But first, she had to tend to the funeral arrangements. As she drove to the mortuary her mother had chosen, she wished she'd tried harder to reconcile with her, to put aside her own anger, and work to get past their differences. She'd been so damn pig-headed about everything. Her mother's anger had apparently been a mask for her fear of losing her daughter, and Dana should have realized that. It was all her fault, and now she'd never be able to put things right.

She signaled, turned left into the funeral home's lot, and parked the car in a slot that faced the front of the building. Sat there.

"Oh, crap," she said after several minutes. "Get a grip, will you? Just go in there and get it over with already."

She got out of the car and headed inside. The wallpaper in the lobby was striped with gray-green and white, and a peaceful landscape hung on the wall. In the corner sat a brass lamp that cast a soft yellow glow across the room. Plush green velvet couches and matching chairs surrounded a beautiful oak coffee table. On it sat a ceramic bowl filled with pink snapdragons, yellow stargazer lilies, lavender statice, and something white she didn't recognize. The flowers were very aromatic, and Dana couldn't resist bending over to inhale their fragrance.

It was all very welcoming. She felt comfortable here. No wonder Mother had chosen it. Dana sat down on one of the couches and waited for someone to appear. It didn't take long.

"Ms. Sinclair?" a petite blonde woman greeted her. Dana stood and nodded. "My name is Patricia Gabriel." The woman extended her hand and Dana shook it. "This way, please."

Ms. Gabriel disappeared through a curtained doorway. Dana followed and found herself in a small office decorated in a cozy rustic Americana motif. Alternating silhouettes of old-fashioned single-spire churches and picket fences were stenciled on the walls near the ceiling. Hand crafted designs in wood and metal hung on the walls. There was even a hand-sewn quilt folded neatly atop a simple wooden quilt rack in the corner.

"So," Ms. Gabriel began. "In looking over our records, it doesn't appear that your mother actually told us what she wanted vis-à-vis her funeral."

"I'll be honest with you, Ms. Gabriel," Dana said, and perched on the edge of an Adirondack glider. "My mother wasn't an elegant woman. She didn't care for anything ornate or overstated. A small service with a few roses, I think, a couple of songs, maybe a nice picture of her if I can find one."

"Do you prefer an open casket?"

"God, no." Even though the trauma was to the back of Mother's head, Dana just couldn't bear the thought of putting her on display. She shut her eyes tightly for a moment to regain her composure.

Ms. Gabriel nodded. "I understand completely." She leaned back in her chair, which was not behind the desk as she'd expected. Instead, the woman had pulled up the twin to the rocker Dana was sitting in and sat down next to her. "When would you like to have the service?"

"As soon as possible, I think."

The woman reached over and briefly touched Dana's knee. "Would Friday be all right?"

Dana crossed her legs and leaned slightly away from Ms. Gabriel. Two days from now. She'd be glad to get it over with. "Yes, Friday would be fine."

"Would you prefer morning or afternoon?"

Unlike Dana, her mother had been a morning person and would no doubt want to be buried at dawn. But it didn't really matter now. "Afternoon. Late."

"Would four work for you?"

"Yes," Dana agreed. "Friday at four."

Ms. Gabriel reached into her pocket and pulled out her smartphone. After fiddling with it for a moment, apparently entering her mother's information into it, she put the phone back into her pocket and walked over to a beautiful mahogany drop-leaf table with brass ball and claw feet. The table was polished to a high gloss so shiny Dana could almost see her reflection in it from across the room. Ms. Gabriel picked up a catalog off the top and crossed back to Dana.

"I know this is difficult, but would you care to pick out a casket for your mother?"

Dana reached for the catalog. "Yes, thank you." She flipped slowly through the pages, not really sure what she was looking for.

When she got to a mahogany casket intricately carved with grape leaves and hearts and lined with dusty rose velvet, the mortician sat down in the rocker again.

"That's a lovely model," Ms. Gabriel said quietly. "One of our most popular styles."

Dana looked at the price and felt the blood leave her

face. "Maybe so, but don't you think sixty-five hundred dollars is a little excessive?"

"May I?" Ms. Gabriel asked, reaching for the brochure. She quickly turned to a page near the back. "This one is just as lovely, Ms. Sinclair," she said and tapped the page. "And likely fits more modestly into your budget."

Dana took a quick peek at the woman's face and found not one ounce of peevishness or mockery there. She relaxed and leaned over to look at the woman's choice. It was beautiful. Simple elegance, her mother would have called it.

"You're right," Dana said. She brushed her hair out of her eyes and jammed it behind an ear. "It is pretty. And much more befitting of Mother's personality." She looked up at the woman. "Thank you for your patience and understanding."

Ms. Gabriel simply nodded. "What was your mother's favorite color, if I might ask?"

That stumped Dana. She didn't really know, but they were Irish and she remembered that her mother used to wear a lot of green. "I believe it was green." They had that much in common, at least.

The mortician smiled, then flipped the page and pointed to another casket. "Just so happens this particular model comes in several different colors." She looked up at Dana. "Will this do?"

The description under the picture of the casket stated that it came in an emerald "tone" which was actually a shade of light green.

"If you like, you can also have either a Celtic Cross or an Irish prayer inscribed on the head panel. For a small fee, I'm sorry to say."

"That would be nice," Dana agreed. "I think she'd like the Celtic Cross."

Once the casket was chosen, they went through the hymns Dana wanted and the flowers she thought her mother would like. No English daisies, though. After Dana made her choices, Ms. Gabriel asked one more question.

"We offer one more service you might be interested in."

"And what's that?" Dana asked.

"If you'd prefer, we would be happy to prepare your mother's obituary for the newspaper."

Dana hadn't even thought about an obituary. But it made sense to her, especially in light of the fact that she didn't really know who all to contact about her mother's death, or who would be interested in attending the service.

"Yes, I think I would like that." Relief washed over her. She wasn't sure she was up to such a dreadful task. It took just a few minutes to provide the mortician with all the pertinent details. She made the conscious decision to leave out any mention of her father. Her mother would have wanted it that way. Besides, what exactly would she say? The truth? She didn't even know what that was. Not yet, anyway.

"I think that's everything, then," Dana said when they had finished. She gathered up her purse and reached inside for her wallet. "How much of a deposit do you require?"

"Your mother came in a few weeks ago and gave us a deposit. I'll prepare the paperwork for the balance. Would you care for some tea while you're waiting?"

"Yes, thank you. That would be nice." Dana wondered at the timing. *Had Mother known she was in danger?*

An older gentleman with white hair, wearing an antiquated butler suit, appeared with a full silver tea service, including cart and all the amenities. "Milk or lemon?" he asked as he poured tea into a bone china tea cup.

"Neither, thank you." She sipped her tea and understood why her mother had chosen this particular mortuary. The old-fashioned and compassionate service Dana had received was certainly not what she'd expected. Nothing about the day was what she'd expected.

Ms. Gabriel returned after Dana had taken a few sips of the tea and took care of the deposit then escorted her to the front door.

"I'll need to bring you the clothes I'd like Mother to be buried in."

"Whenever is convenient for you, but sooner would likely be better."

"I'll bring something over as soon as I can." Even if she had no idea what that would be.

CHAPTER 25

Dana dreaded her next two tasks: deciding what to bury her mother in, and finding out where her father was and how he figured into all this. He'd murdered once. What would stop him from killing again? She had to know for sure.

On the way home, she toyed with going over to Steve's but quickly thought better of it. More than anything, she needed time to sort everything out and clear her mind. She didn't have time for a relationship right now. There were more pressing things to think about. Like trying to figure out where the hell Finn was and why he hadn't returned her call. Didn't he understand how much she needed him right now?

Maybe he'd lost his cell. Not bloody likely—he kept such a tight hold over his possessions he wouldn't even loan out his books—but she supposed it was possible, so she drove to his house and knocked on the door. His wife of four years opened it.

"Hi, Helen."

"Hello, Dana." A lukewarm greeting at best. "How are you?"

"Not too good, I'm afraid." They'd never been especially close, but Dana thought it strange the woman didn't even invite her in. "Is Finn around?"

"No. He's on the road." Helen cleared her throat loudly. "Again."

"On the road?" Finn was a CPA. Why would he be traveling?

"He's been taking off for several days at a time for the past six months or so."

"Where'd he go?"

"Your guess is as good as mine."

"Hmm." Dana frowned. "Damn."

"Yeah, that's what I said."

"Do you know if he's on his cell?"

"Beats me. Damn fool won't take my calls."

Something was definitely wrong. The Finn she knew adored his wife. "He won't?"

"Nope. Goes straight to voice mail."

"Okay, well, if you do hear from him, tell him to call me, will you? It's important."

"You do the same, okay?" Helen sounded more pissed off than worried, and that wasn't like her. "Bye." She closed the door almost before she'd said it.

Dana walked slowly back to her car and wondered why Finn wouldn't answer his phone, especially when he knew it was Helen calling. She tried his cell, hoping he was merely dodging his wife's calls and that nothing was wrong. That's all she needed, one more thing to worry about. But the call went straight to voicemail. Again.

"Dammit, Finn," she swore while she waited to leave her message.

"Michael Finnegan MacDermott here. Sorry to miss your call. I'll get back to you shortly."

"Finny. What the hell? Call me, will you? Like I said last time I called, Mother's been killed. Murdered. Funeral's Friday at four." Her voice caught a little. "Don't make me come and get you."

That should get some sort of response. She drove home with the radio blasting and tried not to think about anything. When she got home, Charlie was standing in the kitchen. Or rather, bouncing. The dog was part pogo stick.

"What is it, girl?" She dropped her purse on the floor and strode over to her. "Do you have to go out?"

The dog stopped leaping and gave her one of those looks that told her she just wasn't getting it. "What, Charlie? What are you trying to tell me?"

Dana examined the room, looking for any sign that something was amiss. It didn't take long to find the note, taped to the refrigerator. There was no mistaking who it was from. It was bright pink with a pink-and-black checkerboard border. At the top it said *From the desk of* and at the bottom, in big black letters, SALLY.

"What in the world?" Dana took down the note and looked over her shoulder. Disquiet settled in around her.

"'Came by to talk about the wake,'" she read aloud. "Did you forget about me? Hope it was something important. Call me. Sally."

"How the hell did you get in here?" Dana angrily crumpled the note and tossed it into the trashcan. "You better not have a key. And you can bet we're going to have a little chat about the rules." She opened the door and peered into the fridge. Grabbed a low-fat yogurt, looked at the expiration date, then put it back and pulled out some shredded cheese and the flour tortillas she picked up at the market. Anger burned around the edges of her apprehension.

"How dare that woman break in to Mother's house? What gives her the right?" She sprinkled cheese inside a tortilla and put it in the microwave. While her snack was nuking, she went to the front door and opened it, then inspected the lock to see if there were any signs of a break-in. Nothing. No scratches or marks out of the ordinary. Damn woman must have a key. *Did she actually get inside the other day, too?*

The microwave dinged. Dana went back into the kitchen and pulled out her quesadilla. She bit into it without thinking, and promptly spit it out into her hand.

"Hot!" she yelled, waving her hand in front of her open mouth. "Damn." She gulped down half a bottle of water. When she took a second bite, she tested it to make sure the cheese had cooled off. Then she ate it so fast, it gave her heartburn. Or maybe it was thinking about having to deal with Sally, on top of everything else she had going on, that burned in her chest. She winced and put a fist over her heart, waiting for the pain to subside.

Once it did, she marched outside, jumped into her car, and drove the few miles to the diner. When she got there, she took a moment to collect herself before she walked inside. Dorothy stood behind the counter, and smiled when she saw that it was Dana. Her smile quickly faded when she looked at Dana's face.

"May I speak with Sally? Please."

"Um, sure."

Dana tapped her foot while she waited. Crossed her arms. Glanced up at the clock behind the counter and watched the seconds tick by. She had just started pacing between the register and the front door when Sally finally appeared.

"Dana?" she croaked. "Hi!"

"Hello, Sally." She struggled to keep her voice calm and level. "I wanted to talk to you about your little note."

"Oh, hon," she gushed. "I'm sorry about that. It was rude of me. No one should go inside someone else's house unbidden and leave a nasty note. Your mama gave me a key, you know, but I should probably give it back to you now."

"I think that would be best."

"Hey," Sally continued as though she hadn't heard. "Let me make it up to you. How about coming over for dinner tonight?"

"Thanks, but I don't think so." That was the last thing she wanted to do tonight. Or any night.

"Nonsense. You have to eat. Come on," she wheedled. "I want you to meet my new beau." This last she sing-songed, as if that was a big inducement. Dana sighed and tried not to roll her eyes. Again. This woman seemed to bring out the petulant teenager in her.

"Well, I guess I could spare an hour or so. But no more than that," she added quickly. "I have so much to do before the funeral on Friday."

"So it's Friday, then?"

"Yes, at four o'clock. Now, may I have my mother's key back?" Dana held out her hand expectantly.

"Sure. I'll bring it tonight." They settled on meeting at the diner at six thirty and said their good-byes.

Dana had a few hours until then and intended to make good use of them. With any luck, she'd not only find the right clothes for her mother, but also the information she craved about her father.

಄಄಄

The bedroom closet was packed with clear plastic boxes, all neatly labeled in her mother's compact handwriting, each letter perfectly formed. As Dana rummaged around, pulling boxes down off shelves and inspecting the contents, she remembered her mother's spring-cleaning ritual. Growing up, the first Saturday of every April was devoted to it, no matter what else may or may not have been going on at the time. Mother expected Dana and Phil to get rid of anything and everything that was worn out, outgrown, or unused. That included toys, clothes, favorite books, just about anything you could think of.

Dana had already gone through seven boxes and held no hope that the last one, marked "Christmas," would contain what she was looking for, but she pulled it out and opened it up anyway.

Inside, there were the usual red, green, and white pull-over sweaters. When she pulled out the final item and unwrapped the tissue surrounding it, Dana gasped and sat down heavily on the bed.

One day, when Dana was about thirteen, her mother was browsing through the Sears catalog and happened upon a royal blue sweater dotted with rhinestone sequins in the shape of snowflakes. She'd commented that it certainly was interesting, and Dana decided then and there that she was going to buy that sweater for her for Christmas.

She'd spent her entire summer vacation working at odd jobs around the neighborhood: babysitting, mowing lawns, selling lemonade and chocolate chip cookies she baked herself. She'd even cleaned out Mrs. Simmons's nasty rain gutters for a measly ten bucks. The sweater had cost Dana seventy-five dollars. Her mother had worn it on Christmas day, but had never worn it again.

Dana brought the sweater to her face and inhaled. It smelled faintly of White Shoulders, the perfume her mother wore to church and on special occasions.

"Oh, Momma." Her breath hitched. "You saved this sweater all these years? Never spring cleaned it away?"

The woman would probably always be an enigma to her, but now she held the proof right here in her hands. Her mother really had loved her. She wiped her face with her sleeve then rubbed her mother's sweater against her still-damp cheek.

After a few minutes, she collected herself, repacked the box with everything but the treasured sweater, and put all the boxes back in their assigned spots in the closet.

She picked up the sweater and held it against her chest. "Well, Chuckles, old girl," she said, glancing at her watch. "Mission accomplished. Mother will be buried in the Christmas sweater. She'd like that, I think." She paused and looked around the room. "That's about everything there is in here. How's about we head out to the garage and see what's up out there?"

Charlie ran down the hall ahead of her. When they got to the garage, Dana marveled at its neatness. It was lined with shelving units, every shelf crammed full of cardboard boxes. Each box on one entire wall was labeled with the letter D and a number. The boxes on the other side were similarly labeled with the letter P. Dana and Phil. Her mother was nothing if not organized.

She hunted around on the workbench and found an X-Acto knife. Starting with the rack closest to the door, she pulled down each box, sliced through the tape that held the lid and rummaged through it. She didn't expect it to take more than a couple of hours.

But she hadn't counted on memory. On how the past could draw you in. Her mother had saved everything, every school report, every childish drawing, every crude clay pot, macaroni necklace and painted Mother's Day plastic coffee cup Dana had ever made. How ironic that she'd made her children spring clean things away but had obviously been a pack rat herself with every last piece of their childhood.

Growing up, things had been tough, but they weren't always bad. There'd been many Saturday nights filled with popcorn and endless games of Monopoly and Clue, scary movies watched from under cover of quilts and couch pillows, mugs of steaming hot cocoa with whipped cream. Phil would often sneak back into the refrigerator, spraying extra whipped cream into the cocoa until it was piled so high it would coat their noses when they drank. She smiled at the memory of how it never failed to make Mother laugh.

Rummaging through her current box, she pulled out something wrapped in wrinkled tissue paper. She folded it back, stunned to see a ceramic bunny ear. It was her Easter mug, the one she'd broken in a teenaged fit of rage about something or other. All these years she'd harbored such resentment and anger toward her mother, and only now, when it was too late, was she beginning to know her, to find out what a remarkable woman she really was. *Had been.*

She'd been so sure her mother didn't love her. Why hadn't Mother ever done anything to correct that impression?

Standing in the middle of the garage, she sipped her Diet Coke and looked at all the boxes she still had to go through. Shaking her head, she walked out to the driveway and sat down next to Charlie. The little dog dozed in the warm sun. Even Dana found it a struggle to stay awake. She lay down, laced her fingers behind her head, and closed her eyes. Heat permeated her body, pelting her from the sun and the warm asphalt, but it felt so good. *I'll only lay here a minute or two. Got too much to do to take a nap.*

Sometime later—she wasn't sure exactly how long, but she noticed the sun seemed a little cooler, the shadows a little longer—she awoke with a start. Her eyes flew open, and she bolted upright.

"Charlie?" The dog was gone. "Charlie! Here, girl."

Dana ran into the street and looked up and down the

block. She glanced at Steve's driveway and noted that his car was gone. A dog barked down the street.

"Charlie?" The barking continued, high-pitched and frantic, and Dana sprinted toward it. Half a dozen houses down, she spotted a man climbing into a blue Honda— the same blue Honda she'd seen twice before. She was sure of it. Charlie stood a few feet away, barking her head off.

"Charlie!" She ran to pick up the dog, but Charlie snarled and growled so viciously that when Dana did, the angry animal actually nipped her in the webbing between her thumb and index finger. "Ow! Damn it, Charlie," she said as she brought her wounded hand to her mouth. "What's gotten into you?"

Turning to the man to apologize for Charlie's behavior, she watched, puzzled, as he scrunched down in his seat, yanked his cap down over his eyes, and drove off. His tires screeched. The car fishtailed.

"What the hell?" She tried to get a good look at the mud-splattered license plate, but it was impossible to read. "Daddy?" she whispered. "Is that you?"

のそのそ

She stood in the middle of the street, scratching her head. *Could that possibly have been Daddy? But why wouldn't he have stopped and talked to me?* If it wasn't her dad, who was it? And why would someone just take off like that? While she'd believed what Brian had told her about her father, she hadn't wanted to accept the fact that everything she'd ever been told about him, everything she'd held dear, everything she'd loved about him, was a lie. That she'd based her entire life on a lie.

As they turned up the walkway toward the front door, something caught her eye. The low-lying sun glinted off an object on the first step, and she squatted down for a closer look. It seemed to be some sort of ceramic figurine, about two inches tall. She picked it up and turned it over. It was a funny-looking little man with a bulbous, misshapen nose, crouched atop a rock and wearing an odd square hat.

"Did Daddy leave this here?" she asked Charlie, showing the figurine to her. "Is that why you took off like that?" She tucked the figurine into her pocket, set the dog down, and headed for the garage.

It was time to get back to work. There were still a lot of boxes to sort through. She was so focused that she didn't hear the footsteps behind her until it was too late.

"Still looking for those shoes?"

"Shit!" The corner of the box she was shoving into place caught on the shelf and bounced out of her hands and onto her foot. "Ow, shit," she repeated, whirling around. Steve was grinning at her. "You scared the crap out of me."

"Sorry." He reached out and took her hand in his. "Are you okay?"

"Yeah, I'm fine." She pulled her hand away so she could bend down and scoop up the mess on the floor.

"You sure?"

"Positive." She dumped everything back into the box and reached for the lid.

"I really am sorry." His smile widened and quickly turned into a chuckle. "Didn't mean to sneak up on you like that."

She hitched the box up on a hip. "Maybe we need to put a cat bell around your neck."

"Maybe." Still smiling, he ran his hand through his hair then leaned over and kissed her on the cheek before she realized what he was doing. His voice softened. "Missed you today."

She pushed the box back into place and looked around the garage, suddenly aware that it was a filthy mess—and so was she. Grime stuck to her face. She tried to rub some off her cheek.

"You missed a spot." He reached over and stroked her neck with his finger. His eyes drew her. When he put his arms around her, she let him pull her close. And when his lips found hers, she closed her eyes and lost herself.

But only for a moment. She put her hands on his chest as she took a step backward. "Why don't we go inside? I think there's a couple of sodas in the fridge."

"Sounds good to me," Steve said.

"Don't get any funny ideas," Dana told him. "I'm really busy right now." She gestured toward the boxes that lined the garage. "As you can plainly see."

ↀↀↀ

"Hungry?" They sat in the living room. Dana had cleaned up and changed into jeans and a simple pink tee. Barefoot, she sat at one end of the couch and ran her hands through her damp curls. Steve sat at the other end, his arm resting on the back of the couch, his fingers rubbing the top of Dana's shoulder. Charlie lay in a chair on the other side of the room and glared at them. Two sodas sat on the coffee table before them.

When Dana's stomach growled loudly enough for Steve to hear, he chuckled.

She snorted and rubbed her stomach. "Does that answer your question?"

"Why don't we go over to my place?" Steve asked. "I've got some chicken breasts I can toss on the grill, throw together a salad—"

The man certainly loved his barbeque. "Sorry." She shook her head. "Can't."

"Sure you can," he said and flashed a grin.

"No, I mean," she said, tapping her watch. "I have other plans."

"Oh." He shrugged. "Well, you could come over after."

She reluctantly declined. "Naw, better not. I should get to bed early." He leered at her, and she struggled to appear serious. "To sleep," she emphasized heavily. "I have so much to do before Mother's funeral Friday and all—"

"Wait, what?" Steve looked puzzled. "The funeral's on Friday?"

Had she forgotten to mention it to him? "Yes, at four." Dana tucked her legs underneath her and leaned her head on the back of the couch, eyes closed. She was so tired. Steve switched from rubbing her shoulder to rubbing the side of her neck. "Are you planning on coming?"

"I'd like to," he said. "Would you like an escort?"

She opened her eyes and smiled at him. "I would. Do you have one in mind?"

"Very funny." They sat there for a moment and grinned at each other. "Seriously, though, I would like to escort you."

"I'd like that," Dana replied. "I thought I'd leave about two-thirty or so. I should be there early. Make sure everything's done right." She pulled herself up off the couch as an indication that it was time for him to leave. He hesitated a moment then stood and smoothed down his pants legs.

"Sure you don't want company tonight?"

She reached out and took hold of his hand. "I'm sure." For some reason, she couldn't say why, she didn't want to tell him that she was seeing Sally. "I've got a short meeting, then I'm just going to grab something quick for dinner and hit the sack." He grinned wickedly and raised an eyebrow at her. She caught the look and tried her best to ignore it. "Alone."

At the front door, they stood in the doorway, the warm night breeze light upon their skin. Steve leaned over and kissed her on the cheek. "I'll check on you to-morrow." And then he was gone.

CHAPTER 26

Six-ten. Twenty minutes until she was supposed to be at the diner. Even though it would make her a few minutes late, if she hurried, she'd have time to drop off the sweater at the mortuary. She snatched it and a pair of her mother's black polyester pants off her dresser where she'd left them, pausing long enough to bring the sweater to her face and inhale her mother's scent one last time, and grabbed her purse and keys.

Neither Ms. Gabriel nor Kevin, the tea-welding butler, were at the mortuary, so she left the clothes with the young man who greeted her in the lobby, secured a promise that he would see to it that Ms. Gabriel knew she'd dropped them off for her mother, and headed over to the diner.

The thought of spending even an hour with Sally and her new boyfriend made Dana groan. She couldn't help but wonder what kind of man a woman like that would attract. But if Dana was lucky, the guy might have known Agnes, and she could quiz them both.

When she pulled into the parking lot, she glanced at the strip club where those three men had loitered. Was that only three days ago? It seemed so much longer than that, an entire lifetime, almost. Dana snorted. "Stop being so melodramatic," she chided herself. It had been a long three days, true enough, but it was still only a matter of days, for God's sake.

She slid the car into a slot underneath a light standard, turned off the ignition, climbed out of the car, and locked up. Adjusting her tee shirt, she took a deep breath and marched across the parking lot.

Angry voices greeted her when she walked into the restaurant. The dining patrons didn't seem to notice, and that had Dana wondering if it was a common occurrence. She shot a quick look at the waitress standing behind the register trying to look busy.

"Hey, Dorothy." Dana motioned toward the kitchen. "What's going on in there?"

Dorothy rolled her eyes. "Sally's having some trouble with Eddie."

"Eddie?"

"Her new fella."

"Yeah," Dana replied. "Sally wanted me to meet him tonight. We're all supposed to have dinner together."

"Don't think there's much chance of that."

"Why? What's going on?"

Before Dorothy could answer, there was a loud crash. Dana bolted around the counter and through the swinging doors into the kitchen. Sally stood next to several pans that were scattered on the floor. Her arms were folded tightly across her chest and her face was the same bright pink as her blush. A cool October breeze blew in from the back door, which was standing wide open.

Dana carefully approached the angry woman. "Sally? You all right?"

"Yeah, honey, I'm fine." She popped her gum loudly then turned and waved her hand in the general direction of the back door.

"Men," she explained. "Can't live with them, can't find a decent place to hide the body." She cackled and flashed an awkward smile.

It was an odd thing to say to someone whose loved one had recently been murdered, and it made Dana even more suspicious about her mother's supposed friendship with the woman. "Sure you're okay?" She looked from Sally to Dorothy, who'd run into the kitchen behind her, and back to Sally.

Sally nodded. "Yeah, but looks like it'll be just us girls for dinner tonight. For some reason, Eddie blew a gasket when I told him I'd invited you for dinner."

Dorothy turned to go back out into the diner, but not before Dana saw the smirk cross her face. She wondered what that was all about and made a mental note to speak to Dorothy about it when Sally wasn't around.

"That's okay, Sally. I'll meet him some other time."

"Well," Sally said, rubbing her hands together, "we might as well go out front and sit down." She ushered Dana out of the kitchen.

"Where do you want to sit?"

"How 'bout in the back?" Sally asked. "Dorothy can cover for me while we chat."

Dorothy brought a couple of glasses of water and plunked them down on the table. Dana expected her to pull her order pad out of her skirt pocket, but instead, she adjusted her tiny black hat and asked, "So, Sal, what's up for tonight?"

Sally looked across the table at Dana. "Go ahead, have anything you want. The Steak Diane is on special tonight."

Dana scanned the menu. "Not really in the mood for steak." She looked up at Dorothy. "How's the Chicken Maxwell?"

"It's delicious," Sally replied before Dorothy had a

chance. Dana couldn't miss the exasperation on Dorothy's face.

"Okay, I'll have that, but could you ask the chef to put the Hollandaise sauce on the side?"

"Sure."

"Oh, and no broccoli, okay?"

"Allergic to our veggies, are we?" Dorothy teased.

"Just the gassy ones," Dana shot back, and they both smiled. "And a Diet Cherry Coke, please."

"Make sure she gets an extra cherry." Sally didn't even look up at Dorothy, which was probably a good thing. "I'll have the Sloppy Joe Bake. And tell Carlos to make it extra crispy for a change."

Dorothy smiled at Dana, flashed Sally another irritated look, and headed for the kitchen and, presumably, Carlos. The cook hadn't been there earlier, but maybe he'd been on a break or in the bathroom or something.

"Ice tea, too," Sally called out. Dorothy made no response. Sally turned back to Dana. "So, I thought we could talk about the wake."

For the next several minutes, Dana tried to stay alert as Sally droned on about the menu, the songs and even who she thought would attend. Dorothy couldn't bring their food fast enough for Dana. When she did, Sally finally came up for air and Dana took the opportunity to ask about her relationship with Agnes.

"Sally," Dana said hesitantly, smiling up at Dorothy as she set her chicken on the table. "How did you meet Mother?"

"Oh, let me see." Sally speared a section of meat and pasta, blew on it, then shoveled it into her mouth. She grabbed her iced tea and gulped it down. "Hot. I'm not really sure, it was so long ago."

Dana lifted a piece of crab meat off the chicken breast, dunked it in the tiny container of Hollandaise, and sampled it. It was surprisingly good. "Mmm, this is really good. My compliments to the chef." She took a sip of soda, then picked up her knife and cut into the chicken. "Do you remember how long ago?"

"Must be, oh, about six, seven years back. Some committee or other, I'd imagine."

Dinner progressed slowly. Every time Dana asked a question, Sally hedged. She couldn't seem to get a straight answer out of the woman.

When Sally excused herself and went to the ladies' room, Dana took advantage of the break and motioned for Dorothy to join her.

"I love that woman dearly," Dorothy told Dana. "But she sure can suck all the oxygen out of a room in nothing flat, can't she?"

Dana smiled. "Can I ask you something?"

Dorothy glanced toward the ladies' room before nodding hesitantly.

"Did you know my mother?"

"I'm afraid not. Never had the pleasure."

"Do you know how Sally and my mother met?"

She shook her head. "No, not really. I do know that they used to be friends, not so long ago."

"Used to be?" Dana frowned. "You mean they weren't when my mother died?"

Dorothy snorted. "Hardly."

Dana sat on the edge of the seat and leaned her forearms on the table. "What happened?"

"Well, I'm not really sure." Dorothy paused, a far off look in her eyes. "I think it had something to do with the park, and—" She stopped suddenly and slid out of the booth. "Got to go. Talk to you later."

She walked down the aisle at the same time Sally came out of the ladies' room and headed toward their table. "Hey, Sal, more tea?"

"No, thanks." Sally slid into the booth and Dana could tell she'd re-applied her make-up. "How about some dessert? Apple Spice Cake, Banana Split, Bread Pudding?"

"Oh, nothing for me." Even if she'd wanted to stay and chat, which she didn't, there was no way she could eat another bite.

"You sure? My bread pudding is killer. I drench it with warm whiskey sauce and lots of whipped cream."

"Sounds great, but I really should go." Dana stood up and reached for her purse.

"Too bad. I was hoping we could spend the whole evening together."

"I'm sorry." Dana rubbed her temple. "But I have a splitting headache. I really need to get home and lie down." She turned and headed toward the door.

Sally walked with her. "Well, I hope you feel better. See you Friday morning."

"Yeah," Dana agreed as she reached for the door. "See you."

"Let me know if you need anything," Sally called after her as she crossed the parking lot. "Anything at all."

Dana hurried to her car, got in, and drove away as quickly as she could. After spending an hour with Sally, she really did need to lie down.

ඐඐඐ

The next morning went by fairly quickly. Dana was able to go through the remaining boxes on her side of the garage in a couple of hours. There were forty-eight boxes in all, everything from the first crayon drawing she'd ever made to term papers she'd written in high school. *Amazing.* She stood back and looked at the wall of boxes that held her entire childhood. She had no idea what she was going to do with it all.

She turned around, wiped her forehead with the back of her hand, and looked at the boxes that lined the other wall. If what she'd just gone through was any indication, she was about to go on another trip down memory lane. It just wouldn't be her memories, so with any luck the job would go smoother and not take her nearly as long.

Well, Phil, welcome to "This is Your Life." There were about fifty boxes. She pulled down the one marked "P1" and got started. Unlike when she'd gone through her own boxes, few items held her attention. She paused over a childish drawing of Daffy Duck she'd made for her brother when she was about six, amazed that he'd actually kept it. There was also a pencil holder she'd made him from an old orange juice can the one time her mother had let her attend a Girl Scout meeting, but nothing else really meant anything to her.

After an hour and a half, she'd finished most of the boxes, except the last half dozen or so, which were labeled with a happy face. This puzzled her, and she pulled the first one down off its shelf with a little trepidation.

Inside, she found meeting agendas and flyers for the "Save the Park" thing Maracella had alluded to. She'd never thought of her mother as a philanthropist, yet here was proof that she'd participated in a neighborhood clean-up and actively worked not only to keep the park, but to beautify it as well.

The agenda for what appeared to be the last meeting listed the motivation for rallying the neighbors and others together under the heading "Our Kids Deserve a Safe Place to Play."

Dana read aloud. "'Do we really want outsiders coming into our neighborhood to eat at some highbrow restaurant that we can't even afford?'" She paused. "Who'd want to put a restaurant in here? That's ridiculous."

She dug deeper into the box. More agendas and some handwritten meeting notes in her mother's tiny, perfectly formed writing. She leafed through the pages, but nothing seemed out of the ordinary.

Putting the notes aside, she reached into the corner of the box and pulled out a few photographs. Her mother at the groundbreaking ceremony, cutting a large red ribbon with an even larger pair of scissors, her mother standing with four others in front of the new park sign, her mother surrounded by laughing children, all looking adoringly up at her.

Had she ever looked at her mother like that? She didn't think so. Why couldn't she have been the kind of mother for Dana that it seemed she'd become for the strangers in the picture? She started to put the photo back in the box when something caught her eye. Could it be? Yes, she was sure of it. A little boy with spiked black hair and startling blue eyes stood next to Agnes, holding her hand. He wore the same yellow shirt with bright green frogs she'd seen that day at the park. Steve's little nephew. Hank.

"Mmm," Dana said to the picture. "I thought you said you barely knew her." She set the picture back in the box and turned toward her neighbor's house. "Maybe so, but Mother and Hank look awfully cozy here, and you yourself said Hank was over a lot. Seems like you knew her a lot better than you said you did."

What happened to her internal early warning system? Pissed off at herself and a little embarrassed, she nevertheless realized that Steve wasn't actually in any of the photos. Maybe he had told her the truth. Maybe Maracella was lying when she claimed not to know Mother very well. Dana would have to do some more investigating, uncover who was lying and who was telling the truth.

She put the photo back in the box, put the lid on it, and started on the next one. Nothing special, mostly junk as far as she could tell. Same for the next two boxes. They contained several certificates of appreciation and a very nice oak and bronze plaque from something called the "Friends of the Library." Yet another pet project of her mother's, it seemed.

"I haven't been to the library since I was a kid. Maybe I'll just go down there and check it out, see what I can see." Dana turned to Charlie, who listened with her head cocked and her ears sticking up. "I'm pretty much done here anyway. Only two more boxes. What do you think? Take the time to go through them now, or save them for later?"

Charlie responded by yawning and smiling sleepily up at her.

"Yeah, thanks for that." Dana chuckled and decided she needed to get out of the garage and get some fresh air anyway, so she put everything back into the open box, except one of the certificates, and shoved the box back onto the shelf. She folded the paper and stuck it in her jeans pocket then went inside to get her purse and keys. She'd find someone who really knew her mother and hope that person would be able to shed some light on the mystery of her murder.

CHAPTER 27

*T**he park isn't the only thing that's changed.* Dana walked inside the library. What had once been rather dark and dingy was now brightly lit and very inviting. There was a rose garden outside the front door, and a beautiful bronze fountain just inside that depicted children at play.

Had her mother been responsible for the renovations here as well? It seemed she'd been a truly amazing woman.

She walked over to the counter and smiled at the woman who was checking out a little girl with six books under her arm. She struggled to hoist them up onto the counter while her father stood nearby.

"Be with you in a sec," the woman told Dana as she ran the first book under the scanner and handed it back to the girl. "This is a good one, Ginny. I think you'll like it."

The little girl smiled. "Daddy says it was his favorite when he was my age." She turned to her father. "Wasn't it, Daddy?"

Daddy beamed back at his little girl. "Sure was, punkin."

Dana flashed on a similar time with her own father before she looked away and willed herself to stop.

"Miss?"

"Oh, sorry." She moved up to the woman and leaned on the counter. "Do you know anything about the Friends of the Library?"

"Sure. They have a little used bookstore downstairs." She pointed down the hall. "Turn left at the elevator, go out the door and follow the walkway down to the parking lot, then go around the corner, and it's right there." She shrugged. "Sorry, but the elevator only goes upstairs."

"That's okay." Dana slung her purse back onto her shoulder. "Thanks."

She set off to follow the woman's directions, expecting to find some dingy hole-in-the-wall, and was quite surprised when she came upon the little store. The door stood wide open and classical music wafted through it from inside. The scent of jasmine filled the air. Used paperbacks grouped together by genre neatly lined the walls. Several small loveseats surrounded an oak coffee table. On the table sat a vase overflowing with pink and white flowers. It was all very homey, a place she would enjoy frequenting. She imagined her mother would, too.

"Can I help you?"

Dana looked up from the cozy nook to find an older woman with gray hair and eyes to match sitting behind a desk, smiling at her.

"Are you looking for something in particular?"

Dana walked up to the desk. "Hi," she said. "My name is Dana Sinclair, and—"

"Oh, honey," the woman purred. Her eyes shone. With what, Dana couldn't quite tell, but it did not look like sorrow. "I'm so sorry about your mother. When's the funeral?"

"Um, Friday at four."

"Well, you let me know if there's anything I can do for you, hear?"

"Sure." Dana glanced over at the stacks. *Was that someone hiding in the shadows?* Shaking her head slightly, she turned back to the clerk. "Did you know my mother?"

"No, not really. But I hear tell she was a real nice lady. Helped raise the money to renovate the library, including this room here for the bookstore." She gestured toward the rows of books. "Do you like it?"

"It's nice," Dana agreed. "Maybe you know a friend of my mother's, Sally Connor?"

"Oh, sure, she owns the diner."

"Yes, that's right."

"A lovely woman. Hearty stock."

Dana bit her tongue. It was probably best to keep her opinion of Sally to herself. "Do you know if she was a friend of my mother's?"

"Sally's everyone's friend. She's a real people person, that one."

"How did they meet?"

"Got me." The woman looked into the same corner where Dana had seen the shadow move. "Why don't you look around, see if anything appeals to you—Hey, Harry."

A man moved up beside her and dumped an armload of books onto the desk. "How much I owe you this time, Irma?"

Dana wandered over toward the spinning rack at the end of the first row and pretended to study the books while she watched the two at the desk. Why the brush off? What was it the woman wasn't telling her? Dana leafed through a paperback romance as Irma put the man's books in a plastic sack.

"Psst."

The hair on the back of her neck stood up. She patted her purse, comforted by the knowledge that her weapon was nearby.

"Over here," the voice whispered.

She looked over her shoulder, but didn't see anyone. Trying to appear casual, Dana put the book back in the rack and strolled down the row toward the back exit. Her hand went automatically inside her purse, and she gripped her gun.

As she got closer to the end of the row, she stifled a sneeze. So much dust, as if no one ever looked at the books farthest away from the desk. They certainly weren't dusted on a regular basis. She inched closer to the exit door, wondering who was back here and why the person was hiding.

Then she saw a flash of red and turned carefully around the corner at the end of the shelves. There stood Janey Smith, the young woman from Dana's accident. She held her index finger up to her mouth. "Shh," Janey whispered. "I don't want them to know I'm here."

"Them?" Dana asked. "Who's 'them'?"

Janey's eyes darted in the direction of the front of the store then leveled on Dana's. "Look, we can't talk here. Meet me outside the back door tonight at ten."

"Not until you tell me what's going on, Janey," Dana told her. "It is Janey, right?"

"Do you want to know the truth about your mother's murder or not?"

"Of course, but—"

"Ten o'clock." She pushed on the bar to the exit door and opened it.

"Wait." Dana reached out for her.

But she was gone.

e/ɔe/ɔ

Dana checked her watch for the three hundredth time. Nine-fifty. She'd been here for over half an hour, waiting for Janey to show. Early, she knew, but she just didn't want to miss her. Plus the cop in her was curious to see if anyone else would show up. She wasn't about to get caught in a trap, but then again, she needed to find out what the girl knew about what had happened to her mother.

Nine fifty-six. The girl should show up any minute now. As if on cue, a car pulled into the empty lot. Its lights swept across Dana's windshield, momentarily blinding her.

Blinking rapidly several times until her eyesight adjusted, she grabbed her pistol off her lap and jammed it into the waistband of her jeans then climbed out and walked toward Janey's car. As she approached, the passenger door opened. Dana took a quick peek in the back seat before she climbed inside.

"Janey," Dana said as she shut the door. "What the hell's going on?"

"Look, Deputy," Janey said. "Dana. I liked your mother. She was a nice lady. But she had a way of making enemies, you know?" She ducked her head enough to look out the windshield underneath the rear view mirror and scanned the parking lot. "I'm probably being paranoid, but I just don't trust certain people."

"Who?"

"Irma Miklos for one."

"The woman in the book store?"

"For starters." Janey turned in her seat to face Dana. "She and Sally Connor are best friends. Did you know that?"

"No, I didn't."

"Well, they are. And both of them hated your mother."

Dana frowned and turned to face Janey more fully. "Do you know why?"

Janey hesitated, chewing on her bottom lip. Dana shifted in her seat but remained silent. "There's this little kiddie park, you know? Premier Park. More like a family park, really."

"Yes," Dana responded quietly. "I know it." It was the park near Mother's house.

"I went to this meeting one time, at your mom's house," Janey began. "It was a 'Save the Park' pot luck. Your mom was really into that park. She hated what it had become, the gangs and graffiti and all." She reached down by Dana's feet and grabbed her purse off the floorboard. "Everyone was supposed to bring their favorite dish." She dug inside her purse, moving things around nosily. "Afterward, we were going to talk about ways to raise money to fix it up."

"What happened?" Dana asked, wishing the kid would leave the purse alone already and get on with it.

"Well, for one thing, Sally showed up and—" She pulled out a pack of Camels and a cheap lighter, and pounded the top of the unopened pack on her palm. "You mind?"

Actually, Dana did mind being confined in a small space breathing second-hand smoke, but didn't want to discourage the girl, so she shook her head and rolled her window down half-way. Janey opened the box and pulled out a cigarette.

"What happened after Sally showed up?" Dana coached.

"All hell broke loose." Her hands trembled just enough to make it difficult for her to light a cigarette, but once she did so, she inhaled deeply. "She pretended at first that she wanted to save the park, too." Janey rolled

her window down a few inches and blew the smoke outside.

Thank God for small favors.

"We all had a nice time eating and everything. But
when it came time to start the meeting, Sally surprised
everyone." Janey took another long drag on her cigarette.
"Basically, she tried to sabotage it. She wanted to buy the
lot from the city so she could put in some stupid restaurant that no one would want to eat at, much less be able to
afford. She tried to convince everyone that it would be
good for the economy, that it would add class to the
neighborhood, and that we needed it more than the kids
needed a safe place to play. What she really meant was
that it would be good for *her* economy."

"What did people say?"

"Everyone was against it, but, dude, your mom went
ballistic."

"How so?"

"She called her on it. Told everyone that the neighbor kids being safe was far more important than anything
else, and that we couldn't afford to let commerce into the
neighborhood with all its traffic and crime and stuff.
Called Sally a mean-spirited, parsimonious narcissist.
Whatever that means." The girl shrugged. "Anyway, everyone laughed. Sally got *pissed.*"

"So, I guess there was a bit of a strain between
them."

Janey snorted and took a deep drag. "You can say
that again."

They sat in silence for a few minutes. Dana watched
the end of Janey's cigarette as it glowed bright red when
she inhaled, then cooled to a small orange circle before it
enlarged and glowed again with the next drag.

"Can I ask you a question?" Dana asked.

Janey inhaled a last time, flicked the butt out the window, and exhaled. "Sure," she said as she rolled up the window. "Then I've got to get out of here."

"Did my mother ever talk about me?"

Janey nodded. "I remember this one time, she told me that you were a cop, and I'd better be good or she'd sic you on me." The girl laughed. "She was kidding, you know? But you could see how much she loved you."

Dana tried not to let the lump forming in her throat choke her.

"And at the Pot Luck? She told everybody what a weird kid you were, that your favorite meal was meatloaf and mashed potatoes. The potatoes I got, but meatloaf? Yuck."

"She thought I was weird?"

"No, dude." Janey shook her head. "*I* think you're weird. Or at least you were when you were little. Meat loaf? Seriously?"

Dana shook her head. "Yeah. I see your point."

"I've got to go."

"Just one final question." Dana didn't give Janey a chance to respond. "Do you know if my mother ever gave Sally a key to her house?"

Janey shook her head then turned on the ignition and let the car idle. "I doubt it. Look, I'm not sure if Sally had anything to do with what happened to your mom, but when I heard about it, she was the first thing that popped into my mind." She put the car in gear. "I just thought you should know."

"Thanks, Janey." Dana opened the door, got out, and leaned back inside. "I'll be in touch." She'd barely shut the door when the car shot forward, turned left, and sped off into the night.

CHAPTER 28

Dana sat in the darkened parking lot, gripping the steering wheel tightly, and rested her head on her hands. Deep breaths, she told herself. It was all too much to deal with.

Was it really possible her mother had been murdered over a park? A *park*? Could anyone really be that ruthless? With a heavy heart, she turned on the ignition and headed home, feeling like she'd been hit over the head with this new information. She tried to empty her mind and flipped on the radio. Maybe singing would help.

As soon as she recognized the song, she smiled and turned it up. "Shimmy shimmy coco puffs, shimmy shimmy pop," she sang at top volume. How she loved those golden oldies and their silly lyrics. She could play sing-a-long all day. Even if she couldn't carry a tune in a bucket.

After Little Anthony and the Imperials finished, she performed a duet with Jerry Lee Lewis and his "Great Balls of Fire," then ended the concert with a little Witch Doctor chanting. "Ooo eee, ooo ah ah, ting tang, walla walla, bing bang." Talk about inane. Couldn't get much more ridiculous than that. *And just think, people actually got paid to write that stuff.*

By the time she pulled into her mother's driveway, her spirits had lifted, and she wondered if Steve was home. When she'd first left the library, she'd thought about giving Brian a call to pick his brain, find out what he thought about everything. But she really wanted to ask Steve about that picture she'd found, the one with her mother and Hank at the park.

Tomorrow would be soon enough to talk to Brian, especially since he'd be pissed about her meeting an unknown in a dark parking lot after hours. Without back-up, no less. Now that she was home safe, she could admit——at least to herself—that it was a pretty stupid move. Still, she had gotten some useful information out of it.

Dana strolled across the lawn and tapped lightly on Steve's door. She was just about to knock again when he opened it. It wasn't all that late, but judging by his tousled hair and the fact that he rubbed irritably at his eyes, she realized that he'd been asleep.

"What is it?" he asked abruptly.

"Oh, sorry," she said, and turned to leave. "Didn't mean to wake you."

"'S okay," he said, his tone softening, and grabbed her wrist. "What's up?"

"Nothing. Just felt like talking, that's all. But I can come back tomorrow."

"No," he said. "It's okay. Come on in." He led her into the living room and motioned to the couch. "Coffee?"

"Rather have a beer if you've got one."

"Sure thing."

He fetched some beers, and they chatted easily about nothing in particular. The silences between topics were companionable, and Dana felt herself begin to unwind.

Eventually, after Steve had almost finished his third beer and she was halfway through her second and feeling a little buzzed, he took a deep breath and exhaled. "So," he began.

"So," she countered.

"Well?"

"Well, what?"

He gave her that same look Charlie did when she couldn't understand why Dana didn't get what she was trying to say. She laughed. "Okay, okay," she said and launched into a monologue that started with the flowers and the strange visit from Finn then continued with her mother's cryptic dying statement, the photographs, the footprint, the feelings of being watched, and ended with the news about her father.

When she finished, Steve simply stared at her for a few seconds, then silently got up and went into the kitchen. At first she thought he was getting some more beer, but when he returned, he was bearing two more pints of Ben & Jerry's, a tablespoon stuck in the middle of each carton.

"Too much information to process without sugar." He shrugged, looked first at one carton, then the other. "Cake Batter or Brownie Batter?"

She made a face. "On top of beer?"

"Any time's a good time for ice cream."

"Is there anything else in your freezer other than ice cream?"

"I'm working my way through, remember?"

"Fine," she said and sighed as though it were a real imposition. "I'll take the Brownie."

He handed it to her. "Dig in."

She did just that. They ate nosily for a few minutes, oohing and aahing over the creamy goodness.

"Do you know a girl named Janey Smith?"

Steve looked up from his ice cream. "Cute kid? Works at the library?"

"Yeah, that's her."

"Never met her." He returned to his treat, scraping the sides of the carton.

"Ha, ha. Very funny," Dana said. "No, really. I'm serious."

"Sure, she's checked me out several times."

This was another one of those times she wished she could raise one eyebrow. Instead, she just looked at him, deadpan.

He flashed that charming smile at her and chuckled. "Books. She's checked out my books for me several times."

"She told me that she's actually scared of Sally, and that she and my mother most decidedly were not friends."

"Diner Sally?"

"Yes."

"Hey, speaking of which, were you home yesterday, about eleven or so?"

"No. Why?"

"Yeah, I didn't think so."

"Why?" she repeated.

"Because she went inside your house." He turned his attention back to his ice cream.

The hairs on the back of her neck stood up, and the ice cream and beer began a sickening tango inside her stomach. "I know. She left me a really nasty note."

"Most have been one hell of a long note."

"Why do you say that?"

"Because she was in there quite a while."

"She was?"

He nodded.

"How long?"

"Hmmm, let's see." He thought for a moment. "I went outside to get the mail. That was about eleven." He smiled sheepishly. "Overslept."

"Go on," she urged.

"Sally was just pulling up when the phone rang and I ran inside to get it. It was little Hank."

"And?"

"And he wanted to know if you could come to the next family barbeque. Seems he's quite smitten with you."

"He's a sweetie pie. Then what?"

"We talked about twenty or thirty minutes. There's this little girl in his kindergarten class—he goes in the afternoon because they're better readers. Such a smart kid."

Maybe silence was the way to go to get him to finish his original thought. So she resisted the urge to rotate her finger in a "hurry up" motion and nodded in agreement.

"After I hung up, I tossed the phone on the couch and poured myself some coffee. Then I sat down to enjoy it and go on Facebook for a while when it occurred to me that I'd forgotten the mail. So I took a swig of coffee—burned my tongue a little—and went to get it."

"What time was that?"

"That's what's so weird. I remember I looked at my watch because I couldn't believe she was just coming out of your house, and I was pretty sure you'd already left."

She struggled to keep her irritation in check. "What time?"

"Eleven-forty. Dana, she was in your house for almost forty minutes."

eɔeɔ

It wouldn't take a child forty minutes to write such a

short note. So what had Sally been doing in there for so long? Was she looking for something in particular, or had she just taken advantage of the situation and snooped through Agnes's things?

Unsure what to do with the information, Dana concentrated on making sure the Brownie Batter didn't come back up. Steve gave her some space and took the ice cream cartons back into the kitchen as she tried to process what he'd told her. She could hear him washing the spoons and putting them away.

By the time he came back, she felt a little better. While she was gathering intel on Sally, she may as well collect some on Steve. "Didn't you tell me that you barely knew my mother?"

"Yeah. We had coffee a few times, and sometimes she'd wave." He'd been looking directly at her, but then shifted his eyes upward and to the left. Warning bells went off in her head. Either he was lying, or else he was remembering something that happened. It depended on whether he was left-handed or right-handed. She tried to remember which hand he'd eaten his ice cream with. She shut her eyes and visualized him a few minutes ago, when he'd first dug into the carton. Right hand. He'd used his right hand. That meant he was probably lying to her. Why?

"Speaking of coffee, would you like some?"

"Sure," she agreed, and followed him into the kitchen.

As Steve prepared the coffee, Dana watched him closely. He reached for the filters with his right hand, dumped the coffee in with his left, and poured the water with his right.

When the coffee was ready, she had him fill her mug about half-full, and watched him over the top of it. She sipped slowly while he dumped a ton of flavored creamer into the mug and filled it to the rim. When he stirred it, he used his left hand.

"Aren't you right handed?" she asked.

He shook his head. "Ambidextrous."

She groaned inwardly. So much for body language. He gestured to the kitchen table and they sat down across from each other. "So what is it you want to ask me?"

She jumped. "What makes you think I want to ask you something?"

"Because you asked me how well I knew Agnes. Again."

"Oh, yeah, right." She'd been so focused on trying to determine if he was lying or not, she'd almost forgotten what he might be lying about. She was beginning to doubt herself, her ability to be a good cop. Maybe she should resign and apply for a job at Walmart.

"I came across this picture that was taken at the park when it re-opened." How would Steve explain it? "It's my mom and a bunch of kids. They were laughing and having a good time."

"Yeah?"

"Yeah." She licked her lips. "And Hank was standing next to her."

"That so?" He took another sip of coffee, this one a little quieter. Again, she wondered what he was hiding.

"But you said you didn't know her very well," she pointed out.

"I didn't."

"But she knew Hank."

"Yeah, she knew Hank. And Maracella. And Jay." He took another sip. "They were on the 'Save the Park' committee together." He set his mug down and looked directly at her. "I, however, wasn't. Too busy. All year, up until just about a week or so ago." He gestured toward the back yard. "That's why I don't go to the office every day right now. Enjoying a little semi-retirement, as it were."

Boy, did she feel stupid. What was it about this guy that had her all tied up in knots and making a fool of herself all the time? And what about his claim that his sister was the one who knew Mother? She'd made the same claim about Steve.

"What about you?" he asked.

"Mmm? What about me, what?"

"Will you go back to being a cop after the funeral, or will you take some extra time off? Enjoy life, as it were."

She couldn't remember if she'd ever told him about José, or that she'd been placed on administrative leave. Too tired to put on a poker face, and believing that it didn't really matter anyway, she told him the truth. "Afraid not." She closed her eyes. When she opened them again, Steve was looking at her curiously. To his credit, he didn't ask the question that he had to be thinking——why not? "Not long before my mother died, my partner was killed in the line of duty. I shot the perp. So I'm on leave till Internal Affairs rules it a good shoot."

"Oh, Dana." Steve reached across the table and placed his hand on her forearm. Compassion made his eyes shine. "That must have been awful."

"It was."

"I'm sorry about your partner."

"Thank you. We were very close."

"You must miss him a lot."

"I do." She grasped a strand of hair and twirled it around her finger. "But at least his kids live nearby. So there's that."

"Would you like to talk about him?"

"Not really. But thanks anyway."

"You okay?"

"I guess." Little did he know how much she was

struggling to keep her emotions from running amok. Intellectually, she knew she would be wise not to let them hit the surface, and part of her police training was learning to compartmentalize your emotions so the things you saw people do to each other day in and day out wouldn't emotionally tear you apart. But psychologically, she was a lonely woman who found it harder and harder to believe Steve had anything to do with her mother's death.

He leaned across the table and took her face gently in his hands, gazing at her with those dazzling eyes of his. She looked up at him and smiled. Then, without worrying about the possible consequences or even waiting for him to make the first move, she leaned across the table and kissed him. He kissed her back, running his hands through her hair. It was relaxing and stimulating at the same time. He pulled back to look at her as he smoothed her bangs away from her face. Then he rose out of his chair, enfolded her in his arms again and brushed his lips lightly against her neck.

First she gasped then moaned as he trailed his fingertips down her arms. It made her shiver.

"You have the most beautiful hair," he murmured, nibbling her earlobe as he ran his fingers through it.

She caressed his chest and stroked his belly, then moved her hands across his hips and squeezed his buttocks. "You have a great ass," she whispered as her hands traveled up his back and pulled him closer.

He traced her collarbone with his fingertip. "Are you sure you want to do this?"

"I've been alone so long." Her eyes locked on his. She felt as if she could plunge into them, sink down to the bottom of his soul and melt into him, become one with him. "So long," she whispered. "I'd forgotten what passion felt like. When you kiss me, I feel alive again." She leaned into him, her hair falling across his shoulder.

He held her close, running his hands up her back underneath her shirt. She buried her face in his neck and inhaled deeply. He smelled of summertime, a faint musky odor, and tasted of sunlight and new beginnings. She craved it, filled her lungs and memory with his scent.

He peeled her shirt off over her head, and her skin tingled with anticipation.

"Turn off your mind, Dana." He rubbed his thumbs across her nipples until they stood at attention. How could she possibly think when he was giving her so much pleasure she felt lightheaded and near collapse? She couldn't have stopped if she'd wanted to. He saturated her senses, filling her with a desire that burned and made her feel alive.

Her eyes locked on his again and she took her time as she unbuttoned his shirt, kissing his chest after each button. She ran her fingernails across his pecs and down his arms as she pushed his shirt off and let it fall to the ground. Smiling, she pulled his face to hers and kissed him gently at first, then with a growing heat that threatened to incinerate her.

She enjoyed the shock of pleasure that flashed across his face when she began to unbutton his pants, the way his belly quivered when she touched it. He caught her hands in his, but her mission would not be foiled, and she twisted her wrists slightly to get him to release them. She strayed leisurely over his chest, brushing her tongue across his nipples before she began the journey downward, lingering over the tastes and textures along the way.

They worked their way quickly down the hall, kissing, touching, and burning with intensity and passion until she was sure she would explode.

And when she did, everything went white hot, moon-light and sunlight blending together in a cacophony of urgency, quivering, pleasured flesh, and erotic intimacy.

CHAPTER 29

She was lying with her head on Steve's shoulder, her hair splayed out across his chest like a rug. The steady rhythm of his breathing combined with his heartbeat to lull her into a kind of post-coital stupor. If it weren't for her stomach growling, she could have stayed cuddled up to him all night.

Wonder what he's got to munch on? She wormed her way out from underneath his arm and slipped off the bed. *Please let it be something other than ice cream.* She loved the stuff, but it certainly didn't love her waist line. Sad but true, and she really needed to get back into a strict exercise regime if she was going to be ready to go back when the department called. And of course, that would preclude further sojourns into the sugar arena.

Glancing back over her shoulder to make sure Steve was still asleep, she smiled at him and thought how in sleep he looked so much like Hank, with his tousled hair and slightly pursed mouth. She sidestepped the jumble of their clothes lying in a heap on the floor and tiptoed across the room. It was a little chilly, and she rubbed her hands briskly across her arms in an effort to get rid of the goose bumps.

There was a beautiful oak dresser in the corner of his bedroom, and she pulled open a drawer and looked for a shirt to put on. Underwear, boxers and briefs both, all colors. Plain white, V-neck tees. Afraid a tee wouldn't be warm enough, she quietly shut the drawer and opened the one underneath it. Pay dirt—it was full of crew neck sweatshirts, some with the sleeves cut off but most were in one piece. She picked a thick one with the LA Lakers purple and gold emblem silk-screened on the front. As she pulled it out of the drawer, something fell onto the floor. Pulling on the sweatshirt, she squatted down to see what it was.

Frowning, she scooped it up. It was a pewter, heart-shaped locket on a silver thirty inch Byzantine chain. She knew the length because she'd seen it before. In disbelief, she clutched her mother's locket and brought her fist to her mouth.

A hand grasped her by the back of the neck and she jumped. Steve leaned in, swept her hair out of the way and bent to kiss the nape of her neck. She squirmed away and glared at him. *No way. No way did I do something so stupid.*

"What's the matter?" he said sleepily, rubbing his eyes with the back of his fingers. "Can't sleep?"

"Where did you get this?" She extended her hand, the locket lying in her palm, the chain hanging down through her fingers. Steve's eyes went wide, and he shook his head vigorously. He held up his hands, palms facing Dana, and took a step back.

"It's not what you think," he claimed.

"Bullshit. Did you steal my mother's locket before you murdered her, or after?"

"Dana." He took a step toward her, a hang-dog look on his face.

Dana took a compensatory step backward. "Stay right where you are."

"You don't understand."

"I understand plenty." Stupidly, she'd left her purse—and subsequently, her gun—in the living room. Brushing quickly past him, she grabbed her clothes from the pile on the floor and clutched them to her chest. Her eyes never left his. She backed out of the room. "Stay where you are."

"But—" he began, and she pointed her finger at him.

"Don't move, Steve. I'm going to put on my pants, and then I'm going to leave." Dana struggled into her jeans as she backed down the hall. "So why'd you do it?" Steve followed but left plenty of room between them. "Was it for her money? Did you somehow find out that she had a ton of stocks worth a small fortune and when she wouldn't give them to you, you thought maybe you'd murder her and take the locket to have it appraised? See what it was worth? Maybe go back later to look for more?"

"Come on, you can't really believe that."

"No? And why is that?" She'd reached the living room and headed straight for her purse. "Because I let my guard down and was foolish enough to believe you actually cared about me?"

"I do care about you."

"Don't make me laugh." She took her eyes off him for just an instant, so she could pick up her purse, and in that instant he crossed the room and grabbed her wrist.

"Let go of me," she said, determined not to grimace against the pain.

"Not until you listen to me." He bent her arm back far enough that she was forced to drop her purse.

"The only thing I want to hear from you," she told him evenly, "is why you killed my mother."

"I told you," he said, his voice rising. "I didn't kill her." The vein in his forehead had started to throb.

She forced her body to relax, hoping to catch him off-guard. "No, you just stole her locket for the hell of it."

"You're right. I did take it. But not the way you think." He propelled her over to the couch and pushed her down into it. She immediately popped up, and he shoved her down again. "Damn it, Dana, just sit still for a minute. You want to know why I have your mother's locket or not?"

Crossing her arms, she glared at him in response. He stood directly in front of her, effectively pinning her down. "This should be good," she said.

"Didn't you ever wonder why I was there that day? The day after your mother…died?"

"To view your handiwork?" she asked. "To find out if the cops had anything that could lead them to you?"

"I went there specifically to put the locket back."

"Back?"

"Yes, back. I haven't been entirely honest with you, Dana."

"No, really? I never would have guessed." Her eyes darted around him, gauging the distance to the front door. She settled back into the couch, trying to appear as though she were relaxed in hopes that Steve would be, too.

"Sarcasm really doesn't become you, you know."

She twirled her finger in a tight circle. Get on with it.

"So, anyway." He ran his hand through his hair and turned slightly. "Your mother and I weren't exactly friends, that much is true, but we were neighbors, good neighbors. She invited me over for coffee every couple of weeks. Usually had something she'd baked for me to try. Woman made a mean black forest cake." He looked at her then took a few steps away. "She was always talking about you. How much she loved you, what a sweet kid you were, how proud of you she was."

As much as people kept telling her that, she still had trouble believing it. "That's all well and good." She snuck another look at the door. "But that still doesn't explain why I should believe you aren't a murderer."

"Because," he replied, "she made me fall in love with you."

"I beg your pardon?"

"Well, she made me fall in love with your picture, anyway, and the woman you'd become. So when she came over that last time, a week or so before..." He trailed off as he turned away from her but spun back quickly before she could get off the couch. "Anyway, she brought Hank and me a blueberry pie she'd baked for us. After she went home, I sat on the porch and watched Hank play in the yard. I saw something glittering on the ground, so I picked it up. And Dana?" He looked her directly in the eye. "It was the locket. I think it must have fallen off when Hank hugged her good-bye. The clasp was broken so I had it fixed for her. It was the least I could do. I know I should have given it back to her the day I fixed it, but I couldn't bring myself to part with it right away. I just wanted to keep it for a few days."

Dana stood and pulled the locket out of her pocket to inspect the clasp before looking back at him. While the chain itself was a little tarnished, the clasp was shiny. It had obviously been recently replaced. Maybe he was telling the truth.

"Why?" she demanded. "Why would you want to do that?"

"Because it reminds me of you."

She narrowed her eyes at him. *Why would it?*

He continued before she had a chance to ask. "But then when I saw all the cop cars at your mom's place and heard all the commotion, I knew I had to take it back so you wouldn't think it was missing. Then I met you and fell in love with you for real."

She had to get out of here. This guy was a lunatic, delusional somehow. He stood in front of her again, reaching out for her. Just before he grasped her arms, she made her move. She pushed him out of the way and elbowed him in the side as hard as she could. It knocked him back a step, but he quickly recovered and grabbed her arm. She twisted her body around and shoved the heel of her palm into his face.

Steve cried out and released her. "Ow! I tink you busted by nose!"

She scooped up her purse and raced for the door, got it unlocked before he caught up to her, and whirled her around to face him. His nose bled profusely, the blood running down his arms to his elbows, staining his shirt, and she felt a sting of satisfaction.

She lashed out with a forearm roundhouse to the side of his head and quickly followed with two sharp thrusts to his busted nose. As he screamed, she kicked him as hard as she could in the nuts and raced out the door. The last thing she saw was Steve lying on his side, moaning and, she hoped, in intense pain.

Considering what he'd done to her mother, even that was too good for him.

CHAPTER 30

C alm down, Dana," Brian told her. She'd called him after racing home from Steve's, running like her life depended on it. It very well might have. She was glad he was here.

"Okay, sorry."

"Tell me again what happened." He pulled out his notebook and pen. "Nice and slow this time."

"I went over there about ten of eleven."

"What for?"

"Just wanted to talk. Maybe have a glass of wine or a beer and relax."

"Okay." Brian looked at her impassively, and she wondered what he was thinking.

She hoped she could avoid the whole sleeping-with-a-possible-suspect thing, but knew realistically that there was no way around it.

"So we talked for a couple of hours, just chit-chat, really. Nothing important."

"And how did you come across the locket?"

Damn. There was no way she could explain digging in his bureau without admitting what happened. She noisily blew her bangs off her forehead, closed her eyes, and braced herself for the tirade. "I was looking for a shirt to put on."

"Say what?"

"I was cold."

"I see." His jaw muscles worked, and she knew he was struggling to keep his temper in check. "So you found the locket in a drawer. Then what?"

"He woke up and I confronted him."

"He…woke up. Oookay." He pursed his lips, his jaw working overtime now. "And what did he say when you did?"

"He made some lame excuse for why he had it, of course." She took another deep breath and held it briefly before slowly blowing it out. "Claimed he found it in his yard with a broken clasp, that he fixed it but then held onto it for a few days—conveniently until he saw all the squad cars at Mother's—but intended to return it all along. Said that's what he was trying to do when he showed up that day." She turned the locket over in her hand. Now that she really looked at it, she thought it was beautiful, the only ornate item her mother had ever owned.

"Right," Brian said. "The guy on the porch. Tried to get inside before I got there." He scribbled something down in his notebook. "I'll get a warrant, send a car over to pick him up. Charge him with assault and petty theft. We don't have enough evidence yet to charge him with murder, but maybe we can get him to confess. But, Dana?"

"Yes?"

"He's been on the short list since day one."

So she really had slept with a suspect. Hearing it spelled out in black and white made her break out in a cold sweat. She'd blown it big time. Made a grave error in judgment. Career-ending, in fact. Shit.

"There's something else," she said. As if sleeping with Public Enemy Number One wasn't bad enough.

"What, there's more?"

"I met someone in the parking lot at the library last night. She claimed she had information on who might have murdered Mother." She told him that Janey had pointed the finger at Sally. "That's why I went to Steve's afterward. I needed to decompress, to just chill out, and take my mind off things. You know how I get."

"Yeah, I know," Brian agreed. "But I can't believe you were that stupid."

"I—"

He cut her off before she could explain. "You've been a cop for how long?" he asked, and Dana could feel the heat rising in her face. "Did I teach you nothing?"

"I couldn't risk her not showing or leaving if she saw that I wasn't alone."

"But you don't know this girl. You could have been killed."

"True," Dana agreed. "But I'm a pretty good judge of character." She was sincerely glad he didn't comment on the irony of that statement. "I could tell she was harmless."

"Right."

She bit her tongue to keep from blurting out a juvenile "it's true" and remained silent.

"So let me see if I have this right. You didn't tell anyone where you were going or what you were doing?"

"No, I didn't."

"Uh huh." Then, "Let me ask you something."

"Shoot."

"You ever hear of a little thing called back-up?" And before she could respond, he continued. "The least you could have done was to confide in me."

"In retrospect—" she began. She wouldn't apologize,

because if she had it to do over, she would have done the same thing and suspected he would, too, but maybe it would help if she placated him a bit.

"Don't give me that crap. You broke the rules, Dana. Seriously." She braced herself for a lecture, but he surprised her when his voice softened. "And more importantly, you could have gotten hurt."

"But I didn't."

"But you could have," he snapped. "So, is there anything else you didn't think you needed to tell me? A meeting with international terrorists, perhaps? Or maybe just a little ransom drop at a kidnapping?"

Don't smile, she told herself. *Don't you dare. He might not be kidding.*

"No, nothing else," Dana told him.

"Fine." He got up and put his notebook and pen back into his pocket. "I'll check out this Sally..."

"Connor."

"Sally Connor. In the meantime, try to stay out of trouble, will you?" Without waiting for an answer, he left. Dana thought he closed the door a little harder than was necessary, but she couldn't really blame him, she supposed. What she'd done had been pretty stupid.

℘℘℘

She leaned back against the couch, tucking her legs up underneath her, and pulled the waistband of the sweatshirt down over her knees. Then she realized what she had on and who it belonged to, and yanked the thing off over her head. Threw it angrily against the bookcase, knocking something off one of the shelves.

"Stupid, stupid, stupid." She strode down the hallway, banging her fists on the walls as she went. She wanted the feel of him, the scent of him, the whole of him, off her body, and took a long, hot shower, scrubbing her skin vigorously until she felt clean again. After she dried off, she slipped the necklace on over her head and pulled on a sweater and fleece pants, then sat down on the edge of the bed, clutched the locket and slowly brought her hand up to her mouth.

"Mother," she whispered.

She fell back onto her bed, rolled over on her side with her knees drawn up, and pressed the miniscule button on the side of the locket. It popped open and she was stunned by what she found inside. On the left side was a picture of her father, looking very serious. It was his Academy photo. What she found on the right side made her draw in her breath. The same Dodger blue eyes looked out at her as they did from the first picture, in almost the exact same face. This one was also an Academy photo. Hers.

Dana couldn't believe what she was looking at. Mother had always worn the locket, had in fact rarely taken it off. Growing up, she'd often wondered what was inside, but her mother would never say, and even in her rebellious teen years, Dana would not have violated her privacy by sneaking a peek. She'd thought about it often enough, but ultimately could not do it. She'd made a lot of guesses, mostly childish, but never in her wildest imaginings, never in a million years would she ever have guessed its true contents. Not the way her mother had refused to speak of her father all those years. Or to her for the past seven.

Something clicked in her memory and she sat up and swung her feet off the side of the bed before rushing down the hall into the living room. She scoured the bookshelves, searching for the little glass figurine she'd found in the yard. There were so many dust collectors here, and she impatiently shoved them out of her way in an attempt to find what she was looking for. Absorbed in what she was doing, she tripped on the Lakers sweatshirt she'd left in a heap in front of the shelving unit.

"Ow, crap!" She grabbed her foot and hopped up and down. Something under the sweatshirt had put a big dent in the bottom of her foot. Hooking the collar with her toe, she kicked the shirt out of the way. She'd stepped on the very figurine she'd been searching for, and reached down to pick it up. It only took a second or two for her to realize what she was holding.

"Where is it?" She tore through the bookshelves, tossing things out of the way until she found what she was looking for. The mate to the figurine she'd just stepped on. Not an oddly-shaped seal as she'd originally thought, but a very ugly walrus. As in, Lewis Carroll's *The Walrus and the Carpenter*. The glass figurine that had been left on the front step for her was a man in a funny hat. Now she recognized it. The Carpenter.

It had once belonged to her father.

CHAPTER 31

I can picture you as a little girl," Maura said.

They had just ordered a couple of margaritas at Duffy's, a bar that catered to law enforcement. Dana had called her friend the following afternoon and asked if they could meet. She knew it was Maura's day off and she just couldn't sit in that house one more minute. Maura suggested they have a drink early that evening.

"Sitting on the floor, your red hair all curly, listening to your father reading 'The Walrus and the Carpenter.' What book is that from?"

"*Through the Looking-Glass and What Alice Found There.*" Dana took a sip of her drink. "Mmm, good."

"That the one with the little footless oysters walking hand in hand with a walrus and a man who eventually eats them?"

"And the Jabberwocky." Dana sighed. "That's what Daddy used to call Phil."

"Jabberwocky?" Maura asked, and held out her hand. "Gimme see."

Dana nodded and handed her the strange figurines. Maura turned them over and studied them closely.

"I think Daddy brought them home when I was about four or five. I remember he used to let us hold them while he read to us but then we had to leave them on the fireplace mantle. We weren't allowed to play with them." She took another sip and smiled. "Probably a good thing."

"Dana, I think these are jade," Maura said. She handed them back to Dana and pointed to two tiny little spots on the walrus. "See the little black imperfections here and here?"

She looked at the figurines closely. "Jade? Really?"

"Pretty sure. Of course, I'd have to run some tests to be positive."

Dana put the figurines back in her purse. "That's okay."

"So your mom kept the walrus all this time?" Maura asked. "That's really something. She must have loved your dad very much."

"It's so strange. All these years, I thought she hated him."

"And then you find these little mementos and the locket—where is the locket, by the way?"

Dana pulled it out from underneath her shirt, opened it, and leaned forward so Maura could look at it. "I still can't believe she had my picture in it."

Maura leaned across the table to get a closer look and shrugged. "She loved you, silly."

"Too bad I didn't know that while she was alive," Dana muttered. She closed the locket and put it back underneath her shirt.

"Some people are incapable of showing their emotions, sweetie. Doesn't mean they don't have them."

"I know," she agreed. "It just makes me wonder how different things would have been if she'd just shown me how she felt once in a while instead of always pushing me away."

They sipped their drinks in companionable silence. While she people-watched, Dana noticed two men sitting at a near-by table pointing each time a woman walked into the bar. Sometimes they nodded, sometimes they laughed.

"Hey, Maura," she said. "See those guys over there?"

Maura turned around and looked. "The one in the red shirt and the guy in the hat?"

"Yeah. I think they're rating women."

"What?"

"Watch." She nodded at the two women who were just entering the bar. The men sat with their heads together. Red shirt said something and his friend laughed and shook his head.

"See?" Dana said.

"My God, I think you're right." There was a twinkle in her eyes. "Hey, I know. Let's give them a cheap thrill. Come on." She pulled a pen out of her purse, wrote on her cocktail napkin, and showed it to Dana, who giggled and grabbed the pen. She wrote the same thing on her napkin.

"Hey," Dana called over to the men, who turned to look at her. "Hey, guys. Yeah, you." She looked at Maura and nodded. They held up their napkins, gave the men a thumbs-up, and smiled. They'd written the number "10" on their napkins.

Both men blushed deeply, smiled weakly, and fled. Dana and Maura burst out laughing.

"Unbelievable," Dana said. She needed something to soak up the tequila and motioned for a server. "You hungry?"

"I could eat," Maura replied.

"Irish nachos okay?"

"Sure. I love those."

"And a diet soda."

"Make it two," Maura added. When the server left, she turned to Dana. "So, pretty coincidental, you finding the figurines, those pictures showing up on your porch, and finding out your dad was released from prison all happening in the same week, huh?"

"If I was a writer and this was a book, no one would believe it. It's enough to make my head spin. Plus, I can't help wondering if that next door neighbor of Mother's is involved somehow."

"The sexy one?" The twinkle was back in her friend's eyes and she felt her own face heat up. She hadn't told Maura she'd slept with Steve and hoped she'd never find out. As she tried to think of a snappy comeback, their order arrived and instead of responding, she dug into the fries.

She could feel Maura watching her.

"Oh, no, you didn't," Maura said after a minute or two.

Dana hesitated, cramming the three fries she was holding into her mouth. "Didn't what?" she asked around her mouthful of potato.

"You did. You slept with him," Maura said. She leaned forward, looked over her shoulder, and whispered conspiratorially. "How was he?"

"Maura!"

"Was he as good as he looks?" she continued. "I'll bet he taught you a thing or three. Or maybe you taught him—"

"Stop it." Dana couldn't help but laugh at her friend's nosiness. "Yes, I slept with him. And yes, it was amazing." She took a sip of her soda and sighed. "Until I discovered he'd stolen Mother's locket."

"He what?"

"He told me this lame story about having it repaired for her. I didn't believe him at first, but now I don't know. Plus there's the whole he attacked me thing."

"Excuse me? What do you mean, he attacked you?"

"Actually, I think I threw the first punch. I'd found the locket, and we got into an argument about how he'd gotten it. So anyway, we got into this tussle, and I belted him one. Then I called Brian and had him arrested."

Maura patted her arm. "Oh, honey, I'm so sorry. Are you okay?"

"I'm fine." She couldn't help it. She smiled slightly. "I think I busted his nose."

"Seriously?" Maura covered her mouth and laughed loudly. "So, no second date, then?"

That sent them both on another laughing jag that lasted for several minutes. Every time they looked at each other, they laughed harder.

It felt good.

Dana waved her hand at her friend. "But enough about that."

"Okay, I'll stop." Maura winked and grinned. "But at some point, I want a blow-by-blow account." She sipped her soda through a straw and giggled. "If you'll pardon the pun."

Dana laughed again. It was good to have a friend, to spend time with someone who could make her laugh, and forget about things for a bit. But then she turned serious again.

"I just wish I knew how my father fits into all this. Is he trying to tell me something? To let me know he's alive? And why all the subterfuge?"

"Kind of makes you wonder why he didn't just knock on your door in the first place."

"Maybe he's scared. Probably knows Mother told us he'd died, and he wants to break it to me gently?"

"That's as good a theory as any, I guess."

They stayed through another round of Irish nachos before finally saying goodnight. Although exhausted, Dana felt a little lighter than she had since this whole nightmare began. She went home and fell into a dreamless sleep.

CHAPTER 32

When she awoke the next day, the sun streamed in through the window, baking the entire room in hot October sunshine. She glanced at her watch and was amazed to find that it was well past ten.

"Shit." She wished she'd gotten up earlier. Girls' night out ended later than she'd planned, and even though she'd had a good time, she so needed to get her mother's things in order. Very little about her mother made sense to Dana, least of all her attitude. It filled Dana with a noxious case of the if-onlys that threatened to rip out her heart. If only she hadn't been so filled with anger as a teen. If only her mother hadn't been so strict. If only Dana had known how her mother had really felt about her. If only she'd told Dana the truth about her father.

She kicked the blankets angrily off the bed and trudged down the hall, hoping to start some much-needed coffee. Instead, she found Charlie sitting in front of the slider in the living room. As soon as the dog saw her, she barked and raced around the room.

"Okay, all right. Shut up already. You need to go out. I get it." When she opened the door, Charlie bolted outside, but instead of relieving herself, she raced over to the side of the yard where the master bedroom was and barked furiously.

"What the hell, Charlie?" Dana strode over and clapped her hands at the dog in an attempt to get her to stop. When it didn't work, she picked her up and gently set her down about six feet away. "Stay."

The dog almost stayed to the count of one before running back to Dana's side.

"No." She put a hand out to prevent her from getting too close. The dog strained against her hand.

At first, Dana wasn't sure what had her all upset. She knelt down on the grass and inspected the dirt. There didn't seem to be anything unusual, so she pushed her way into the shrubs and took a closer look. It was then that she noticed it and got down on all fours, grimacing at the sponginess of the ground. Charlie poked her head through the bushes and wormed her way in between Dana's arms.

There was a footprint near the window to her mother's bedroom. Difficult to tell how long it'd been there, but it had hardened around the edges so it wasn't terribly fresh. She looked up at the sun, squinting and shading her eyes with her hand. It was fairly warm, but not blazing, and it might take the mud several days to completely dry out. It seemed likely that this was where her mother's peeping Tom had looked in at her three days before her death. It also seemed apparent that this footprint was larger than the one left at the scene of her mother's murder, which meant it was probably also larger than a print left by Steve. The two incidents appeared unrelated, although she couldn't be sure. Was it possible someone had looked in on her last night without leaving a print and that was what Charlie was all upset about? It was possible, she supposed. She'd have to mention it to Brian and see what he thought.

In the meantime, she had work to do before the funeral. Charlie had lost interest in the footprint and was on the other side of the yard, attending to her doggie business. Dana hurried through a late breakfast of toast and coffee, dressed in shorts and a tank top, and was headed back into the garage to tackle the last of her mother's boxes when there was a knock at the door.

"Who the hell is that?" she muttered. "I don't have time for visitors. Shit." *Go away and leave me alone.* But a second knock came, louder and more insistent. "All right, already. Jesus."

She opened the door and was about to yell at whoever it was when she realized that it was Brian. "Oh," she said, surprised. "Hey."

"Hey."

"What are you doing here?"

"Just checking up on you." He narrowed his eyes and tilted his head. "You look like you're in a little better mood today. Mind if I come in for a minute?"

"Sure." She opened the door and let him in. "I am in a better mood. Or at least, I was until..."

"Until what?" Brian frowned.

"Come here." She led him out onto the patio. Charlie stopped smelling a daffodil and bounded over to them. "Let me show you something. Look." She pointed at the footprint. "I found this this morning. Charlie alerted me to it."

"I know. It was in the peeping Tom report."

"Any idea who's it is?"

"Not at this point." Brian reached out and touched her lightly on the arm. "But don't worry. We'll catch whoever did this."

"Any new leads?"

"No, but there are a couple of things I wanted to speak with you about." They headed back inside. "First, I wanted you to know that we arrested Campbell last night for assault and petty theft."

"Good."

"Unfortunately, he made bail this morning."

Even though that didn't really surprise her, Dana nevertheless hugged herself and tried to keep her temper in check.

"Now before you go all ballistic on me, I want you to know that he agreed to a polygraph test. He'll be coming in at eight o'clock tonight." Brian paused then snorted slightly. "Said he wanted to go to your mother's funeral first."

"What?" Dana couldn't believe it. Of all the unmitigated gall. The man was not only impossible, but a menace as well. "You're not going to let him, are you?"

"You could get a restraining order against him, and it would probably be granted, but you wouldn't be able to get it before the funeral anyway."

"I know, you're right, but it doesn't make it any easier."

"Don't worry," he said. "I'll be there along with several of my men. We'll be watching him and anyone else who shows up and acts suspiciously."

"Dammit."

"Maybe I should come over right before the funeral, ride along with you in the limo." He paused, and when she didn't answer, continued. "You didn't order a limo, did you?"

"No, I guess not." It hadn't even occurred to her. She flashed back to that moment of pure hatred from her mother at Phil's funeral.

"Never mind. I'll pick you up."

"Okay, thanks."

"Hey, not to change the subject," Brian said. "But have you seen the paper today?"

"No, why?"

"Well, that's the other reason I came by."

"What?"

"So," he paused again. "You haven't seen the obituary then, have you?"

"No, I haven't," Dana said.

"How's about I read it to you?"

She wasn't sure she was ready for that. She sat down heavily on the couch and ran her fingers through her hair.

"Dana?" Brian's voice was tinged with worry.

"I don't know." What was it her mother always used to say? No time like the present? "Go ahead."

He pulled a piece of newspaper out of his pocket and unfolded it. "'Agnes Evelyn Sinclair,'" he read, "'sixty two, of Stanton, California, died last week as a result of severe head trauma. Her daughter, Orange County Sheriff's Deputy Dana Sio...Sio...I forget. How do you pronounce it again? I never can remember."

It was no use. All her life people had massacred her middle name. As a result, she rarely used it. "It's pronounced 'Zhuh-vahn.' Gaelic for Joan."

"That's right. Now I remember." He cleared his throat. "'Her daughter, Orange County Sheriff's Deputy Dana Siobhán Sinclair, was at her side. Agnes was a founder of the Stanton Friends of the Library organization and was responsible for building the Friends Bookstore into a viable money-making proposition. She also spearheaded the controversial 'Save the Park' campaign, raising over a quarter of a million dollars for the rejuvenation of Premiere Park. She was predeceased by her son, Philip Cal...Help me out here."

"Kahl bahk."

"Don't know why your Mother couldn't have just called you Joan and Charles," he muttered. "Predeceased by her son, Philip Calbhach Sinclair. Her daughter is her only surviving relative. Services will be at the Gabriel Family Mortuary, at four o'clock on Friday, October 12, 2018. Burial to follow."

"I didn't know what else to say," Dana said. "God, I wish I'd known her better." Tears formed in the corners of her eyes and she brushed them angrily away. She was really getting tired of this shit.

"It's okay, Dana. Everything's going to be okay."

If she wasn't careful, she was going to burst into a million pieces any minute now.

"Dana?" Brian's voice sounded tinny and far away. "Dana, are you okay?"

"I'm fine," she said too quickly. "I'm really glad you came by, but I have some stuff to do before…you know."

"I know. You need me to do anything beforehand?"

"No, I think I've got everything covered." They got up and walked to the front door. "Oh, wait."

"What?"

"Sally's supposed to bring over a bunch of food in a little while. For the wake?" Dana always hated it when people made statements that sounded like questions, and yet, couldn't help doing it herself when asking for a favor.

"Sally Connor? She's catering the wake?"

"Yeah. But I just can't face her right now." Which was true, but not for the reason she was leading him to believe. "Could you call her, maybe pick everything up for me so I won't have to deal with her right now?"

"Sure, no problem."

"Thanks." She bit her lip, sniffed, and wiped away a rogue tear before it had a chance to give the all-clear to its cohort. "And thanks for checking up on me. I really appreciate it."

"I know you do," Brian told her. "I'll see you about two-thirty, okay?"

"Okay." She closed the door behind him, went into the bathroom, and splashed cold water on her face. After the funeral, when everyone had gone and she was alone, she'd pick up some Southern Comfort, take a nice long bubble bath with some cucumber slices on her eyes, and just soak until she pruned.

But in the meantime, there were still one or two boxes left in the garage, and if she remembered correctly, there was a scrapbook and something that looked like it could be a diary or a journal in one of them. She hung up her towel, rubbed her hands on her shorts, and headed out to the garage and whatever secrets and truths awaited her.

CHAPTER 33

She'd gone through most of the first of the two remaining boxes, unimpressed with its contents, when she came across a meager document clumsily stapled in the corner.

It seemed to be some sort of template for a business plan. There were a lot of blanks, but from what Dana could piece together after flipping through the pages, it appeared as though someone wanted Agnes to invest $250,000 in their business venture.

A quarter of a million dollars. Dana leaned against the wall, amazed, and wiped the perspiration from her forehead. Who could have known Agnes had that much money in the first place?

On her second flip through, something caught her attention. Her eyes widened before narrowing tightly. A restaurant? Really? The only person Dana knew who wanted to start one was Sally. Sally! A small, hard knot formed in her stomach.

Janey had told her Sally wanted to buy the land the park was on and then build a fancy restaurant. But she could have gotten it wrong. What if what Sally really wanted was Agnes's money? If Agnes refused, could Sally have murdered her so brutally?

Dana's jaw worked back and forth, grinding her teeth and giving her a bit of a headache as she folded the business plan in thirds and jammed it into her back pocket. She would have to approach Sally, confront her with this new information. But she'd have to be careful. At some point, she'd tell Brian about her suspicions and turn the document over to him. *But first, I'm going to do a little investigating myself. Even if it might get me into trouble. I owe it to Mother.*

"Okay, Sinclair." Her mind turned back to Sally and she began to pace. "Calm down. You can't go over there all half-cocked and confrontational. You won't get anywhere that way."

Better to just go through the final box and cool off before she got herself so worked up she did something she would probably regret. She'd have to save their little chat till after the funeral.

The funeral. She still couldn't believe she had to go to her mother's funeral. And in just a couple of hours. Not really paying attention to what she was doing, she yanked the last box off the shelf and realized too late that it had apparently suffered water damage at one time. The bottom had disintegrated, and everything inside dumped out onto her foot. Something raked down her shin and left a trail that immediately beaded up with blood.

"Ow, crap," she said as she looked first at her shin, then at the mess on the floor. It'd have to wait while she cleaned up her leg.

She washed the scrape, dabbed on some hydrogen peroxide with a cotton ball, then headed back out to the garage. The only things left to look at were a beat up scrapbook whose edges were bent, and what appeared to be a diary. She sat down on the garage floor and opened the scrapbook.

The first page made her frown. The second page was even more confusing. After the third, her head reeled. The walls closed in on her. Her heart raced. She had trouble catching her breath. She'd wanted to learn the truth about her father. Now that she had, she wished she'd left it alone.

Consciously, she already knew most of what she'd read. What shocked her was that not only had her mother kept a scrapbook that detailed her father's spiral into hell, but she'd updated it just days before she'd died.

The first article described the beating and his subsequent arrest.

VETERAN STANTON COP ARRESTED FOR MURDER

Stanton, NE—Twenty-year veteran Stanton County Sheriff's Deputy Edmund Charles O'Shaughnessy, 43, was arrested today for murder and aggravated assault in the beating death of another man, thirty-five-year-old Quadrees Rashard. O'Shaughnessy admitted beating the man with his baton although he gave no reason other than he "lost his temper." O'Shaughnessy will be arraigned on Monday.

Sitting on the cool cement of the garage, Dana stared at the clipping. It said so much and yet so little. What fascinated her was that she'd always assumed her father was a Lincoln police officer, not a county sheriff's deputy. Like most cops, she didn't believe in coincidence and doubted it was just a fluke that her mother had left a town called Stanton, Nebraska, and settled half way across the country in another small town named Stanton. Why would she do that?

Dana flipped the scrapbook pages. There was an eight-by-ten-inch glossy picture—her father's Academy photograph, those unbelievably blue eyes staring out at her. On the adjacent page was the article describing the arraignment.

STANTON COP O'SHAUGHNESSY PLEADS GUILTY TO MURDER

Stanton, NE: In a plea agreement with the Stanton County District Attorney's Office, veteran sheriff's deputy, Edmund Charles O'Shaughnessy, 43, pled guilty to second-degree murder in the beating death of Quadrees Rashard, 35. O'Shaughnessy readily agreed to the plea and was taken immediately back to jail, where he awaits transportation to Tecumseh State Correctional Institution. He will serve a twenty-year term in the medium security facility. O'Shaughnessy has yet to state the reason why he beat the man to death, other than to admit that he simply "lost his temper."

Again, no new information, but it piqued her curiosity as to what would possibly make her father so angry that he'd kill a man and then offer no excuse in his own defense.

Dana turned several more pages, but none of the articles gave her anything new. Most of the rest of the book was blank, and she almost missed the article taped to one of the last pages. It was just a few lines, buried in the back pages of the newspaper. Her mother had clipped both the name and the date from the top edge of the paper and taped them above the article itself. "The Stanton Register." She noticed immediately that the tape was clear, not yellow like the tape holding the other articles in place, and looked at the date. September twenty-fourth. Two weeks before her mother was murdered.

*Stanton, NE: Convicted murder Edmund Charles
O'Shaughnessy, a former Stanton County Sheriff's Deputy, was released from Tecumseh State Correctional Institution today. O'Shaughnessy pled guilty to second-degree
murder in the beating death of Quadrees Rashard. He
served twenty years.*

Short, sweet, and to the point. Strangely, she didn't
feel sick any more. Instead, her resolve grew. If it was the
last thing she ever did, she would uncover the truth about
what happened to her family.

As she reached for her mother's journal, something
slid out of the scrapbook and landed on her feet. The
thick envelope was yellowed with age. She carefully
opened it and pulled out a stack of brittle paper. It was
her parents' divorce decree and settlement agreement,
dated a short six months after her father was sent to prison.

"Didn't waste much time, did you, Mother?" Dana
gave them a cursory glance then shoved them back inside
the envelope, ripping it slightly. She jammed the envelope between the scrapbook pages and angrily tossed the
whole thing on the floor beside her.

She picked up the journal and began to read as she
worked a knot in her hair.

*It finally happened. Edmund's temper got the best of
him and he beat someone to death with that damn baton
of his. At least he waited until after Dana's birthday.
Poor girl, she adores her father, even though he's not
always that nice to her. They called to let me know what
had happened, and wanted me to come down to talk to
Edmund tonight, but it's late and I don't have anyone to
stay with the kids. He'll have to wait until tomorrow. The
kids will be in school and I'll go see him then.*

The next entry was dated the following day. There was a smudge on the corner of the page and it was a little warped, as if a single drop of water had spilled onto it. It made her wonder if her mother had cried while writing it.

Went to see Eddie today. He looks like he's aged ten years since yesterday. Wouldn't look me in the eye. Refused to talk to me. I don't understand what's happening. Eddie's always had a temper, but he loves me and the kids, I know he does. How could he get himself into such a mess and leave us alone like that?

Dana looked up from the dusty pages, her eyes swimming. She'd never known her mother to show so much emotion. Or any emotion. The thought that she'd actually cried while writing the entry ate at her. There was just so damn much she'd never known about her mother.

She leafed through the next several pages, which consisted of the daily drudgery of a life in crisis, until she came across an entry that seemed to focus on her.

Dana keeps asking about her daddy. I just don't have the heart to tell her what's happened. That he's going to spend the rest of her childhood locked up in a tiny little cage, like some sort of animal. It breaks my heart to think about the pain she'll be forced to endure when she learns the truth. I have to protect her, protect my little girl from the ugliness that is her life.

Phil, on the other hand, barely seems to notice that his father is gone. Has never once asked where he is, why he isn't home. I can feel him watching me sometimes, through those narrowed, angry eyes of his. Will he accept the truth? Maybe he'll even relish it. I wonder if he already knows.

Her mother had agonized over her children? Over her? It all seemed so incredible. Dana needed a break. She pulled herself up off the floor, clutching the journal to her breasts, and patted the side of her leg. "Come on, Chuckles, let's go inside and have a drink." The dog stood slowly, stretched, and trotted over to the door. She looked over her shoulder and grinned at Dana, who shuffled over to her. They went inside, Charlie disappearing down the hall, and Dana grabbed a Diet Coke. Even though it was a warm autumn day, she felt a little chilled and pulled on a sweatshirt before curling up on the couch. She put the journal down on the coffee table and picked up the ceramic Carpenter. She rubbed her thumb over it, into the crevices, around the tiny hands, the large nose and feet, the square hat. Holding it made her feel closer to her father, somehow.

As she brought the figurine to her lips, shivering slightly at the touch of the cold gem, the doorbell rang. Dana glared at the door, hoping that if she ignored it, whoever it was would go away and leave her alone. No such luck. The doorbell chimed again, followed by three quick raps on the door.

"Dana?"

Crap.

"How you doing?" As soon as she opened the door, Brian wrapped his arms around her in a warm embrace. "You okay?"

Dana rested her head on his shoulder and allowed herself a brief moment to enjoy the feeling of being protected before she gently pushed him away. She closed the door and gave him an appraising once-over. His black suit was double-breasted, which she normally despised, but with his broad shoulders and narrow waist, he filled it out nicely, like a GQ model without the arrogance. She realized she was staring at him and cleared her throat.

"You look nice," she said. *What a doofus.* "Two visits in one day? What's up?"

Brian smiled, one hand flying up to cover his mouth while the other wrapped itself around his waist. His eyes twinkled merrily.

"What?" What the hell was so funny?

"That," he asked, moving his hand up and down to indicate her clothes, "what you're planning on wearing?"

She looked down at what she had on and realized that she hadn't gotten ready yet. She looked at her watch. "Is it two-thirty already?"

"Closer to two-fifteen. Guess I'm a little early. Is there anything you'd like me to do while you're getting ready?"

She shook her head. "No, I won't be long. Charlie will keep you company while you wait." As she headed down the hall, she felt something bounce off her calf and turned to see what it was. Brian was bending down to retrieve it when she realized the business plan had fallen out of her pocket.

"I'll take that," she told him, a little too quickly. Not quickly enough, though, because he'd already opened it up and was looking it over.

"What is this?" As he scanned the paper, he frowned before looking up at her. "Dana?"

It was pointless to deny anything, so she told a teeny tiny white lie instead. "Oh, that? I was going to give that to you. After the service."

"Uh huh," he said noncommittally and went back to perusing the document.

"I found it just a little bit ago in Mother's things. It seems to be some sort of business plan."

"I can see that." He folded it back into thirds and stuck it inside the breast pocket of his jacket. So much for her following up on the lead. But at least he would let her know if it panned out. She hoped. "Any idea where she got it from?"

His eyes burned, and Dana could tell he knew she'd been lying about meaning to give it to him. "Sit down," she told him. They sat on the couch, and Dana told him everything she knew, about Sally's desire to purchase the land the park was on, about her anger at Agnes and the argument they had, about how the woman made her wary.

When she was done, all Brian did was nod. Charlie had jumped up on the couch next to him and licked his hand the whole time he and Dana were talking. When they stopped, he turned to the little dog and said, "Okay, you big flirt." Then he scooped her up and sat her on his lap. "Enough."

He scratched her behind the ears before turning back to Dana, his warm cognac eyes once again sincere and full of compassion. "Go on, get ready. Take all the time you need."

His response certainly wasn't what she'd expected. "Thanks." Charlie plastered his face with kisses and she smiled. "Brian?"

"Hmm?"

"I'm glad you're here."

෧෨෧

She cleaned up and changed into her black pants suit. Standing in front of the bathroom mirror, she ran a wet comb through her hair and scrunched it with her hands to set the waves. She dabbed a little lipstick on her lips and hoped it wouldn't highlight how pale she was. The last thing she did before leaving the bathroom was to slip on her mother's locket, her breath hitching a little.

Brian was sitting with Charlie curled up in his lap, enjoying his attention. "Such a pretty girl," he murmured, scratching her behind the ear. The little dog was enjoying it so much she'd practically bent herself in half leaning into it. "Yes, you like that, don't you? Yes."

Dana smiled and cleared her throat. He gently placed Charlie on the couch before he stood. The dog gave him a dirty look when she found herself booted off his lap. He brushed off the dog hair and ran his fingers down the creases in his trouser legs.

"You clean up nice," he said. "Ready?"

"As ready as I'll ever be," she told him, looking around for her purse. It was on the floor. When had she tossed it there? She couldn't remember but supposed it didn't really matter. She walked over and was about to pick it up when someone knocked on the door.

"That'll be Officer Shaheen," Brian informed her.

Dana looked at him quizzically and wished for the millionth time that she had the gene that would allow her to raise one eyebrow. Brian opened the door. "Mu'tazz is here as a personal favor to me. Come on in, Tazz."

Tazz, a young Arabic man with dark skin and an even darker demeanor, walked in carrying two huge trays of food, one with meats and cheeses, the other with every type of bread she could name, as well as some she couldn't.

"Where do you want these?" Tazz asked. "Suckers are heavy." He paused, then glanced in Dana's direction and nodded. "Sorry, ma'am. No offense intended."

"None taken," she said.

Brian clapped Tazz on the shoulder and pointed. "Kitchen's that way."

"There's three more trays in my car," Tazz told him.

"Just put the meat tray and anything else that needs to stay cold in the refrigerator."

"Yeah," Tazz said, scowling. "Thanks."

Brian leaned over and whispered in Dana's ear. "His name means 'powerful' in Arabic. I thought he'd be a nice deterrent to that neighbor of yours. Or anyone else who shows up uninvited."

"I know I'd think twice about messing with him," she said. She slung her purse over her shoulder. "What is all that?" She nodded toward the kitchen and Tazz.

"Remember? You asked me to save you from Diner Sally and pick up the food."

"Oh, yeah. Sure," Dana said. "I remember."

Brian frowned. "You okay?"

"Not really," she admitted. "But we'd better get going, I guess."

Tazz sighed exaggeratedly and made his way out the door, apparently resigned to getting the rest of the food himself.

"I asked Tazz to follow us in his car," Brain told her. "I hope you don't mind."

"Is that really necessary?"

"With everything that's been going on the past few days, I'd say yes, it's very necessary."

"Fine."

Tazz came in, the three huge trays balanced like a professional server. He grinned sheepishly at Dana. "Did a stint at TGI Friday's back in college." His smile made him far less intimidating.

"Shall we?" Brian ushered her through the door, then held out his hand. "Keys?"

She pointed to where they were hanging on the wall. He plucked them off the hook, waited for Tazz to exit, then locked up and handed them back to her. "This way."

Tazz strode down the driveway ahead of them and climbed into a huge black Hummer that looked like an armored car. Brian propelled her toward a Lincoln Town Car with tinted windows and leather upholstery.

"What's this?" She'd expected him to show up in his shiny yellow Camaro.

"I know you're not into fancy things like limos," he explained. "But you deserve to go in style for a change, so I borrowed this for you. Do you mind?"

"No, not at all. It...it's perfect." She smiled at him and he nodded, opening the door for her. As she climbed in, she looked over the top of the car and felt her heart speed up.

Steve stood on his porch, drinking a beer and watching them. Watching her. He waved. She glared back. As she got into the car, she saw his smile disappear as he dropped his hand.

Brian shut the door and walked around the front of the car. As she watched him, her cell rang. She dug it out of her purse, looked at the display, and turned it off in disgust. Man had a lot of nerve calling her at all, but especially as she was leaving for the funeral.

Brian climbed in next to her just in time to see her shove the phone into her purse. He raised an eyebrow but otherwise made no comment.

CHAPTER 34

The church service went smoothly. Dana was surprised at not only the sheer number of people who attended, but how many wanted to eulogize Agnes. If Dana had had any doubts before about the kind of woman her mother had been, they were all gone now. It seemed everybody loved her, or at least respected her. Everyone, that was, except whoever had brutally murdered her.

True to his word, Brian had arranged for about a dozen undercover officers to attend the funeral, along with several uniforms stationed outside the mortuary chapel as well as graveside. The plainclothes detectives watched the funeral goers with a detached eye while they searched for anything out of the ordinary. The uniforms were there for back up.

As she stood at her mother's grave, Dana pulled one of her mother's hankies out of her purse and kept it crumpled in her hand. It still smelled faintly of White Shoulders.

She was vaguely aware of the people around her, and of the words the preacher spoke over the grave. It was all a numbing jumble to her. Brian and Tazz bookended her, effectively preventing all unwanted company, for which Dana was eternally grateful. Maura stood on the other side of Brian, quietly offering her support.

When the service ended, she took the single white rose Brian handed her and placed it on the casket. "Oh, Mother." She stroked the cold green box into which she was expected to leave her mother forever. "I'm sorry. So, so sorry."

She laid her cheek on the casket and closed her eyes. Brian gathered her into his arms, and she let him lead her away.

As they walked slowly toward the town car, she caught sight of a lone figure standing off in the distance behind a large tombstone. She stopped and raised her head, her body tense.

"What is it?" Brian asked. His free hand reached inside his jacket, alert to the possibility of attack.

"There." Dana looked up at him and pointed at the silhouette.

"Where?"

"There," she repeated. But when she turned back to where the figure had stood, it was gone. "I don't understand. He was right there."

Brian gestured to three of his men, who immediately headed toward the area where she'd pointed. He turned back to Dana. "Who was right there?"

"I...I'm not sure. Someone. A dark figure."

"Well, if there's anyone there now, my men will find him. Come on," he said as he directed her back toward the car. "It's time to go."

She allowed him to put her into the car but her mind raced. Who had she seen? Although the figure had been silhouetted by the sun to the point that there were no discernible features, she couldn't shake the feeling that it was her father.

ღაღა

An exhausted Dana sat on the couch and wished everyone would just go away. She became aware of raised voices and some sort of commotion at the front door. She glanced at Maura. Her friend raised an eyebrow but said nothing. People brought her plates of food she couldn't eat, and she looked at them all lined up on the coffee table, then wearily got up and went to see what was going on.

"I just want to pay my respects." Steve was trying to force his way past Tazz, whose very stance—arms crossed, shoulders back, spine ramrod straight—was intimidating, like a giant Anubis guarding the pharaoh's tomb. But her cocky neighbor didn't appear to be intimidated in the slightest.

"Come on, man," he whined. "I'm not going to hurt her or anything. I just want to extend my condolences." He tried to take a step across the threshold, but Tazz wasn't budging.

"I'd suggest you leave," Tazz said quietly. "*Sir*."

"Dana?" Steve stood on his tiptoes and tried to see past Tazz, who simply adjusted his body to prevent any possibility that the intruder would get past him. "Dana!"

She walked up to Tazz and laid her hand on his shoulder. "It's okay, Tazz. I got this."

Tazz frowned. "You sure? Brian left specific orders not to let this guy in."

"Oh, he's not coming in." She patted Tazz affectionately and motioned with her head for him to go inside. Then she turned on Steve. "You got a lot of nerve showing up here. What the hell do you want?"

He took a step toward her. "Dana, I just—"

"What? Came to attack me again?"

"Please." He reached out as if to take hold of her hand. "If you'll just let me explain—"

"Don't touch me." She held her ground, not about to back down, no matter what lies he came up with. Steve recoiled as if bitten. With his blackened eyes and the bandage over his nose, she sincerely hoped he was afraid she'd cold cock him again.

"Five minutes? Just five minutes, then I'll go."

"Fine." She looked at her watch. "You now have four minutes and fifty-nine seconds. Fifty-eight...fifty-seven..."

"I know you think I killed your mother," he began. "But I didn't. Yes, I kept her locket when I should have returned it." He pointed at the locket around her neck, his eyes flashing down to her breasts before looking her in the eye again. "Have you opened it yet?"

She clutched the locket protectively.

"Then you know why I kept it," he continued. "I was sure that I'd never have the chance to meet you. So I kept the locket to have a memento of you. Then I saw you sitting there on the porch. You were so pale and upset, I just wanted to take you in my arms and never let you go. When I introduced myself to you, I had the locket in my pocket. I didn't know how to put it back without being caught. And anyway, it didn't seem like such a big deal. I didn't think it would be missed, to be honest with you."

"Honest?" Dana laughed. "You don't know the meaning of the word. Your five minutes are up. Now get out."

She turned as Brian walked up behind them.

"There a problem here?" he asked.

"No problem," Dana told him. "We're done."

She returned to the couch.

"What was that all about?" Maura whispered.

"Oh, that?" Dana gestured at the front door, now

closed. Brian and Tazz were huddled together. "Just the neighborhood cockroach." She was too tired to explain further, but Maura probably realized who it was even without an explanation.

Dana closed her eyes and rubbed her aching head. *It will all be over soon,* she told herself, but didn't really believe it.

"You okay, ma'am?" Tazz loomed above her, but instead of feeling menaced, she took comfort from him. His face was full of concern, as if he'd known her for years instead of mere hours. She could see why he and Brian were friends.

"I'm good," she replied. "Thanks, Tazz."

"Can I get you something? Coffee? Tea?" He gestured at the plates of food that littered the coffee table. "Something to eat?"

She couldn't help but smile. Yes, they were going to be fine friends. "Could you just make everyone go away?"

"Done." He disappeared. She couldn't tell where he went, but people immediately began walking up to her and insisted on shaking her hand.

"Sorry for your loss."

"Agnes was a fine lady."

"We're all going to miss her."

Dana murmured her thanks to everyone, glad when the line of condolence-givers was nearing an end. The last person she had to deal with was Sally.

"Honey," she said, smothering Dana in an overly-dramatic bear hug. Dana could smell Sally's perfume and nearly gagged on its cloying scent. "I'm just so very sorry. Are you all right?"

"Yes." Dana stiffened. "I'm fine." She gestured around the room at the plates full of half-eaten food the mourners had left, hoping Sally would get the hint and leave. She'd talk to the woman later, after things calmed down. "And thanks for everything."

Sally grasped her hands gently. "Just let me know if there's anything, anything at all, that I can do."

Dana shot a pleading look Tazz's way. "I will. Thanks."

Tazz caught her look and swiftly walked over to intercede. He put his hands on Sally's shoulders and gently but firmly turned her away from Dana and ushered her toward the door. "This way, ma'am," he said. "I'm sure she'll be in touch."

Once she was gone, Maura took Dana's hands in hers. "Look," she said, "you call me if you need me. Or even if you don't, if you just want to talk, whatever. You hear me?"

Dana smiled weakly and nodded. "I hear you. I will."

"Promise."

"Yeah. I promise."

"Okay then, I'll be going too. Unless you want me to help clean up?"

"No, you go on. Get home to your family." Impulsively, Dana put her arms around Maura and hugged her tightly. She smiled as she felt Maura hug her back. Yes, she was a good friend, a valuable friend, and Dana was sure they would stay that way for years to come.

"See you soon, honey," Maura told her.

"Bye, Maura. And thanks."

Tazz, Brian, and a few other officers were all that remained. They gathered in a corner, speaking in hushed tones. She watched as Brian directed them, and then as they broke formation and began picking up the remnants of the wake. Everyone but Brian, who walked over and stood next to her, watching his men.

"Would you like to lie down?" he asked after a time, still watching the other officers.

"Actually," she replied, "what I'd really like is to finish reading my mother's journal."

He turned to look at her. She expected him to quiz her about it. Instead, he simply asked, "Where is it?"

She couldn't say for certain. "Hmm, I think I left it in the garage." She looked around the living room. "Or maybe in here somewhere."

"Tell you what." Brian put his arm around her and turned her toward the bedrooms. "You go relax. I'll hunt for it and bring it in when I find it. What does it look like?"

She described it then headed on down to her mother's bedroom. So far, she hadn't slept there, but she thought tonight would be a good night to start. Reading her mother's journal in her mother's bed would certainly help ease the pain, lighten the sorrow she felt at having lost her with so many things left unresolved between them.

After changing into her favorite sweats and tank top, Dana gently pulled down her mother's comforter and lie on top of the blankets.

Charlie jumped up on the bed and curled up beside her. She threw her arm across her eyes, swollen and tender from crying, and listened to the sounds of the men cleaning up. She dozed until there was a soft knock on the door.

"Dana?" Brian whispered. "You asleep?"

"No." She struggled to sit up and settled for propping herself up on an elbow. "Did you find it?"

He entered the room with the journal underneath his arm and something in his hand. "This it?"

She took the journal and set it on the bed.

"This was sitting on top of it," he said, holding out her father's glass figurine. "Did you want it, too?"

Smiling, she took The Carpenter and held it in her

hand. She patted the bed. He sat on the edge, looking uncomfortable. Dana put her hand on his knee.

"Thanks for everything, Brian. I couldn't have gotten through this without you."

Brian cleared his throat. "You get some rest now." He pushed her bangs off her face, then bent and kissed her forehead, being careful not to touch her still-sore goose egg.

"I'll be right down the hall. You call me if you need anything, you hear?"

She nodded and watched him leave. Then she turned her attention back to her mother's journal. It had fallen open at the half-way point, and she started to read.

Tried many times to get Eddie to talk to me. Didn't expect today to be any different, but it was. He finally told me what happened. Then he told me to divorce him and take the kids far away. Tell them he was dead, make up some story about how. I don't want to, God how I don't want to, but Eddie's right. They don't need to grow up with the stigma of having a father in prison. Particularly little Dana. She worships her father so.

Dana let the book fall open on the blanket. She still didn't know the truth about what happened, but at least she understood her mother's motives a little better.

She hadn't taken Dana and her brother away from their father as she'd always assumed. On the contrary, her father had sent them away. If only her mother hadn't been so pig-headed, if only she'd been honest with them, maybe she and Dana would have had a better, more open and fulfilling relationship.

She picked up the book and read the next entry.

Dana was crying for her daddy today. I couldn't calm her, so I dug out the old standby and read her fa-

vorite poem, the one Eddie and the kids used to read to-
gether. "The Walrus and the Carpenter." I let her hold
The Walrus. She went right to sleep. Precious angel. I sat
at her bedside for over an hour until I could pry the thing
out of her hand. Then I sat for another hour just looking
at it, turning it over in my hand, thinking about Eddie,
and how much we all miss him.

Dana looked at the Walrus and tried to remember
how life was before her father went to prison. She fell
asleep that way, sprawled across the bed, one hand
clutching the figurine, the other lying across her mother's
journal.

CHAPTER 35

Dana couldn't get over the fact that her mother had never stopped loving her father. It filled her dreams for nearly three hours before she woke up, feeling more refreshed than she had since this whole thing started. She rubbed her eyes and sat up. The Carpenter was still clutched in her hand, and she smiled as she realized the significance of the two little statuettes. Her father had kept The Carpenter, her mother, The Walrus. They'd still been in love, despite the divorce and the way her mother hadn't allowed her and her brother to speak of him. They'd kept the statuettes as reminders of each other. She wasn't sure why her mother had pretended to hate Edmund, but she thought maybe talking about him or hearing his name was just too painful.

This realization made her feel better than she had in a long, long time. The feeling didn't last, however, as she recalled the solitary figure she knew she'd seen at the funeral. Had it been her father? It must have been. Who else could it be?

"Steve," she said aloud and wanted to hit something. Was it possible that he really had lurked in the background, true to his word to Brian that he would attend come hell or high water? Now that she knew the truth, she'd almost rather it was her father.

In her mind, Dana ticked off what she knew. One, the Fairy Fire. She was convinced her father had sent them, now more than ever. Finn was the only other person she knew who might have, but his reaction when he'd seen them had been one of caution, maybe even fear, and she doubted he'd been responsible for them. It was possible he knew the truth about her father, she supposed, but the thought dissolved as soon as it formed. That was impossible. How would he have known?

Two, the phone calls. She didn't remember her father having a raspy voice, but a man aged a lot in twenty years.

Three, the photographs, and four, The Carpenter. The photos had her father's fingerprints on them—a sure sign he'd left them—and the statuette was one-half of a set her parents had shared.

It might have been her father who'd been watching her, but she refused to believe he'd run her off the road. She didn't know who had, but it was for damn sure not her father. It could have been Steve. He had a work truck for his landscaping company that was very similar to the one that had hit her. She was certain her father meant her no harm.

There could be no other explanation. Everything pointed to her father trying to make contact with her.

"Hey, what're you doing up?" Brian stood in the doorway. She'd been so absorbed in her thoughts she hadn't heard him come into the room. He crossed to the bed and sat down on the edge then laid his palm on her forehead and frowned.

"How come you're still here?" Dana pushed his hand away. "What're you doing? I don't have a fever."

"Just checking. You look like shit, you know."

"Again with the sweet talk."

He gestured at Agnes's journal. "Interesting reading?"

"Actually, yes." She didn't offer any specifics, and he didn't ask for any. Instead, he cleared his throat, smoothed his tie, which was already loose with the knot hanging half-way down his chest, and smiled. "Can I get you anything? Tea? Something to eat?"

She shook her head then immediately pursed her lips. "Well, as a matter of fact…" What she really wanted was the number of her father's parole officer, or at the very least, the Tecumseh State facility where he'd spent the past twenty years. Unsure if she should make such a request right now, she decided to keep quiet. She could always Goggle it later.

Brian grinned at her and pulled out his wallet. "Is this what you want?" He held out a slip of paper. She took it between her thumb and forefinger and looked at him questioningly. A name and phone number were scribbled on it. "I meant to give it to you the other night, but it plain slipped my mind."

"Who is this?"

"Fred's a friend of mine. He runs the prison your father was housed in."

"Is *everyone* in law enforcement a personal friend of yours?"

"Networking, kiddo," he told her with a straight face. "It's all about networking. Who you know is where you go."

Dana rolled her eyes. "Oh, brother."

Brian's tone turned serious, but his twinkling eyes belied his humorless voice. "Hey, you're in no position to argue, little missy."

"Little missy?" she asked. "Seriously? Quit calling me that, will you? No one's called me that since I was twelve, and that was when my mother yelled at me for going to the store without permission."

He patted her arm and smiled. "I'm going to bring you some hot tea." He reached over and patted Charlie, who looked up at him. "And this pretty little girl a cookie." Charlie's ears perked up and she licked her lips.

Dana checked her watch. Nearly four a.m. That would make it six o'clock in Nebraska. Too early? After pondering the situation for about ten seconds, she decided to call anyway. Worst case scenario, she'd have to leave a message. Best case, she'd finally get some answers.

೧೨೧

Dana called the warden's office and paced while she suffered through some especially horrible easy-listening Muzak.

The warden's assistant seemed perturbed at having the phone ring so early, and she suspected he'd put her on hold to spite her.

Finally, at six o'clock on the dot, the warden came on the line. "This is Warden Benson."

"Warden." She sat down on the bed then popped back up and paced some more. "My name is Dana Sinclair. I—"

"Oh, yes, Miss Sinclair. Or is it "Ms."?"

"Actually, sir, it's Deputy."

"Well, honey," he said. "I stand corrected."

She bit down on her tongue and prayed for the strength to keep her temper from getting the best of her and screwing this up.

"I've been expecting your call, little lady." She couldn't help but wonder just how much Brian had shared with him. "What can I do for you?"

She unclenched her jaw as best she could. "I wondered if I could get some information on a former inmate?"

"That depends on who it is and when he was here."

"His name is Edmund Charles O'Shaughnessy."

"Ah, yes, Mr. O'Shaughnessy. He left our establishment several weeks ago."

"Do you happen to know the name of his parole officer?" It would be in his file, she knew, and hoped that the warden would cooperate.

"May I inquire as to your interest in a man like O'Shaughnessy?"

"I believe him to be my father." *You nosy old fart.*

There was a long pause. "O'Shaughnessy talked about a daughter, but he called her Dee Dee."

Her father was the only person who ever called her Dee Dee. He'd started calling her that after the one and only time Phil had called her Tweedle Dum. Daddy had corrected him sharply, telling her brother to never, ever call her that again. But the next day, her father had started calling her Tweedle Dee, which then was shortened to Dee Dee, and she'd always wondered if that was his silent nod to Phil's humor.

"That was my father's nickname for me," Dana reluctantly told the warden.

"Oh? That so?"

A headache had formed behind her eyes, and she rubbed them gently. "So, can I get that name from you?"

"Mr. O'Shaughnessy came up for parole, oh, let me see..." She could hear papers rustling. "Three or four times. He always refused."

What kind of man refused to be let out of a cage? "Refused? Why?"

"He said he didn't mind paying his debt to society, but he'd be damned if he'd report to some little pipsqueak—that's the word he used—when he was out. He insisted that when he left here, it would either be in a body bag or when he'd served his full sentence and was a free man."

Damn. Now what was she going to do? Not having to report to a parole officer meant her father could be anywhere, and there was little that she could do to track him down. "Do you have any idea where he might have gone?"

"You need to be very careful, young lady."

"Why is that?"

"I'm looking at a report written by his psychiatrist. It seems that O'Shaughnessy took the news of his son's death very hard. He was treated for depression and anxiety."

"Is he dangerous?" She hadn't wanted to ask it, wasn't sure she wanted to know the answer, but the question was out before she realized she'd even been thinking it.

More paper rustling. The warden cleared his throat. "'O'Shaughnessy never fully recovered from his son's death,'" he read. "'But it made him somewhat fixated on his only remaining child. May take extreme measures to get back into her life.' Deputy Sinclair." He was no longer reading. "You need to be extremely careful. If O'Shaughnessy really is your father, he may use force if he feels it's necessary. Do you understand what I'm telling you?"

So it had been her father who'd been watching her. Originally, she'd thought it might have been Steve's footprint she found under her window the other day, but now she wasn't so sure. It was looking more and more like her father was the peeping Tom.

"Did you hear what I said?"

"Yes. I heard you."

"Watch your back. O'Shaughnessy has killed a man

in anger once before. He's obsessed with getting back into your life. No telling what he might do this time around." He paused, and Dana could almost hear him debating with himself about what to say next. "Or to whom."

CHAPTER 36

Mmm, good." Dana took another sip of tea. "Relaxing." Hopefully, Brian would believe that she really could sleep all day. What she actually wanted to do was to delve further into her family history, try to piece things together. That would be impossible as long as he hovered over her, and she knew he wouldn't leave until he was sure she was all right. Trouble was, she wasn't all right. Far from it. But she'd have to do her best to convince him otherwise.

"The secret is to only use real tea, never a tea bag," he explained. He handed Charlie a puppy cookie, who took it gently and chewed it delicately.

"But all I know how to do is dunk," she said. "Who uses real tea anymore anyway? It's so much easier to just dunk in the tea bag, dunk the biscotti into the tea, and the donut into the coffee. You know." She mimed dipping something into her cup. "Dunk."

"Are you hinting?" he asked, standing up and pointing at the door. "Do you want me to get you some cookies or something?"

"No, thanks." She shook her head, put her cup on the nightstand, and burrowed down into the covers. "I'm a little tired." She yawned, hoping it looked real. Brian seemed satisfied. "Think I'll see if I can get some more sleep."

"Not on your life, Sinclair."

She peeked an eye out of the covers and batted her eyelashes at him. "Huh? Whatever do you mean?"

"Don't give me that innocent routine. I know you called Fred. You going to tell me what he said, or am I going to have to pry it out of you?"

Dana sighed. She never could pull anything over on Brian. "Basically," she said, pushing back the covers and sitting up. "He said that Daddy had been released and might want to get in touch with me at some point."

Brian made no comment, his face inscrutable.

She stared back at him.

He continued to look at her, not saying a word.

She shifted. Pulled the blanket up and smoothed it down. Folded the top of the sheet down over the edge of the blanket.

Brian didn't move.

"Fine." She blew her bangs off her forehead, pissed at herself for letting him get to her. "He told me to watch my back, and that Daddy might try anything to get back in my life again. But it's okay," she assured him. "Daddy would never hurt me."

"Yeah, right."

She frowned. "You know he won't."

"Well, let's just hope that's the case." He picked up the mug and walked to the door. "I'm going to wait out in the living room."

"Brian," Dana called.

He turned and looked at her, his face a knot of worry.

"I'm just going to sleep. Please don't wait around for me to wake up. I'm sure you have better things to do with your time."

"Well…"

"Really. I'm already asleep." She rolled over onto her side and pulled the covers up underneath her chin. "See?"

"All right," Brian agreed with a laugh. "You convinced me. But I'm going to post a uniform outside."

"I don't need a sentry, Brian. I have Charlie." She patted the dog on her head.

"Yeah," he snorted. "Fat lot of good she'll do. Either I post a sentry or you have a permanent roommate. And I don't mean your mongrel there. At least until we find your father."

"But—"

"I mean it, Dana."

She sighed dramatically. "Fine." It was no use arguing.

"Now go to sleep."

She dutifully closed her eyes and faked a snore that rumbled like an LA earthquake.

"But you call me when you get up, okay?"

"Mmmm," she agreed sleepily.

She listened as he walked down the hall and into the kitchen. He turned on the water, presumably to wash her cup, then opened and shut a cabinet before she heard footsteps again. As soon as she heard the front door close, she'd planned on getting back to the journal. Instead, she really did fall asleep. She slept all day and didn't wake up until early evening. She couldn't believe she'd slept so long but had to admit she felt much better.

After tending to Charlie and getting a quick bite, she felt strong enough to return to her mother's scrapbook, and find out what it might reveal.

Expecting to find all the stuff from that last box on the garage floor where she'd left it, her heart lurched when she entered the garage and found that the space was clear. She looked around the garage in a panic, shifting boxes from side to side, until she'd worked up quite a sweat.

She'd given up and was heading back inside when she found what she was looking for. A small smile touched her lips. *Brian.* He must have picked everything up off the floor when she'd asked him to fetch the journal and stacked it neatly on the workbench.

When she pulled her mother's scrapbook out of the middle of the pile, a small tin box fell onto the floor. It was an old cigarillo box, tarnished and beat up, and she wondered why she hadn't noticed it before. Curious, she put the scrapbook back on the workbench and tried to open the tin. It was rusted shut, so she searched for a screwdriver and pried it open. The hinges broke and the lid clattered to the floor. She pulled the stool out from underneath the workbench and sat down, withdrawing the contents of the box.

The first several items were pictures. Mother, Daddy, Phil, and Dana that time they'd traveled to Colorado and the West Pawnee Butte, a rustic cabin in the background. The four of them at the one and only county fair they'd ever gone to. A tanned Dana and Phil, arms slung around each other, laughing and playing along the Elkhorn River.

That was one of her favorite family vacations. They'd spent two weeks in the summer camping along the shore. Daddy had let the kids sleep in their own tent, and they'd laughed and had a great time. She ran her finger over Phil's face.

"I miss you so much," she said. Her voice wavered. Without warning, she was launched into the past, into a memory as vivid as a psychic vision.

Shortly before her twenty-fourth birthday, the phone rang while Dana was getting ready for her shift.

"Dana Sinclair."

"Hey, Tweedle Dee Dee." It was Phil. "How's the cops 'n robbers biz? Still loving it?"

Dana laughed. "Sure as shootin'." It was something their father had always said. "Right through the bull's eye."

"More like the bullshit." Ever the eloquent one, her brother.

"I'll ignore the sarcasm, if you don't mind." It was always so good to talk with him. "So, what's up, big brother?"

"Just called to wish you happy birthday and let you know your present will be a little late this year. If you feel up to a visit, that is."

"Hearing your voice is all I need." But inside, she was doing a happy dance. She couldn't believe he was coming out, and hoped he'd be able to stay at least a few days.

"That's the biggest load of crap that's ever come out of your mouth. You love getting presents. What was it you called them when you were little?"

"I don't remember."

"Yes, you do. Come on," he teased. "What did you call them?"

"Prezzies," she mumbled.

"Sorry, I didn't quite catch that." He was laughing at her, and she knew he wouldn't be able to contain himself for very long.

"Prezzies."

"Yeah, that's it." His laughter exploded through the wires and Dana had to pull the phone away from her ear. How she loved him. "Prezzies. That's priceless."

"If you're quite done with all your mirth and merriment, I've got to get going. Some of us have places to go, citizens to save."

"Yeah, yeah. My busy little sister. Always wants to

be where the action is." She could hear the hesitation in his voice, and frowned.

"Something wrong?"

"No, no."

"You sure?"

"I'm sure. I'll let you go now."

"Okay, then. If you're sure nothing's wrong—"

"Bye."

"Bye."

"Hey, Dana?"

She brought the phone back up to her ear. "Hmmm?"

"Love you."

Dana didn't have a chance to say it back before he hung up. He had settled in Chicago after graduating from the Honors College at Chicago State University. His visits home were rare. That's what made this one so highly anticipated.

Several days later, she'd gone to pick him up at LAX and laughed when she'd first caught sight of him. He was wearing the gaudiest purple, lime green, and yellow Hawaiian shirt ever made. His way of poking fun at her and her fellow Californians. He was, and always would be, a Midwestern boy.

"Phil!" she cried as she leapt out of the car and ran toward him. A huge smile on his face, Phil hurried toward her, weaving in and out of slower pedestrians lugging their souvenirs and suitcases.

He'd just stepped off the curb when a loud shot ripped through the commotion. Dana ducked without thinking about it. She scurried around the back of the car, drawing her weapon from its hiding place in the small of her back.

"Get down," she shouted. "Everybody get down." Things had seemed to be moving in slow motion except the sleek black Mercedes that screeched past, trying to zigzag its way through the traffic. Taking careful aim over the trunk of her car, she'd squeezed the trigger and shot out one of the tires, then watched as the Mercedes swerved before it crashed headfirst into one of the terminal parking structures.

She rushed to the vehicle, accompanied by several airport police officers, just as the front doors flew open and the driver and passenger stumbled out.

"Sheriff's deputy," she shouted, raising her gun again. "Freeze." The passenger immediately stopped, arms raised in surrender, but the driver took off, racing through the traffic that had slowed to rubberneck the accident. "You two take him," she said to the closest airport cops, gesturing with her gun. "I'm going after the driver."

Followed by a third airport officer, she sprinted through traffic, spotting the driver as he disappeared into a second parking structure. "Stop. Sheriff's deputy," she shouted.

They caught up to the suspect and Dana tackled him. He panted heavily and barely resisted. She sat on his back while the other officer pulled out his handcuffs and tossed them to her. She'd put on the handcuffs, a little rougher than was really necessary, and hauled the driver up off the ground.

As they walked back to the terminal, Dana felt uneasy. Something was wrong. She quickened her step until they were practically race walking.

"Hey, what's your hurry?" the driver asked, still wheezing. "Not like I'm going anywhere. Besides," he added, "my head hurts."

"Shut up." For the first time, Dana saw that the man's forehead was bleeding, and hoped he'd hit his head on the dashboard when he crashed, not on the pavement when she tackled him. That's when she noticed the crowd standing on the sidewalk in front of the terminal doors.

"Here, take him." She practically shoved the driver at the other officer and ran to the edge of the crowd. As she pushed her way through, she caught a flash of purple. And red. So much red.

"Oh, no," she groaned. "No, it can't be."

She'd broken through to the front of the crowd and fallen to her knees. There lay Phil, bleeding heavily from a chest wound. An airport security guard sat on her brother as he performed CPR, his olive green trousers soaked with Phil's blood. But it was no use. Although CPR continued all the way to the hospital, once Phil arrived and was examined by emergency department doctors, her brother was pronounced dead.

Dead. All because of her. While she hadn't recognized either the driver or his passenger, who turned out to be the shooter, it didn't take long for their identities to be discovered. They'd killed Phil as a warning to prevent Dana from testifying against the leader of their drug cartel.

No wonder her mother had blamed her for Phil's death. She was right. It was all Dana's fault.

ᘉᘓᘉᘓ

Dana ran her thumb over her brother's face, smiling up at her from the Elkhorn River photo, and sighed wistfully. Things were so simple back then, so uncomplicated. Then her father had gone to prison, they'd left everything and everyone they'd ever known and moved two thousand miles away, and things were never the same again. Mother had even changed their last name. Dana tried to understand why. According to her journal, she'd left Nebraska still in love with her husband. She'd held on to The Walrus for over twenty years even as she'd severed every connection they had to him. They hadn't even been allowed to speak his name. So what could her mother possibly have meant when she'd said she'd done it for her own good?

Dana had to accept the fact that she may never know. It didn't make any difference, anyway. She loved her mother and had discovered how very much her mother had loved her. Ultimately, that was all that really mattered.

Her father, however, was a different story. She wasn't sure just how she felt about him.

Outside, the sound of footsteps approached, seemed to hesitate just outside the garage door, then continued across the driveway and around the corner. Someone was about to ring the doorbell, probably to pay their respects. As the bell sounded, she thought about ignoring it, hoping whoever it was would go away. She wasn't up to making nice-nice with someone right now. But her mother had ingrained her Midwest sense of propriety into her at an early age, and Dana reluctantly gave in to it and went to see who it was.

"Who's there?"

"Dana, it's Bill Moore. Lieutenant Jackson told me to watch the house and check out anyone who comes near. There's a guy here, claims he's a friend of yours."

"Open up, peaches, it's me."

It's about time. She opened the door. Charlie rushed past her and gave Finn the warm greeting he wasn't going to get from her.

"Looks like your dog knows him, anyway," Bill said.

"Yeah." Dana ran her fingers through her hair. "It's okay. Thanks, Bill."

"Okay," he replied. "I'm right across the street if you need me." He gestured to his cruiser. "Night."

"Night." Dana watched Finn coo over Charlie. When he was done, he peered up at Dana with one eye. "So."

He scooped up the dog and held her close. "What's that all about?"

His eyes darted back and forth, and Dana thought he looked like a perp shielding himself behind a hostage, expecting to be shot at any moment.

"Nothing," she said tersely. "Just routine."

"Oh." He busied himself with petting Charlie.

He's really pushing it. He had to know she was angry and hurt that he hadn't gone to Mother's funeral, or even returned her calls. He'd better have a damn good excuse if he expected her to forgive him. She cocked her head and glared at him.

"So," he repeated. "You're probably wondering what I'm doing here."

Again she said nothing.

He shifted from one foot to the other. "Why I didn't call you back."

Arms still crossed, she simply stood there and glared.

He tucked the dog under an arm and used his other hand to gesture. "I wanted to come to the funeral, peaches, I really did. But, well, you see…" He trailed off, looking uncertain. "Can I come in? Please?"

She opened the door a little wider, but didn't move. He had to turn sideways to get around her. "Got any bourbon?" he asked, once inside.

"You know Mother doesn't allow any alcohol in her house. Didn't," she corrected herself. "Diet Coke's the best I can do." She wasn't about to share her SoCo with him. At least not until he explained himself.

"Great. Thanks."

She went to get the soda while Finn and Charlie got comfy on the couch. It'd been a long time since Finn had visited her in this house, and Dana wondered if it felt as weird to him as it did to her.

"So, are you going to tell me what's going on? Helen

said you've been acting really weird lately. Even for you."

Finn opened his soda and took a big gulp. "Well," he replied, setting the soda can down. Dana pulled a coaster out of the little wooden holder on the end of the table and handed it to him. He wiped the wet ring left on the table with his fingers and set the can down on the coaster. "The shit's really been hitting the fan lately."

Dana sat down next to him. Watched his clasped hands as he rubbed one thumb across the top of the other, his knuckles as white as a freshly groomed West Highland Terrier. She put her hand on his and tried to calm him. Something was definitely wrong. "Hey, Finn. What is it?" When he jerked his hands away and looked at her with tears in his eyes, her heart nearly broke. "Whatever it is, we'll get through it together," she told him. "But I can't help you unless you tell me what's going on."

"Oh, man." Resting his elbows on his knees, he put his face in his hands and rubbed vigorously. Then he clasped his hands together and tapped his lips. "I've made such a mess of things." He turned to Dana. "I think Helen's going to leave me."

That saddened Dana, but didn't really surprise her. She'd seen it coming for a while now.

"Can I stay with you for a few days?"

"Of course." There was still a lot to do and she'd really prefer not to have a houseguest, but as angry as she was at him, she just couldn't say no. "You can stay in my old room."

"Oh, so you're sleeping in your mom's room, then?"

"Yeah. What's wrong with that?"

"Nothing, I guess. It's just that…" He shrugged. "Never mind. I'm just being stupid."

"No," she prodded. "What is it?"

"Dude, if it was me, and my mom had just been

murdered, I think it would give me the creeps to sleep in there. That's all I'm saying." He stood, smiling at Charlie when she peered up sleepily at him. "I think I'll call it a night, then, if you don't mind."

"Actually, Finn," she said. "I do mind. What is going on with you? You show up here without calling, you miss Mother's funeral—I really needed you, by the way—and you have your poor wife all pissed off because you won't return her calls. What's up with that?"

"Can we just wait till morning?" he whined like a four-year-old. "Please? I promise I'll tell you everything."

"Seriously?"

"It's been a really long week."

"What. Ever." He thought *he'd* had a long week? What a drama queen. "Just get your stuff, then, and I'll pull out some clean sheets. You can make the bed up yourself," she added a little tersely. "Just pull the dirty ones off and throw them in the laundry hamper. I'll take care of them later."

"Thanks, Dana. I knew I could count on you."

Yeah, too bad it's not mutual. As she pulled sheets out of the linen closet, she mulled over her friend's comments and what his predicament could possibly be. Truth be told, Finn had always been a little flaky. His marriage to Helen had been unexpected and sudden, but seemed amicable. He had to have done something really stupid to make her threaten divorce. Surely, he hadn't slept with someone else. He was far too loyal for that. But if not an affair, then what?

The front door slammed and Finn appeared in the hall, lugging a large suitcase, an overstuffed backpack, and a laptop. The backpack threatened to slip off his shoulder, and he clumsily shoved it back up, banging the suitcase into the wall and nearly dropping the laptop. He stopped to get a better hold on things, grinning at her sheepishly. "Still down there?" He gestured down the hall toward her bedroom.

"You know where it is." She tossed the sheets at him and chuckled lightly when he bobbled the backpack trying to catch them and then dropped everything except the laptop.

"Hey!" He scrambled to pick things up, while Dana stood there laughing.

"Oops. So sorry."

"Yeah," he muttered. "Sure you are."

"See you in the morning." As she entered her mother's bedroom, she peeked around the doorjamb just in time to see Finn hurl his backpack inside her old room. Charlie eagerly followed him, but to Dana's surprise, he yelled at her to get out. The little dog did, head down and stubby tail covering her backside. When she saw Dana, she trotted down the hall and promptly sat on her foot. Dana picked her up, murmuring that it was okay, she was a good girl. Finn had never before spoken harshly to Charlie, yet tonight, he had her trembling against Dana's chest.

What was that all about? Why was he so angry? Just what was going on here?

CHAPTER 37

Snuggled in next to Charlie, a Maggie O'Dell novel on her lap, it took only half a chapter before Dana's eyelids grew heavy and she was forced to stop reading. After putting the book on the nightstand, she pulled the covers up, turned off the light, and arranged herself around the sleeping pooch beside her. It was amazing how such a tiny animal could take up what seemed like five feet of bed.

Within moments, she was asleep.

When she awoke sometime later, the room was flooded with moonlight. Charlie stood at the edge of the bed, growling. Dana crept next to her and rested her hand on her neck. The little dog was trembling, all the hair on her back standing on end.

"What is it, girl?" Dana whispered. The dog looked briefly at her, teeth bared, then turned back and continued to growl softly.

A barely audible thud came from the other end of the house. What the hell? She grabbed her gun and a flashlight out of the top drawer of the nightstand then walked quietly to the door and opened it a crack. Charlie leaped off the bed to follow, but Dana blocked her with her foot. "Not this time, little dog. You stay here and be good."

She stuck the business end of her weapon through the crack and opened the door a bit more. The hall was empty so she slipped out and shut the door softly behind her.

As she passed her old room, she checked inside, expecting to find Finn snoring away. The room was empty. His bags were strewn all over the place. His laptop was open on the bed. The clean sheets she'd pulled out for him had been tossed on the floor.

More confused than ever, she continued down the hall, tightening her grip on the gun. The living room was full of shadows, and Dana flashed back to that night, not so long ago, when she'd encountered her mother's killer in this very room. Moonlight forced its way around the window blinds, and Dana half expected some night creature to jump out at her. She forced herself to breathe slowly, in through her nose and out through her mouth.

The main difference between then and now, she realized, was that before, fear had gripped her so intensely she'd allowed the intruder to get past her. Not this time. Adrenaline coursed through her veins, but she was ready for anything. In the short time she'd been here, this had become home like it never was before, and she'd die defending it.

She peeked out between the blinds. The cruiser was parked across the street, but the shadows were so thick she couldn't tell if Bill was still there. But she figured he must be. He wasn't one to leave his post.

She loosened her grip on her gun just long enough to wipe off her palms on her sweats. When another muffled thud came from the garage, she debated going and getting Bill. *But what if it's nothing? A squirrel or a possum or something?* She'd be a laughingstock around the department. Bill was a nice enough guy, but she didn't kid herself that he'd be the first one to spread a little gossip if he could. No, better to check first and call for back-up if she needed it.

She crossed to the garage door and leaned against it, listening. Someone was definitely in there, all right.

She slowly turned the knob and prayed that the hinges wouldn't squeak when she opened it. Unfortunately, the door opened into the garage, which meant that she wouldn't be able to see whoever was in there as she opened it. To avoid early detection and possibly drawing fire, she'd have to leap blindly into the garage.

Pushing open the door and stepping inside in one smooth motion, she aimed the gun and flashlight at the file cabinets. And was so shocked by what she saw, she almost dropped them both.

There, with his hands inside the top drawer, a penlight in his mouth, stood her best friend since childhood. Someone she'd thought would always have her back.

"Dana." Finn smiled from around the flashlight, and she was chilled. "I thought you were asleep."

"I could say the same thing about you," she said, noting the way he pulled one hand out of the drawer but kept the other one in it, as if he were marking his place. Or hiding something. "Looking for something?"

"I can explain." He shook his head. "It's not what you think."

"No? Then what is it?"

"Can we go inside, talk about it?"

"We can talk about it right here."

He shaded his eyes against the light from Dana's flashlight. "Can you at least turn on the overheads and stop shining that thing in my face?"

"Fine." The instant she moved to flip on the lights, he leaped at her. His body slammed into her. She was knocked to the ground. A knife sliced her forearm. Her skin opened up. The pain was immediate. White hot. Her blood splattered the wall.

Finn straddled her. Gripped her wrists. Tried to squeeze her gun free. She struggled against him. He leaned in close.

"I really hate to have to do this, peaches." He grimaced as he slid his hand into the slice in her arm and applied pressure. She cried out at the pain. "But I can't let you leave here. Not now."

Adrenaline surged again and overtook the pain. With the speed of a rattlesnake, she threw herself upward and bashed her forehead into his face. His eyes went wide as the pain started to register. She shoved him off and struggled to her feet. He wrapped his arms around her waist and brought her to her knees. She twisted around and shoved him away.

His nose bled profusely, mixing with the blood emptying out of her arm, and her hands slipped. She fell heavily onto her side. Finn clung to her. Her gun clattered onto the cement floor. He raised his arm and tried to stab her again, but she blocked him and squirmed away.

"Finn, stop it!" She scrambled for her gun. "What are you doing?"

He grabbed her ankle, and she wriggled around and slammed her other foot into his face. She heard his nose break again. Blood poured from it, and she'd split his lip, too. He dropped the knife and covered his face with his hands.

"Son of a bitch!" he exclaimed. "I'm going to kill you."

It was a race to see who could get to their weapon first. When Dana reached hers, she turned and aimed it at the spot where Finn had been. But he was gone. He had to be hidden among the boxes she'd filled with her mother's things.

"Finn, don't be stupid," she said. "I know you're in here."

"Yeah," he replied with a snort. "But you could never shoot me."

She inched her way around the boxes, heading slowly toward his voice. "Don't be too sure," she replied. She took another step and adjusted the grip on her gun, aiming slightly left of the spot where she believed her old buddy was hiding. He was left-handed, so he'd probably move to the left. "Why'd you do it, Finn? Why'd you kill Mother?"

"Stupid, stupid old woman," came his reply. "If she'd just given me the money, none of this would have happened."

"So you did kill her."

"I came to her with my hat in my hand. I needed her help, and she laughed at me. She actually laughed at me."

Dana couldn't believe what she was hearing, and yet, the pieces all fell into place. She moved a little closer to the sound of Finn's voice. "Did you embezzle funds from the partnership, Finn? Is that what this is about?"

"I tried to pay it back," Finn whined. "I would have paid your mother back too. Eventually. Stupid, antiquated old dinosaur. Tried to get her passwords off her computer, but the bitch didn't even do any of her banking online."

That explained the missing computer. "But why'd you have to kill her, Finn? I mean, couldn't you have figured out some other way? You could've come to me. I would have helped you." Another step or two closer, hidden by mounds of boxes.

"Do you think I'm stupid?" he yelled. "You don't have any more money than I do. And I doubt Agnes shared her financial situation with the likes of you."

"The likes of me?"

"Little Miss Goody-Two-Shoes. So smug and self-satisfied. Think you're better than me just because you're a cop."

"When did I ever treat you like you were beneath me? You've been my best friend since second grade, you jerk."

"Bet you didn't even know your father spent the last twenty years busting up rocks on a chain gang. Yeah, that's right, you holier-than-thou bitch. Your hero is a common thug, a real-life murderer."

Dana was devastated. How on Earth did Finn know about Daddy, and when did he find out? More important-ly, how had she completely missed his hatred of her?

If she'd seen the knife a split second earlier, she could have deflected it. It hurtled out of the shadows, tumbling end over end, a flash in the darkness. She saw it at the last second and tried to dodge it, but it sank deep into her shoulder just under her collarbone. She screamed. The pain was tremendous.

It also pissed her off. She took aim at her friend and squeezed the trigger.

The shot hit home.

Finn fell to the ground.

Dana used the back of her gun hand to brush her bangs out of her eyes then let her hand fall to her side. Her shoulder bled freely. She brought her hand up to the wound and winced as the gun bumped into it.

She crawled across the garage with her gun still drawn and peered around the boxes. Finn's face was white. There was a hole in his side. His shirt was soaked with blood.

"Help me," he wheezed.

"You'll live, I'm thinking." As soon as she said it, it

felt like a lie. As she knelt beside him, a man rushed in, skidding to a stop when he saw Dana. She lifted her gun and crouched down into a tiny ball.

The man raised his hands, palms facing Dana. "Don't shoot, Dana," he said. "It's me."

"Stop right there," she responded then frowned and took a closer look at the man who stood over her. His hair was gray, close-cropped, and thinning. His rugged face was deeply lined, as if gouged by giant claws. There was a grayish pallor to his skin that accentuated the smattering of freckles tossed haphazardly across the bridge of his nose. There was something familiar about the man's stature, his meager chest and the way he puffed it out. But it was his startling, icy blue eyes that she actually recognized. "Daddy?"

Finn moaned, and she turned her attention back to her friend, the one who had just tried to kill her. The one who killed her mother.

"Here." She grabbed one of her mother's blouses out of the nearest box and pressed it to the hole in Finn's side. "Keep pressure on it."

Edmund knelt and did as he was told. When he saw the knife sticking out of Dana's shoulder, he moved as if to touch it. "You're hurt."

"Just stay with him," she said, "while I grab my phone and call for back-up."

Dana tried to stand up, but felt a little shaky and dropped back to the floor. "Where's Bill? The officer in the squad car out front." She narrowed her eyes. "What did you do to him?"

"For God's sake, Dee Dee. There's a knife in your shoulder, and your arm's a bloody mess, too," Edmund said. He pulled his cell phone off its belt clip. "Just sit still for once in your life, will you? Let me call the paramedics. Then you can call your cop buddies."

She leaned back against a box and did her best to apply pressure to her own wounds. It was agony, and she grimaced, especially when she remembered her first aid training and tried to keep her arm elevated.

While Edmund dialed 911, she tried to take her mind off the pain in her shoulder and arm and focused on his long, talon-like fingers.

"Yes, we have an officer down and the guy who knifed her has been shot." He gave the address then covered the phone with his hand. "What's the name of your lieutenant friend?"

She felt something on her knee, and looked down to see Edmund touching her.

"Dana," he said sharply. "Name."

"What?" She felt fuzzy, and shook her head in an effort to clear it. "Oh, um, Brian. Bri—Brian Jackson."

She couldn't make out what else her father said, but when he finished talking on the phone, he slid it shut and clipped it back onto his belt.

So tired. I'll just sit here for a few minutes, just until the medics get here. She watched as her father left Finn and went to the workbench, yanked open one of the drawers, and pulled something out. Her eyes were so heavy, she just had to close them. Just for a second.

Then everything went dark.

CHAPTER 38

A high-pitched, steady *beep, beep, beep* interrupted her sleep. Dana groaned and reluctantly opened her eyes. Everything was white. And blurry. She blinked her eyes several times and tried to focus. A face appeared above her, and she squinted and brought her hand up to swipe at her eyes.

Something rough rubbed against her face and she drew her hand back to see what it was. A bandage covered her forearm.

"What…" She tried to sit up, but it took too much energy, and she fell back onto the pillow.

"Hey," a disembodied voice said. It must belong to the floating head above her. "How you feeling?"

After squinting a second time, the face above her cleared. She smiled in spite of herself.

"Brian." She smiled weakly. "I'm fine." Foolishly, she tried to sit up again. The pain in her shoulder flared, and she moaned, falling back onto her pillow.

"Well, Sinclair." He returned her smile. "You look like shit."

"You kiss your mama with that mouth?" They both laughed. Hers trailed off into another moan, and she reached for her shoulder. "Don't make me laugh, okay?"

"Oh, quit whining, you wimp. You'll be up and dis-obeying orders again in no time." Brian caressed her cheek and smiled at her again, and she was glad he was there.

"How long have I been out?" She gently touched her fingertips to the bandage that covered her shoulder.

"About twelve hours, more or less. You were on the table for about five."

"Table?" She looked around at the sterile room with its beeping monitors and plain walls and understood she was in the hospital.

"Took that long for the doctors to sew you up." He took hold of her hand, careful not to jostle her shoulder too much. A wadded-up pillow hung over the arm of the chair.

Dana frowned. "Have you been here the entire time?"

"Huh?"

She nodded at the pillow.

"Oh. Yeah. That." He shrugged. "Figured someone from the department should be here."

"Yeah," she said, grinning. "Sure you did."

He grinned back, clearing his throat. "Seriously, though, you couldn't have kept me away." He nodded toward the door. "And I wasn't the only one."

"What?" She was getting tired and licked her lips in an attempt to stay alert. "What are you talking about?" Her eyelids were so heavy she could barely keep them open. She thought she heard the door to her room open and wanted to ask Brian where he was going, but she just couldn't keep the blackness at bay, and she slipped into a post-surgery slumber filled with images of her childhood, of her parents, her brother, and Finn, her best friend through thick and thin.

ᥱᕽᥱᕽ

The next time she opened her eyes, the chair beside her bed was empty. She shifted slightly, and the pain in her shoulder flared, then settled into a nagging ache.

"Good, you're awake."

A nurse was changing the IV bag that hung from a pole next to her, and looked down at her while she fiddled with the switches on her tubing. "Are you in pain?"

Dana tried to push herself up a little higher in the bed and grimaced. "Not too bad."

"You up for a little company?" The nurse wore a busy print smock filled with purple teddy bears and bright red balloons, and Dana wondered briefly if they'd put her in the pediatric ward by mistake. The nurse looked at the beeping machine next to Dana and wrote something on her chart.

"Not really."

The nurse took the stethoscope from around her neck, stuck the ends in her ears, and pulled down the neck of Dana's hospital Johnny. "Oh, I think you'll want to see this guy. He's been here since they brought you in. Just about..." She studied her watch again. "Eighteen hours ago."

She put the stethoscope to Dana's chest and listened. When Dana tried to ask who she was talking about, the nurse shushed her.

"In fact," she continued, taking the stethoscope out of her ears and wrapping it back around her neck, "you've had *two* admirers here the whole time."

"I have?" Dana asked. "Who?"

The nurse simply smiled and left the room. Dana couldn't imagine who she meant. She knew that Brian had been here, but who could the other be? Surely not Finn.

Brian poked his head in the door. "Good, you're awake. Feel up to some company?"

"Um, I guess." She wished she had a toothbrush.

He came in carrying the biggest bouquet of flowers she'd ever seen, a crazy conglomeration of white roses, red carnations, and sunflowers. When he put it on the nightstand next to her, he had to move the phone over and put the water pitcher on the rolling table in the corner.

"Those are...unusual. But beautiful." Her shoulder really smarted, and her arm throbbed. She wondered how long it would be before the nurse came back to give her a pain pill. "Thanks."

"So." He pulled the chair up next to the bed and sat down. "Do you remember what happened?"

She shifted and used her good arm to push herself up, then reached for the controller, studied it for a second, and pushed the button to raise the head of the bed. The pain in her shoulder flared again, but this time, it stayed with her and she winced.

"Are you in pain?" He got up from the chair. "Should I call a nurse?"

"I'm fine." A big fat lie, but he already looked so worried she couldn't bring herself to tell him she hurt like hell. "Charlie? Is she okay?"

Brian rubbed her arm. "She's fine. I left a little while ago and fed her then took her for a nice long walk. Don't worry," he reassured her. "I'll take care of her."

Dana smiled. "Thanks. Now, what did you ask me? Oh, yeah, what I remembered." She hesitated. "Before I tell you, you need to tell me something."

"What's that?"

"Finn?"

Brian shook his head slowly. Dana closed her eyes and almost allowed herself to sink down into the pain, but at the last moment, pulled herself back. Finn had betrayed her. Murdered her mother. Tried to kill her. She owed him nothing. Certainly not her grief.

Brian shifted in his seat.

"What?" she demanded

"Later," Brian said.

"Tell me."

He gave her a strange look she couldn't figure out. "We did some investigating into your friend's life. Seems he'd been embezzling funds from his firm. Nearly a quarter mil."

"So he told me, although I didn't know it was that much. But it makes sense." She was silent for a moment, trying to soak it all in. "The business plan I found. Wasn't it for a quarter mill?"

Brian nodded. "It was just a ruse."

"So because he was her accountant, he knew she had money and figured she'd be an easy target, a quick way to replace the money he'd stolen?"

"Yep. And when your mother refused to give it to him…"

"He killed her. He killed my mother." Dana closed her eyes. "When he found out she had no passwords for online banking, he pretended he needed to talk to me so he could find a way to go through her things and get the money that way."

"Looks like it." He took her hand in his. "We found her computer in his hotel room."

"Guess he forgot she only just learned a few years ago how to use a computer in the first place, and still did all her banking in person."

Brian smiled at her. "Guess so. Oh, and we found a brass vase in a dumpster behind the Hotel MacDermott he was staying at, that we believe is the murder weapon."

Dana pursed her lips and looked up at him. "Does it

look like an anchor and Aladdin's lamp spent a wild night together and produced a child?"

"Sure does," Brian said with a chuckle. "How'd you know?"

"Phil gave that hideous thing to Mother when we were kids. Found it in a thrift store. I think he paid about four bucks for it." Dana shifted to a more comfortable position and tried not to grimace as she did so. Closed her eyes in an attempt to camouflage her discomfort. "I bet Mother threatened to turn Finn in when he confronted her, and he must have grabbed the vase and bludgeoned her with it."

"Probably. You okay?"

Dana sighed. She was getting a little tired of him asking her that, but she knew it was just because he was concerned about her. "I'm fine." She opened her eyes. "Hey, whatever happened to Bill Moore?" Once she'd discovered Finn rummaging through her mother's things, she'd completely forgotten about the officer Brian had posted outside the house. Now she wondered why he hadn't heard the shots and rushed in to see what was going on.

"Oh, yeah. Him." Brian's brow furrowed deeply. "Seems he fell asleep."

"He fell asleep?" Dana giggled. She couldn't help it. "You *insisted* I needed a babysitter, and then picked someone who falls asleep on the job?" Her giggles trailed off into a slight moan as more pain flooded into her.

"Yeah, well...he'll be writing parking tickets and helping little kids and old ladies cross the street for a long, long time." He leaned toward her. "Dana, I'm so sorry..."

Dana waved her hand at him dismissively. "Forget it."

They each looked at different corners of the room for a several seconds until Brian snapped his fingers.

"Hey, before I forget, that accident you had? Remember? When the truck hit you?"

"Yeah." She rubbed her forehead. On top of everything else, she was getting a bit of a headache. "What'd you find out?"

"Totally unconnected to anything. Just a dumb kid out for a joyride in her stepfather's truck."

"So my father didn't try to kill me?"

Brian shook his head. "Nope." He chuckled. "Drama mama."

"It could happen," she said. Relief flooded through her, and as quickly as it'd come, her headache faded away. "You don't know."

He smiled and shook his head again. "What do you remember about what happened in the garage?" He brushed her bangs back from her forehead and listened intently as she explained how Finn had come for a visit under the guise of separation from his wife, how Dana had caught him searching through her mother's files, and the ensuing battle.

"And then the funniest thing happened," she told him hesitantly once she had finished.

"What's that?"

"Um...I thought I saw my father."

"You did."

"What?"

He stood up. "Hold on."

She watched as he walked to the door and pulled it open. He was gone for less than ten seconds before he reappeared with someone in tow.

"Hello, Dana."

So it wasn't a vision. There stood her father. Twenty years older, thinner, road-weary certainly, but she'd know him anywhere. He wore a beat-up Dodger's cap that exactly matched his eyes and a baseball jacket two sizes too big.

"Father." Glaring took too much effort, so she simply lay there and looked at him.

"Feeling okay?"

"Just ducky." She turned her head away.

The door opened again and she wondered if he'd left. When she turned to look, she groaned. Sally had barged inside.

"Eddie, there you are," she said. "Why didn't you wait for me?"

Edmund frowned and shook his head slightly. Sally brushed past him and stood by Dana's bed. She grabbed Dana's hand and patted it. Dana winced as Sally mashed the IV tubing into her flesh. "How you doing, honey?"

So Sally's new boyfriend, Eddie, was her father? Life just kept getting weirder and weirder.

"Sally, do you mind?" Edmund said harshly. "I haven't seen my daughter in twenty years. Could we have a little private time?"

"Of course," she said. She smiled weakly and turned back to Dana. "Hope you feel better soon."

"Hold on a minute." Dana used the bed controller to raise her head a bit more and levelled her gaze at Sally. "That day I caught you coming out of Mother's house. What were you doing there? Were you looking for something in particular, or were you just planning on ransacking the place?"

"Oh," Sally said, her eyes darting from Dana to Edmund and back to Dana. "It's silly, really."

She's stalling. This should be good.

"Tell her," Edmund said.

Wait...what?

"You sure?"

Now it was Dana's turn to look from her father to Sally and back again. "What? What are you two hiding?"

Sally shifted her weight onto her left hip and popped her gum. Looked at Edmund again.

"It's my fault," Edmund said. "When I realized she had a key to Agnes's house, I asked her to use it to go in and find something for me."

Dana exchanged glances with Brian, who had edged noticeably closer to Edmund. *What the hell?*

Edmund sighed. "I wanted to get your mother's journal. Get rid of it before you read it and discovered the truth about me."

"Oh, Daddy," Dana said, her heart softening immediately. "Why?"

"Why? Because I couldn't bear for you to find out that way. I wanted to tell you myself. In time…"

"Find out what, exactly? That you loved your family so much you were willing to sacrifice your freedom, to give up your life for us?"

Edmund jammed his hands in his pockets and shrugged.

"Well, isn't this nice?" Sally said over-enthusiastically. "We…"

"I think we're done," Edmund mumbled.

"What's that, honey?" Sally slipped her arm through his and hugged it tightly.

He made a show of extricating himself from her grip. "I said, we're done here. Good-bye, Sally."

"But…" Sally teared up and looked from Edmund, to Brian, to Dana, and back to Edmund.

It was a rotten way to tell her that it was over, that she'd just been a means to an end, and in spite of everything, Dana felt a little sorry for her.

"If that's the way you want it," Sally whispered and headed for the door. She stopped in the doorway and looked back at Edmund, who refused to look at her. "Feel better soon, Dana." Sally sighed heavily, took a deep breath, straightened her shoulders, and left the room.

"Well, that was fun," Dana said.

Edmund crossed his arms and shrugged. "She'll get over it."

"Yeah, maybe. Speaking of telling me the truth, how about you tell me what really happened that day, back when I was seven?"

Brian rubbed his index finger along the collar of his shirt. "This seems like family stuff. Maybe I'll—"

"Don't you dare. You *are* my family." Dana motioned to the chair. "Sit." She turned back to her father and shifted a little. "Spill it."

Edmund closed his eyes as if mentally collecting himself. When he opened them again, she noticed that they had darkened. Gone from the color of his favorite baseball team to the color of midnight. "Twenty years ago, I was supposed to testify in a murder case. Some rich banker type decided that a good way to increase his wealth would be to finance a drug deal. Then he tried a double-cross and they killed him. I was eating dinner at Carlucci's and saw it all go down. Tried to catch the shooter but he was too quick for me. So he sent his hoodlum cousin to pay me a little visit, told me that if I testified, my whole family would be wiped out."

Dana listened intently. It almost made sense. There were just a few holes in his story that needed to be filled in. "The cousin?" she asked. "Quadrees Rashard?"

Edmund nodded. Brian whistled softly.

"So. You made Mother divorce you, change our last name, and move away." She hesitated, hardly able to believe it all. "Because you loved us and wanted to make sure we were safe?"

Edmund nodded again and shoved his hands deeper

into his pockets. Tears welled up in his eyes, and Dana was deeply touched. Was this the same man who'd ruined her birthday by humiliating her when she'd spilled her ice cream on him? It was all so hard to believe. And yet, it made perfect sense.

"The only thing I ever asked your mother to do was to send me a letter now and then, let me know how you and your brother were doing," he explained. "All she asked in return was that I never contact you, at least not until I got out of prison. Then we were supposed to get together and break it to you both about what happened. But then Phil died, and then your mother, and, well…"

"Oh, Daddy," she said. Her voice trembled and her lower lip quivered uncontrollably. She reached out to him, and after a brief hesitation, he crossed the room and took her by the hand. He patted it roughly, looking around the room as if for a means of escape.

The nurse came in and stood with her hands on her hips. "Okay, time for the patient to get a little rest."

Edmund immediately let go of Dana's hand and turned to leave.

"Daddy?"

He hesitated before he looked back at her over his shoulder, eyebrows raised in question.

"Come back later, okay?"

"Sure as shootin'." He slipped out the door and was gone. She smiled at the familiar phrase and couldn't wait to see him again.

Brian handed her a tissue, and she realized she was crying. And this time, it didn't even matter.

About the Author

After sixteen years as a paralegal, Lisanne Harrington staged a coup and left the straight-laced corporate world behind forever. Now she panders to her muse, a sarcastic little so-and-so who delights in getting the voices in her head to either all speak at once in a cacophony of noise or to remain completely silent. Only copious hamburgers and Diet Cherry Dr. Peppers will ensure their complicity in filling her head with stories of serial killers, were-wolves, and the things that live under your bed.

When not writing, she watches reruns of *Gilmore Girls*, horror movies like *Sharknado* and *Fido*, and *Investigation Discovery* crime shows. She likes scary clowns, coffee with flavored creamer, and French fries. Lots and lots of French fries.

She lives in SoCal with her beloved husband and persistently rowdy but sweet miniature pinscher, Fiona.